"*Ruin* is a captivating romantasy that masterfully blends steamy tension with breathtaking world-building. The enemies-to-lovers trope is perfectly executed with a delicious slow burn that keeps you on the edge of your seat, making every interaction between Ren and Oralia sizzle with anticipation...a must-read that will leave you bewitched and eager to read the next book."

— **Amanda Richardson, *USA Today* Bestselling Author**

"A debut romantasy that truly set itself apart and was completely memorable. I was fully enraptured from start to finish and I never wanted *Ruin* to end. Especially with the yearning between our two main characters, absolute heaven."

— **Laura @elitereading**

"*Ruin* is a mesmerizing retelling of the Hades and Persephone that will pull you in from the very first page. The romance between Ren and Oralia crackles with tension and undeniable chemistry, but it's their individual journeys—of healing, self-discovery, and transformation—that truly make this story unforgettable... *Ruin* is a book you won't want to put down once you start."

— **Angie @thebiglittlelibrary**

"*Ruin* is like Beauty & the Beast meets Hades and Persephone. There is a beautiful darkness about the story that pairs perfectly with its endearing charm. I am blown away by the depth of Gillian's writing—her immersive world and heartfelt characters had me emotionally invested from page one."

— **Farrah @hellodarknessdarling**

"*Ruin* is a wonderful debut for Gillian Eliza West and it left me panting for more. I am also terrified about what's coming next but Oralia and Ren had me in a choke hold by the end. I will be waiting anxiously for book two."

— **Jenn @thebookrefuge**

"*Ruin* is going to have fans of dark, immersive, sexy fantasy screaming. Incredibly well paced world-building that isn't overwhelming, paired with complex characters, and a sizzling, angst-filled, slow burn romance that pays off!"

— **Whitney @whitneybrownreads**

"Oralia and Ren are my new Feyre and Rhys. I am that level of in love with this world, story, and characters that Gillian has created. The world is interesting, but not overly complex. Her writing is lyrical and romantic, but not overly flowery. The characters are multifaceted and endearing, but not perfect. In short, Gillian has created a world that I didn't want to leave and cannot wait to return to. *Ruin* has easily risen to my top five (if not the top!) reads of the year."

— **Jordan @abluenest**

RECKONING

RECKONING

THE INFERNIS DUOLOGY
BOOK TWO

GILLIAN ELIZA WEST

Immortality can be a horrifying thing...

ERA

Eastern shore

IAPETOS

Oralia

Once, I found this place beautiful.

The vast and endless blue sky.

The dappled sunlight through the branches of the orchards.

The river of gold reflected from the castle, threading through the kingdom like veins.

But now the light hurt my eyes, burning my skin until I wanted to scream. My hands itched to destroy everything before me—to turn it all to ash.

"Welcome home, Lia," Typhon, the Golden King, murmured, skin bright in the sun.

My knees buckled. I caught myself in the deep green grass with splayed hands, and I heaved. Acid swam through my veins, and I welcomed the tears as they spilled over, swallowing back the bile as I pressed my lips to the tops of his gilded boots before lowering my forehead to the ground.

The scent of wildflowers filled my nose, cloying in its sweetness.

The gurgle of a stream rang in my ears, the neighing of the horses in the stables. It turned my stomach even as a warm breeze skittered across my skin, catching on my hair and swirling the strands around my face.

Power throbbed within my chest, rushing through my blood, desperate for a way out. I grit my teeth, finding some vestige of control from the weeks of training before my power could seep through my pores and shatter all our plans. Another whimper slipped through my lips, and someone shushed me. A ribbon of light spilled across the back of my white gloves as my adopted father lowered to a knee.

"You are home, and you are safe."

Another sob wrenched its way up my throat. Typhon could not have been more wrong. My home was through the forest, into a wall of mist, and across a vast river one could not swim. My home was a castle made of bones and a city full of souls. My home was in the arms of a god who had ruled the kingdom of the dead with ice in his heart and sorrow in his soul—though not any longer. I was anything but safe in this kingdom with Typhon, but then again...

Neither was he.

CHAPTER
ONE

Oralia

The library was quiet. Familiar and yet foreign.

I stood only a few paces from the door with my hand wrapped around one of the chairs scattered around the large hearth. The tang of copper slid across my tongue, the inside of my cheek throbbing as I bit the skin raw. At my back, armor groaned as Hollis, one of Typhon's guards, shut the door with a *click*.

But I found I could not spare a glance for the soldier at my back, not at the sight of the wings hanging upon the mantel. The afternoon light shimmered off silver talons, catching on the membranes stretched and pinned against the white backing. Nausea roiled within my stomach, and I dropped my trembling hands to my sides to hide in the skirts of the lilac gown I'd dressed in the moment I stepped into my old rooms.

My king's, my *mate's* wings, hung like a trophy above the roaring hearth.

I had not lied all those weeks ago when I'd told Ren they were beautiful, night black, and terrifying—like him. Now, I wanted to shatter the glass, to slide my fingers across the velvet skin and send them back to Infernis to reunite with their master. And though I could sense his magic within me, the soft slide of his power shifting against mine, I could no more call his face to my mind than his body into my arms.

No, I could only recall him in the abstract. His dark wavy hair and the way it tangled in his long lashes in the ever-present breeze of our kingdom. The pale glow of his skin, the curve of his lips, the sharp planes of his cheekbones. How his rumbling voice sighed with contentment as his hands slid through my hair, as he buried himself deep within my body and my soul. I ached for him as I had never for another in my two-and-a-half centuries of life. He had been reunited with the lost pieces of himself, but I feared what would happen in my absence. Would he lose the warmth and compassion he had only recently regained?

My magic shimmered and, reluctantly, I turned as the door swung open, banging against the far wall. More and more, my power was growing, alerting me to changes in my surroundings or flexing beneath my skin like an animal ready to protect. Armor glinted in the sunlight, temporarily blinding me before a helmet clattered to the floor and a soldier fell to their knees in front of me.

No, not any soldier.

"Drystan..." I murmured, grief catching in my throat.

His head bowed, the tightly woven locs of white hair messy around his crown, but he merely pressed his hands to his face, the exhale of relief so loud in the room my ears rang with the silence before weeping slipped through his fingers. My palms tingled with the urge to comfort him, to draw him into my arms, and yet the divide gaped between us. I was no longer the lonely god I'd been

4

before I left Aethera, but I could not show it. And so, I dropped to my knees as well, clutching my hands to my chest and leaning to catch my guard's eye.

His words were harsh as if ripped from his throat. "I failed you."

Shaking my head, I gave him a watery smile, heat pricking at the corners of my eyes. "You did no such thing."

Drystan, my guard for as long as I could remember, let out another sob before sliding his hands over his head. The blue-black skin of his cheeks glimmered in the light as if the sun made a mockery of his pain. "I abandoned you in my fear. I did not protect you at the hour in which you were most in need."

I hated that I could not embrace him, I wished I could gather him in my arms and reassure him all was forgiven. My hands clenched tighter around each other until I was sure the leather of my gloves would rip. Gloves which had once been my salvation and now were a reminder of the prison I had willingly walked back into.

"I do not blame you," I breathed, cutting across him when he made to retort. "Listen to me: I do not blame you, and you did not fail me. What has befallen me is in the past, and we cannot change it."

And I would never want to.

My guard blinked with shining gray eyes, his thick brows pulled together in confusion. Striking, his resemblance to Dimitri—Ren's second-in-command—down to the freckle beneath his left eye. But he wiped at his face, heaving another sigh.

"You are unharmed?"

I nodded, sliding my hands over the bodice of my gown, the high neck tight at my throat.

Drystan's lips pursed as he gazed upon me, assessing. "Unharmed... but changed."

Biting the raw part of my cheek again, I exhaled slowly. "Time changes us all, regardless of if we wish it."

And how true it was. The last time Drystan saw me I had been full of anger, bubbling over with rage, my power volatile. I had been unable to control myself or my emotions and was so fearful of what I might become if I gave in. Now, my power roiled within me, and, though I had moments of uncertainty, I did not fear.

The darkness nourishes, the darkness strengthens, the darkness protects.

I pushed myself to my feet, unable to resist glancing up at Ren's wings on the wall. Drystan rose as well, his armor groaning at the movement. Shimmers reflected onto the white marble of the hearth.

"Hollis, you may go," Drystan commanded, turning toward the red-haired demi-god stationed at the door.

"I am under orders to keep Oralia safe, lest the Under King return to take her once more," Hollis answered, his voice a hollow monotone.

I turned, brows furrowing, but it was Drystan who stepped forward, swiping his helmet from the ground. "She has been under my protection since she was a child, well before prime. I do not—"

Hollis's blue eyes flicked to me with an obvious dismissal. "The king requires a word with you, my lady."

Drystan let out an indignant scoff, but I did not look at him. Instead, I dipped my chin. "Of course. I would not want to keep His Grace waiting."

My fingers tangled together in front of my gown before picking at the edge of one of the frayed cuffs of my gloves. It was a tic that had once been subconscious, one I'd found soothing in times of great stress. Now it was merely a distraction from the satisfaction roiling beneath my skin, another piece in the charade I had to play.

Both men tracked the movement before Drystan came to stand at my shoulder. Hollis opened the door, turning in a swirl of his white cloak to guide us from the library and through the halls. Strange to be back in this castle, the only home I'd known for so long. Foolishly, when Ren and I had made plans for me to return to Aethera, I believed it would be easy to slip back into this role. Now that I was here, however, I found it was much like slipping into a once-beloved garment only to find it two sizes too small.

The dining room was the antithesis of Ren's, with its long rectangular table and gleaming throne at the head. Gold dripped from every surface, threading through the white marble beneath our feet. Typhon sat at the head of the table, knife cutting an apple into pieces and white wings flaring to allow him room to lean.

Mecrucio and Aelestor were seated on one side of Typhon, the former's chestnut curls clean and shining around his face, the latter's copper curls plaited back behind his shoulders. On the other sat Caston, Typhon's heir, outfitted in his travel armor, the muted gray of Aetheran soldiers across our borders with the sun sigil bright across his shoulders.

Hollis and Drystan stayed back as I approached, the three of us lowering with practiced movements to our knees to press three fingers to our brow.

"My king," I murmured, the title ash upon my tongue.

Silence stretched throughout the chamber, save for the rustling of Typhon's feathery wings as they stretched when he rose to his feet. My knees ached with the echo of the pain of childhood, the memory of the countless days and nights on the throne room floor crawling up my spine like a chill I could not shake. The helplessness, the fear, had been a constant companion. Now, it settled like a hand around my shoulder in comfort.

I was no longer so weak, no longer a slave to the fear I believed would keep me safe. And though I rounded my shoulders and dipped my chin as the light reflected off Typhon's golden skin and hair, I was anything but small.

I am a wolf within the flock, I reminded myself. *I am the thing that weaker men fear.*

"Why did you run, Lia?" Typhon's tone was measured—a mere whisper of the fury which lived within him, as volatile as the sun fashioned in his image.

With a steadying breath, I gazed down at my tangled fingers. "It was not a choice, Your Grace. Merely instinct. I fled in horror of what my power had wrought..."

The image of the night I'd left Aethera flashed within my mind, so clear when Ren's face was not. *Caston's intended mate face down on the table, blood trickling from his ears. The human servant sprawled upon her back, eyes wide and blank in death.*

"And yet you did not stop when my men called out to you."

I licked my lips, searching for an answer.

"Any god would be frightened of a battalion of soldiers barreling down upon them, Father." Caston's voice rumbled through the room, punctuated by the thud of a goblet on wood.

Typhon hummed, running a hand down his beard as he gazed down upon me. I flushed, chin dropping to gaze at the floor.

"You lost control."

Anger prickled at the back of my neck. I had found control from my time in Infernis, but those words would once have scratched the old wound within my soul. My brows drew together, mouth tightening, however I did not respond, only allowed a soft flare of shadow across my shoulders as they might have come when I lacked understanding of my magic. Typhon merely nodded.

"Tell me what happened."

I took another deep breath, eyes fluttering closed against the memory of Ren in those woods. The cold mask upon his face, the slither of his shadows across my skin. He had been my enemy then, one I'd believed was there to bring about my destruction.

"The Under King was waiting on the other side of the boundary line," I explained slowly, fighting back the curl of my lip at Ren's title within Aethera. "My power had taken over, cutting a path through the wards, and he...he did the rest. Before I could turn and run back to the castle, he compelled me to sleep and..."

My voice trailed off, gaze sliding to the trunk of the tree the far wall had been built around. The wide branches of the oak caressing the ceiling shivered at my look. I heaved a sigh, heart heavy with longing and I hoped Typhon would read it as fear. Because Ren had shown me kindness when I had expected cruelty—he had wrapped me in power when I'd thought I would be wearing chains.

"I woke in a chamber meant for my mother, and there, I remained."

Typhon gazed at me with an expression similar to the one Drystan had worn, yet without the paternal affection. Once I would have said it was due to the burden upon his shoulders. I was a physical reminder of the loss of his wife, a constant source of pain. Now, I knew better. It was a monster who stood before me in the guise of a king. A murderer who paraded as a savior.

"You do not remember the journey to Infernis?"

I shook my head. "No, Your Grace. One moment, I was outside the wards, and the next, I was in a bedchamber."

A muscle ticked in Typhon's jaw. "And the Under King, what did you see of him?"

Images of Ren flashed before my eyes, clear and strong. The ice cold expression which cracked with time, warming until there was heat within his midnight gaze. His lips softening each day into a smile, curving around the letters of my name.

And if I want you until the end of time?

Then it will still not be enough.

My heart ached, reaching out within our soul bond that had only recently been threaded through our magic. I thought I could find the tang of pomegranate upon my lips, the language of Infernis heavy on my tongue.

"Once he was satisfied I knew nothing of consequence, I rarely saw the Under King. But he is exactly as you said, Your Grace."

Typhon raised a brow biting down on a piece of apple. "And what is that?"

I lifted my chin, the words leaving my lips an assessment of the god before me:

"The king is a murderer, a tyrant, a *monster.*"

CHAPTER

TWO

Oralia

How odd it was to smell the blossoms of the orchard, to walk through the rows and rows of trees, and feel as though nothing had changed. It was as if my time in Infernis had merely been a dream and I had woken to find myself right back where I started. The only reminder that everything was different was the bond connecting me to Ren, the subtle shift of his magic within my own, and the memory of his lips on mine.

"Did you miss this?" Drystan asked as we walked, gray eyes assessing.

Can a bird miss its cage?

I frowned, gazing up at the bare branches of the tree withering in my absence. Ilyana had been beside themselves with joy when I had hesitantly ventured from the castle and onto the grounds this morning. The crops had not given forth what they'd hoped during the winter months, and my return meant all would surely be well— or so they said. It was why we were pacing the orchards now. Ilyana and the other gardeners observed from a respectful distance, waiting for my magic to fix what my absence had wrought.

"Yes," I answered, drawing a small smile to my lips. "Though I missed you most of all."

That was the truth at least. I'd missed Drystan each moment I was gone. I missed his paternal love and care, the quiet questions he cast my way, and how he pushed me to think outside of myself.

"Have you ever met the Under King?" I asked, chancing a glance in his direction.

It was Drystan's turn to frown. Would this gulf between us always be so wide? He rested his hand on the pommel of his sword—so similar to another soldier I knew who served within Infernis—and settled his attention on a particularly sad-looking tree.

"I have not met him, no," Drystan murmured, placing a gloved hand on the bark. He opened his mouth to say more before he cleared his throat and dropped his hand.

The loss of the Under King's wings. Do you not contemplate the cruelty of it?

I wanted to press him on it, to ask him why he always wanted me to consider Ren's suffering. Because, *stars*, had Ren suffered. Even now, Ren bore the scars of the torment and yet he continued to hold on to the hope that one day he might be reunited with that severed part of him—his wings. But I knew it was not fair for me to force Drystan to speak of things he could not bear to, especially when I refused to lay my own truth at his feet. The truth was dangerous within the wards of Aethera, and there were ears everywhere.

"Best not keep them waiting," he said after a moment, looking over my shoulder to the crowd gathered at the edge of the orchards.

I pressed my lips into a thin line, and a soft smile tugged at his cheeks, a reminder of who we'd been before I'd left. And so, I nodded, taking a deep breath and rolling my shoulders back. It was easy now to call forth the power, to allow the hum of my song to brighten until the entire orchard was swimming in the song of life. Magic danced across my skin, reaching out to touch the trees with a sigh with relief, leaves shuddering and branches spreading wider with blossoms.

There, within the light, was the dark. But unlike the last time I was here, I did not fear it. Now, I understood its purpose. My shadows observed with a careful eye as the life swept through my body. There was a danger that lay within. If I was not cautious, I could be reduced to nothing but light and life to begin again in something new. Therefore, I stoked the power carefully, pushing it through the trees.

"Great Mothers," Drystan murmured, his exclamation mixing with the riotous sound of joy from those observing beyond.

I grimaced. I'd left this kingdom with a brittle hold on both my powers, one feeding into the other. Gritting my teeth, I came to a stop before one of the large trees with the heaviest fruits. This would get back to Typhon if he was not already observing out of sight. A small twang echoed through my chest as I gazed at one tree, forcing my breaths into faster pants.

Wings rustled, and a bird landed on a nearby bush within my line of sight. I stared at the raven for a long moment, magic humming through my veins.

"Oralia…" Drystan's voice was a quiet warning which echoed of a time long ago.

I called the shadows, invited them to twine around my shoulders, to push the gloves from my hands, exposing the deadly power living within my palms. The raven stared back with all the awareness of a god, understanding in its black eyes. With the slowness of dreams, my arms outstretched and I placed a bare hand on the trunk.

It crumbled to ash beneath my touch.

Someone screamed. Before I could have blamed it on my lack of control, but now, I could only stare upon the tree with a strange sort of satisfaction, mixing with the shame that my power had brought those behind me distress.

I wondered if it would be enough—if my charade could continue for another day. The last few nights, Typhon had called me into the throne room, asking the same sort of questions he had the first day. Each time, I gave the same answer as before. Each night, I swore my allegiance to Aethera and its ruler. Each night, I forsook in words my people and my mate.

The wind swirled the ashes of the apple tree up into the sky. Through the dust, I could barely make out the raven as it took flight, its soft feathery wings brushing over the top of my head in a caress before it disappeared, reminding me of my true purpose here.

I was not here to bring prosperity to this kingdom.

I was here to make sure it burned to ash.

CHAPTER

THREE

Renwick

This kingdom held no beauty now.

For a brief moment of my existence, Infernis had blossomed like the spring, blooming into shades of green and whites and purples. The scent of death and decay had been replaced by fresh breezes and happy sighs. The souls had blossomed, too, turning Rathyra into a true city as I had always dreamed. But now?

Infernis was as empty as a tomb.

I slid a hand over the smooth white stone of the throne before me, thumb tracing a carving of an asphodel flower. A week ago, I'd had Oralia in my arms. Only a week ago, I had been here, kneeling before her, hands traveling up the fabric of her gown.

"There is no time," Oralia breathed, fingertips raking through my hair.

I hummed, pressing an open-mouthed kiss to the inside of her knee, gazing up into her dark green eyes. Her hair was a mess of sunset waves around her cheeks, the obsidian crown of stars nestled within her curls. Our inner circle had only recently left, and we were set to depart in the morning for Aethera. Horror was already taking root, dread knocking at the door, and I could find it there, reflected in her gaze.

"Then I will make time," I murmured, wrapping my hands around her hips and dragging her forward to the edge of the seat.

Her knees widened to allow me to slip between them, the pale skin of her creamy thighs dotted with constellations of freckles. I traced them with a fingertip, smiling when they prickled beneath my touch and a shiver ran up her spine. Her scent deepened, swirling around me with whiffs of sage and wildflowers.

Oralia's laugh was soft but hollow. "Time is untouchable."

It was true. After the Great Mothers had created time, it had been an unreachable magic. No god possessed the power to alter it.

She traced the line of my cheekbone with her fingertips as if I were beloved. With a pang, the truth of the thought hit me. My chest was full of warmth and love and contentment, but it was threatened even this night. And yet I would give up all my warmth if it meant having her return to the safety of my embrace.

My lips pursed over her thumb, leaning into her touch. I could not get enough. Even now, I wanted to pull her closer, to climb inside her skin and live within her heart. To be parted now, so close to the soul-bonding ceremony, was beyond agony—it was cruelty. Yet we must, for the good of our people.

"I offer you my service," I whispered, pressing a kiss to her inner thigh, dragging the thin fabric hiding her from me to the side. The words mimicked the vows those within our inner circle had offered her tonight one by one. "I offer you my sword." I leaned forward, inhaling the scent of her arousal. "I offer you my body." Slowly, languorously, I licked up her center, gathering the taste of starlight on my tongue. "I offer you my soul."

She whimpered, tangling her fingers in my hair, holding me to her. Her
hips tilted up to meet my face before I slid one finger through her need.
"My queen," I finished, before devouring her whole.

"Ren." Dimitri's voice cut through my reverie, tugging me back into empty awareness.

Oralia was not here. I could not pretend she was in the next room, training with Horace or wandering the grounds with Sidero.

"I heard you." My voice was flat, but I did not turn to look at them and see the worry hidden behind smooth façades, as mine was. I knew it was there, as I knew Horace stood with his arms crossed over his wide chest, chin dipped in contemplation. As I knew Dimitri stood with his hand on the pommel of his sword, white hair tied back at his neck. As I knew Thorne would be leaning against the window, lips pursed and quick eyes assessing, looking for a solution for an impossible problem.

There was an ascension in only a few days. Twelve souls who were ready to give their magic back to the world to begin again, whether in this realm or the next. I blew out a breath, running my hands through my hair before turning to them with a grind of my heel.

"I will be in Aethera until then," I answered. Already I was itching to make my way through the mist. To stretch the only wings I had left to me and glide through the wards to see what I could through the gilded glass of the castle of nightmares.

Even if it was only to catch a glimpse of her.

Dimitri shifted uncomfortably, but it was Sidero who answered, stepping forward with a slither of gray robes.

"She will survive," they said, the fervor of belief suffusing their words as they slid a hand down their thick black braid.

"You serve her better by not straining your—" Thorne began.

I let out a roar of frustration, fire careening through my chest until I was sure I would spout flames.

"I cannot feel her." My voice rang through the room, each god and soul stumbling back a step save Horace, who merely reacted to my temper with something like relief. "The distance is too vast. I only know that she is alive. All else is lost and silent, and there is nothing I can do."

My power was nothing in the face of the mountain we must climb. I might have been a timeless god, one of the most powerful within our world, and yet all I could do was pace the castle like a predator in a cage and beg the universe for her safe return. The helplessness was acid eating through my bones, like the golden fire of my half brother, Typhon, searing my skin. I was not sure if I could endure it.

The moment Oralia had stepped through the wards of Aethera, our soul bond had pulled taut. Even when I shifted into my raven form and glided through the boundary, I could not feel her as I had before. There was only the hollow echo of her heartbeat in my chest and the soft shimmer of her magic tangling with mine. But it was as insubstantial as the mist wafting around the dark windows of the throne room.

"The only one who benefits from your fury is Typhon," Horace said, ruby-flecked eyes boring into mine.

I took a breath to calm the furious rhythm of my heart. He was right. Of course, he was. But after centuries of ice hardening in my chest and the cold eating away any semblance of feeling, these emotions were overwhelming. I was as volatile as a god hitting prime and ascending into their power—unable to control my temper and my sorrow. But what a gift to feel such things. A gift Oralia had given to me.

My wife.

My soulmate.

My queen.

"What news from Mecrucio?"

But I was not truly listening as Dimitri explained that no word had reached them yet as to how Oralia had fared once received within the castle. Neither Mecrucio nor Aelestor would return until it was safe. Instead, I was searching through my power for the small glimmer of her.

Are you there, eshara? I wanted to ask, though I knew no response would come.

One hollow note of her heart.

Then another.

Faster and faster, until my heart was beating in time with hers. Until my hand was covering my chest, my eyes wide and unseeing as they stared into the blue flames of the chandelier overhead. Panic spiked through my veins, our hearts reaching a fever pitch. I pushed my magic to her in a desperate attempt to help her overcome this silent struggle.

Voices murmured my name, but I could not see them. I could not hear their questioning cries or the hands shaking me. I could only feel my mate's heart as it beat within her chest, the terror thrumming through our soul bond as tangible as the air in my lungs. And the only thing I could speak in response as I careened through the throne room and out into the night air was her name before the bond echoed once with a hollow thump.

Before I could feel her no more.

CHAPTER

FOUR

Oralia

The dappled morning light danced across the veins of gold marble in the throne room. I tracked its slow progress toward my feet at the bottom of Typhon's dais over the hours I stood there.

Unending streams of soldiers entered the throne room, carrying with them crates of offerings from the outlying regions of Aethera, from Severa to the Western Reaches and the Eastern Shore, all under Typhon's rule. "Gifts of goodwill," they repeated again and again as they uncorked wine and tugged open barrels of grain. It was a ritual I'd seen more than once in my time in Aethera growing up, but now I experienced it with fresh eyes.

The soldier currently standing in the center of the receiving circle appeared haggard with smudges of gritty dirt on his golden-brown cheeks, and he panted as he placed the crate before him and bowed.

"Fruit, my king, from Severa."

Typhon hummed, flicking his fingers, and the soldier opened the lid. Bright red apples and smaller boxes of berries caught the waning afternoon sun. This was the fourth crate from Severa. They had also supplied grain and meat. I couldn't help but wonder how they could afford to send so much.

"This is a smaller offering than last," Typhon mused, chin resting on his fist.

The soldier cleared his throat, brown eyes flicking to Caston and away again. "They have offered all they can."

Fear fluttered around the boy—I couldn't truly call him a man. This was someone who was nearing adulthood, perhaps nineteen or twenty, and soon, he would learn if he had inherited magic from whichever parent had made him a demigod. But for a boy, a demigod, he was not so foolish as to not realize the danger lurking in the space between him and his king.

Typhon pursed his lips, assessing the boy as I did, before he nodded, dismissing the soldier with a wave of his hand. Golden armor creaked as the soldier's shoulders dropped. Without a word, he grabbed up the crate, bowing so low the rough wood skimmed the tops of his boots, before backing up a few paces and rushing out of the room.

"Perhaps those in Severa should be reminded to whom they serve. They grow lazy. I should send you there instead," Typhon said softly, leaning toward Caston standing on his right side.

From the corner of my eye, I was able to make out Caston raise a shoulder and drop it. "They are working hard, Father. Last season, they gave double what you asked. It must count for something."

Typhon hummed again. "Perhaps...perhaps."

Nausea crawled through my stomach, and I swallowed back the acid threatening to rise. I did not know how I could have been so foolish for the first years of my life as to believe the god seated above me was anything other than a monster. For so long, I had mistaken his cruelty for compassion and the cracks in his façade as merely signs of worry for his people.

"You may approach." Mecrucio's voice rang out across the throne room from the other side of the dais, his chocolate curls wild after the long day.

Hollis was the next to step into the gilded circle, but he did not hold a crate like the rest. Instead, a small black box rested between his hands, the corner of his mouth tilted up in a satisfied grin.

"The offering, Your Grace."

Slowly, he lowered to his knees, sliding the box onto both palms and lifting it overhead. When it caught the light, intricate markings found their relief: star-like blossoms and tangled vines dancing together across the lid and sides. Typhon froze, mouth popping open before he rose to his feet, bright wings flaring wide.

The smile breaking across his face was blinding. This must have been what had enraptured my mother in the beginning, if there had ever been a courtship before she had found true love in my father. But I could see the glimmer of the timeless god he pretended to be, the skin he tried to wear but did not fit. Quickly, he descended the steps of the dais. White feathers slipped across my throat as he passed, swirling the skirts of my gown.

"They have accepted?"

Hollis nodded. I'd heard whispers that he had left shortly after my first morning back in Aethera on some business for Typhon. Usually, it meant he'd been sent to find a weakness in the mist of Infernis. Though perhaps with the way through already found, he'd been sent elsewhere.

"And the other half?"

"The other half is waiting on your signal, Your Grace," Hollis answered.

Typhon lifted the box reverently, staring down at it for so long the silence grew thick. Mecrucio rocked onto the toes of his boots, brows furrowing together, and even Caston looked confused.

"You all may leave us," Typhon murmured, not lifting his gaze from the box.

My knee slid to the floor with a practiced curtsey while I pressed three fingers to my brow along with everyone else in the room. Drystan's warmth curled around my shoulder as he approached, guiding me with a gesture toward the double doors leading out into the palace.

In front of me, Aelestor and Mecrucio exchanged a look before the former chanced a glance over his shoulder at me. I hadn't seen the God of Storms much in my time back in Aethera, save for the chance meetings in the halls or at Typhon's table. But we had not spoken, not when the animosity between us had only broken weeks ago in Infernis when I returned his mate, Josette, her memories.

"Oralia." Typhon's voice boomed, echoing across the marble and shivering the leaves of the gilded trees set into the walls. "Stay."

I caught the worried look passing between Aelestor and Mecrucio as I froze. There was the barest shimmer of alarm in Aelestor's eyes before he disappeared down the hall, followed by Mecrucio. I moved back toward the circle in the center of the room and lowered to my knees the same way I'd done for two and a half centuries.

"This meeting is not for you," Typhon said.

Caston stood stubbornly between us, armor shining in the afternoon light, his rose-gold skin flushed. A muscle fluttered in his jaw. "What is it you need her for, Father?"

My adopted brother had been present for each evening I'd been questioned, speaking up in moments of uncertainty or strengthening my responses. Discomfort skittered across his heart the same as mine, it appeared. He did not want me alone with Typhon any more than I did. From the way Drystan hovered at my shoulder, it was clear he felt the same.

Typhon's voice dropped low, though his face betrayed no hint of emotion. "I have told you to leave, Caston. I will not ask again."

The rose gold of Caston's cheeks flushed brighter, but he bowed all the same, backing a few paces before turning. His eyes caught mine, widening until I could see the entirety of his irises, before he was gone in the next heartbeat.

I was alone with the Golden King, save for Drystan. Alone with the god who had murdered my parents. Alone with the god I had come back to destroy. Yet my hands did not shake, and even the discomfort I'd experienced only moments ago smoothed. My magic hummed as if it could sing to me the way Ren's mother, Asteria, had from her prison within the first kratus tree when I'd been small. A prison Typhon had put her in.

"I never told you about my father," Typhon mused.

"No, Your Grace, you did not." Though I knew enough of his father from Ren, who shared the same lineage. The god who had grown hungry for power—who had lost himself to it in the end.

When I looked beneath my lashes, it was to find Typhon standing at the base of the dais, weighing the black box in his hands. A strange sort of energy threaded around the room, ominous and fearsome. He flicked it open with a *snap*, and I blinked in confusion. There was no weapon within, nothing so outwardly menacing. Merely a dark metal ring. The band was crafted of two snakes woven together and on top sat a bright red gem. And yet the temperature of the room grew colder as he slipped it onto his index finger.

"My father was a brilliant god"—he extended his hand, admiring the ring—"though a short-sighted one. He created merely to control and consume and nothing more. But in the final years before he found his end, he began to fear Renwick and his magic. He regretted giving the gift of dominion over Infernis to him after it took too much of his magic to maintain on his own."

At the mention of Ren, my pulse flared. It was the first time Typhon had referred to him as anything other than *the Under King*. When Typhon's gaze slipped to me, there was an approximation of understanding there as if I'd been a soldier in the same war. But it was odd, not a perfect fit.

"Death is not merely a weakness, Oralia. It is the great equalizer on a battlefield. And as you have now seen with your own eyes, my half brother has no such leveler. He is a threat, a plague upon the world which spreads without end."

Typhon took a step closer, snapping the box shut. My confusion and fear washed across my face for his benefit while I pushed away the shadows threatening to curl around my shoulders like the snakes on the strange ring. Beside me, Drystan stiffened, and I caught the barest twitch of his hand toward the pommel of his sword.

"He taught you control, didn't he?"

I blinked, the corners of my mouth turning down. "No, Your Grace, the Under King did not."

He clicked his tongue. "Morana, then."

Shaking my head, I opened and closed my gloved hands in front of me, my neck aching as I craned it up to look at him. "I do not know who that is."

Morana, the God of Night, the powerful and terrifying timeless god whom Ren used the formal *mother* for in the old language— *maelith*. The god who'd taught me how to listen to the whisper of my magic and not to fear it.

The heavy pounding of my heart sounded in my ears alongside Ren's steady one.

Typhon loomed over me, face in shadow. A rough hand shot out to grip my chin, sizzling fire spreading across my skin. A scream tore from my lips, ringing through my ears, as his magic tore through my veins. It was a burn I knew all too well, the sunlight he wielded, the power his father had created in his image at the beginning of the world. Ribbons of it wrapped around my throat with my shoulders, pinning my arms into place.

With each breath I took, I pushed my shadows down. Some small intuition told me not to fight—I would survive this.

"Show me your power," Typhon demanded.

Corrosive tears slipped down my cheeks, another scream rang around the sickeningly gilded hall. I shook within his hold. My skin bubbled and blistered beneath his burning touch. Metal scraped against metal, another cry deeper than my own echoed across the marble, and the pain vanished in an instant, leaving in its wake a humming through my skin and ears.

The haze of my vision cleared as I panted, hands spread wide across the floor, before the same cry sounded again. Drystan laid sprawled at Typhon's feet, sword tight in his hand, a wreath of flame around his neck, tightening with every breath. And as the Golden King tortured the only person in our entire cursed world I'd ever loved as a parent, those gilded eyes were fixed on me.

"Show me or he dies."

CHAPTER
FIVE

Oralia

Drystan screamed. The sound was a thousand knives piercing my heart.

I did not hesitate—did not stop to weigh the cost—I could not allow Drystan to die. Shadows exploded from my chest, sharp and deadly, zinging toward the Golden King.

Perhaps the smile on his face should have prepared me.

Or maybe the dread pooling in my chest should have instead.

The moment my shadows reached him, primed to strike, they disappeared as if they had never been there. But Drystan's screams quieted into soft heaves. I sent another bout of shadows forward, intent on finishing what the first had not, but Typhon merely raised his hand. The same smile sliced across his face.

The shadows turned, shooting back at me and barreling through my skin. Like rabid dogs, they twisted around my arms, my throat. I knew these shadows—they were mine, but they were *wrong*. As if they did not know to whom they belonged. Drystan was crying my name even as Typhon laughed, as the shadows wrapped around my throat and squeezed.

The magic in my veins roiled, loosening its grip only to falter, surging higher but holding back on instinct. I gasped for air as the demented magic jerked me up to the tip of my toes. My head fell back to gaze unseeingly at the curved ceiling of the throne room. The last thing I thought before the world went black was that I hoped Ren would not come.

The world was wrong.

My skin itched, too tight across my bones. Each breath ached, and the fabric of my gown was stuck to my skin. I groaned, head rolling, and hissed at the sharp slice of pain in my throat.

"Do not move," Drystan groaned.

As I blinked slowly, the throne room swam into view. The marble of the floor dug into my knees. My arms were spread wide, and as I jerked, the grunts of two soldiers reached my ears. Dark metal cuffs circled my wrists, unearthly metal I had never seen before biting into my flesh. The soldiers held the ends of each chain, keeping my arms spread, and a third held one hanging between us, attached to a collar at my throat.

I reached for my magic and came up empty. There was nothing but the absence of it as if it had evaporated like mist in the sun. My lips moved without words, calling without sound to a power no longer present. Even now, I could only barely feel the tug of the soul bond in my chest, connecting me to Ren—his heartbeat a frantic rhythm beside my own.

"Breathe, Oralia."

Drystan was kneeling beside me, strung up as I was, though his arms were around his back. Blood pooled on the floor beneath him, streaming from gashes beneath his eye and lip. He was wheezing, a hollow whooshing with each breath hinting at a puncture in his lung.

I tried to breathe, but though there was air, I found it did nothing to satiate the need, not without my magic. The dark metal cut into my skin, rivulets of blood sliding into my gown, dripping onto the floor, and they did not heal. It had to be kratus resin worked into the metal—the only thing able to pierce a god's skin, yet it did not *feel* like kratus resin. This felt wholly new.

"The king requests your presence," Hollis intoned as if this were all a game.

He stood a little farther back, elbow resting on the pommel of his sword. An amused smile curved his lips. When Hollis jerked his head toward the door, Drystan was wrenched to his feet. With a tug, I was dragged onto my stomach as the soldiers holding my chains surged forward. I grit my teeth against the scream building in my chest while Hollis observed in fascination. Drystan stumbled, shoulders jerking as if he might break his chains.

"Pick her up, Vion, *please,*" he begged one of the soldiers. "Do not do this."

But whichever soldier he was entreating paid him no mind as the doors opened. I was dragged down the hall, a dark smear of blood left on the marble floor in my wake. Each breath was agony, and it was not merely the slice of pain through my wrists and throat, it was the absence of the magic I'd come to love. My power had turned on me, *abandoned me.* When I closed my eyes, I saw those shadows rushing back at me, felt their bite against my skin.

Dying sunlight streamed across my lids, and I was wrenched to my feet, tugged down the stairs on shaky legs, and into the grounds. We rounded the palace to the field of wildflowers, the rays of the fading sunset spilling over a sea of purple and white blossoms. And there, gathered within the beauty, were Typhon and his men. Caston stood beside his father, the corners of his eyes tight with worry before they widened, tears brimming in his eyes and slipping down his cheeks.

But it was Aelestor that had his hand closed over the pommel of his sword, outrage wild on his pale face. Mecrucio wore a similar expression beside him. Though it was muted as if shock had taken hold. And like any common prisoner, I was dragged through the grasses and thrown at the feet of the Golden King.

"I am willing to forgive your treason if you agree to serve me, and in exchange, I will reward you with power beyond your wildest dreams."

The edges of my vision pulsed, and bile coated the back of my tongue. It was as Ren had always feared, and I could do nothing but stare up into the face of a monster.

"I would rather return my magic to this world," I spat.

He nodded, tongue clicking in contemplation. Caston gazed in horror at his father, lips parting to speak before Typhon silenced him with a look. The Golden King's hand closed over the pommel of the young god's sword, sunlight glinting off the strange metal ring.

"You are nothing with him," Typhon commented mildly, weighing Caston's sword in his palm. "But you could be something with me."

I shook my head. "I would be nothing but a puppet."

Beside me Drystan fought harder, a growl slipping through his teeth before one of the soldiers kicked him in the stomach. He pitched forward, hanging heavy on his chains and gasping. The world swam in and out of focus, the darkness of night melting across the sky a strange comfort.

Typhon hummed. "Better a puppet than a consort thrown out into the cold the moment he is done with you."

My lip curled at the idea that I could be so insecure. That I would crumble beneath insinuations of being nothing but a plaything to Ren. A hollow laugh slipped through my lips.

"You do not know who I am, do you?" I asked as he raised the sword high above his head.

Typhon smiled placatingly, as one might to a child. "Who is that, Lia?"

There was a hiss of wind as the sword swung down. Right before it hit my neck, a deep voice rang out through the clearing.

"*Lathira na Thurath*," Ren answered in a swirl of shadow and smoke.

Dread dropped deep into my stomach as the sword was wrenched from Typhon's grasp before he could make the killing blow.

CHAPTER
SIX

Renwick

This was a trap.

My power pulled me from the castle to the river, from Vakarys's boat to the shore. I shadow walked through the in-between to find myself at the line of Aethera, ready to shift, only to realize there was no tang of Typhon's magic on my tongue. Only the sounds of clanking chains and ragged breath I knew all too well rang through the silence.

Unease curled within my gut, my instincts roaring to turn back, to find another way. But then I caught sight of Oralia kneeling before a gilded god, the scent of her blood on the wind flooding through my senses. Typhon questioned her worth within my heart and kingdom. Yes, this was absolutely a trap.

But there was no other choice. Not when Typhon raised Caston's golden sword above his head, the dying light of the day glinting on the blade. Oralia did not look afraid, and it scared me more than my half brother wielding a sword above my mate. No, she merely looked resigned.

"You do not know who I am, do you?" Her voice in my ears after so many long days apart was a balm to the open wound of my heart.

Her hair was wild in the breeze, a few strands sticking to the blood sliding down her throat. Did she know I would come for her? I pulled the shadows to me, reappearing only a few paces away from them and, with a flick of my fingers, wrenched the sword from Typhon's grasp, all but shouting her true title for Aethera to hear.

"*Lathira na Thurath*—you remember our old language, do you not?" My voice was cold, an imitation of what it had been before Oralia's power had stitched me back together. "*Myhn lathira na thurath: nat urhum rhyonath.*"

Typhon's lip curled in distaste, but I knew he understood the words even as he abhorred the old language we'd shared since before time. The language he'd turned his back on the moment he placed a golden crown upon his head and began ruling Aethera with a gilded fist.

"Not you?" he asked, a golden brow raised with the first words he'd spoken to me in centuries.

I shook my head. "Not me. Her."

The wind blew through the field, her scent mixing with the wildflowers and other gods'. Only a glance, I told myself, but when our eyes met, I could not tear my gaze from hers. Blood was splattered across her cheeks, sliding down her throat beneath the collar digging into her skin and pooling in the thin fabric of her white gown as if she were the kind of sacrifice the humans in their realm offered to their gods. Fire ignited in my veins. My hand closed over the sword until the metal cracked within my grip.

They would all pay for this. I would raze this kingdom and allow a new one to rise from its ashes. My shadows flared, spooling out. Golden soldiers cried into the wind before falling to the ground.

"Ren," she breathed, eyes wide.

I tore my gaze from her and back to Typhon. But his expression was not one of fear or uncertainty, merely satisfaction and amusement. I had played right into his hands. But if Oralia survived, I would not regret it—not for a single moment.

"What will you do when you destroy the only two gods who might rule Infernis, Brother?" I asked, rolling the sword over my wrist before catching it again.

Typhon smiled, the expression so akin to the one he'd worn when our father announced the murder of my mother it forced another tide of fire to burn beneath my skin. Once, we had fought as brothers did with playful boasting and competitions to prove who was worthy of the title of heir. I had even thought he loved my mother, revered and respected her as I did and it had made his betrayal all the more bitter. But our father had twisted Typhon and his insecurities, molding him in his image until the bond between us was as poisoned and tainted as daemoni venom.

It had been countless millennia since I had recognized the god before me as anything other than an enemy.

With a shrug, he gestured to Oralia at his feet. A glimmer of red flashed on his hand, there and gone before I could fully see it. Yet ice cracked through my veins. It couldn't be, not after so many thousands of years. I blinked, inspecting the chains again, noting the way they ate the dying orange light in the sky. Oralia could not call her magic any more than she could move.

Those chains were the work of our father, Daeymon, who had

thirsted for other gods' powers to be his own—to possess all the power of the universe.

Typhon was truly smiling now, and the expression was nothing like the one he'd worn when we were children. His hands spread wide. "I have all I need right here. Her death is merely another step on the road to power."

Behind him, soldiers shuffled. One fought against bonds that required four demigods to hold him. Aelestor placed his hand upon his sword, gray eyes fixed intently upon me, waiting for a signal. But I had none to give.

"And me? How will you destroy a timeless god who cannot die?"

Not truly. Typhon knew death would not take hold—I would merely rise again. Yet I dreaded the next death and what I might lose. Would it be my mercy, my hope, my ability to love? And would Oralia be there to put the pieces back together again? But perhaps I did not want those things if she was not in this world any longer.

My magic pressed against the barrier barring me from Oralia, searching for any cracks. But there was nothing, merely the empty shell where she should live within my heart. The only thing left was a mere shimmer of our soul bond connecting our hearts.

"I suppose you will have to wait and see," Typhon answered, flicking his fingers.

A faint hiss slithered through the air.

I slid a foot back, knees bent and ready to spring. My shadows snapped out, catching the first arrow before it could hit its mark, crushing it into dust. I grinned, lips parting to tell Typhon he would have to do better.

Blinding pain exploded across my shoulder. My shadows flickered, but I grit my teeth, forcing my gaze to remain steady on him. One step, then another.

"Ren!" Oralia screamed.

Another shooting pain sliced through my abdomen this time. I wrapped my hand around the arrow only to find it would not budge. But I leaned forward, intent on my goal before my torso was wrenched backward, white light shooting into one thigh, then the other. My tongue thickened with the kratus resin bleeding into my veins, stifling my strength and my magic. I could remember so clearly the last time I'd experienced this numbing pain, two and a half centuries ago when Typhon had shot me through the heart with an arrow hewn from the tree in which my mother's magic lived.

But I would not give in. I jerked, reaching for the arrow embedded in my skin before another shot through the air and into my hand. I staggered, falling to my knees, arms spread wide. My magic pulsed within my veins as I sought her out. Oralia was clawing at the earth, pulling against her shackles, blood pouring furiously from her throat and wrists.

How could we have gone so wrong?

According to my spies, Typhon had not known she was anything other than a prisoner. We had been reassured again and again that she would be welcome back into the kingdom with open arms. He could not penetrate the mist, though a few of his soldiers had slipped through. But we had dispatched them with quick efficiency—unless we had missed some in our haste to ready Oralia for this fool's errand.

Typhon strode forward, another sword hanging loosely in his grip, but I did not spare him a moment's notice. I leaned to the side, testing the strength of my bonds, unwilling to lose sight of Oralia for even a heartbeat while I drew up the last of my power. Pale lips, pale cheeks, wide green eyes, more beautiful than the clearest sunset or the brightest dawn.

She was as beautiful now as she had been when we knelt before our kingdom and placed the pomegranate seeds upon each other's tongues. When we had spoken the words of the old language to bind our souls together. But it was not her beauty calling to my soul, it was her strength—her fire.

Oralia would survive this. I knew it. I did not believe anymore in the power of the Great Mothers or the universe, not the rightness of magic or the workings of the so-called fates from other realms.

No, the only thing I believed in was her.

"*Eshara*," I breathed, sending out the last of my magic, slicing through the bonds at her throat and wrists—weak points in the chains I knew were there because I'd watched Daeymon craft them with his own hands.

Hot agony ate through my shoulder followed by a heavy, sickening wrench. Then the other, nausea rippling through my gut. But my eyes did not leave her. Her lips silently formed my name over and over. She was frozen to the ground, even as the collar and shackles fell around her.

"I lay my heart in your hands." The words, the echo of our soul-bonding vows, rasped through my lips—the final thought I had before the golden sword caught the fiery light of the sun.

Then blackness.

Oblivion.

Mist and shadow.

And so many stars.

CHAPTER
SEVEN

I lay my heart in your hands."

The words floated to me like mist on the breeze, and yet, I could not process them. Not when he was strung up with those dark chains. Not when his blood wept from each wound, pale face growing wan with each beat of his heart.

My magic woke slowly, stretching within my bones. I reached for it, welcomed it, begging it to respond as Typhon raised his sword. All eyes were fixed on the two timeless gods as I rose shakily to my feet, shadows pulsing around my palms. But I could only see Ren, lips parted on an exhale, darkness shooting from his lips and barreling straight toward me.

Typhon swung.

A sickening crack.

A hollow thump.

A bloodcurdling scream.

And an explosion of darkness.

I blinked, a rasping breath tearing through my lungs. Water lapped at my ankles. Mist curled around me, wiping at the tears on my cheeks and the blood from the wounds at my throat and around my wrists. Black, jagged sand crunched as I shifted my weight, a soft negation slipping from my lips, growing louder with each breath.

"No...*no, no, no*," I wheezed.

Ren's power had done this. His last piece of magic before Typhon's blow had not been to defend himself but to save me. I stumbled, falling to my knees in the damp bracken at the river's edge, slipping in the dirt.

Arms banded around my middle, heavy breaths at my back as someone struggled to lift me. I recognized Drystan's grunts of pain as he tried to hold me steady, so I did not claw at him as I wanted. His forehead pressed to the back of my head as I hung limply in his arms. The fight left me with another wave of exhaustion.

Waves lapped at our feet. The wide bow of a black boat sliced through the thick mist. Ren had sent me with the one person he knew he could trust most: the demigod who had willingly laid his life on the line to save me. Drystan froze, his grip loosening around my waist as I steadied myself on my feet, his hands rising to rest on my shoulders.

"Are we dead?" he murmured as the boat turned to dock.

I shook my head, my voice coming out in a rasp. "No, we are not dead."

The blue light of the flame over the bow of the boat swung, illuminating the sunken features of Vakarys as she dug her punt into the water, anchoring to the shore.

"*Myhn lathira*," she croaked, placing a hand over the ruined shell of her heart and dipping her head.

I thought perhaps I knew how she felt now as I stumbled aboard, barely managing to greet her in the old language. The mist thickened around us. My nostrils flared as I breathed deep—as if I could imbibe this small piece of Ren's remaining magic the space where my heart had been. The bond we had only recently forged was brittle, weaker than it had been even when I crossed the threshold into Aethera. My power was aware that Ren's soul hung somewhere in the balance between life and death, waiting for his resurrection, but I could not reach him.

"*Myhn Lathira...*" Drystan whispered, stumbling over the language as he followed with a heavy limp. "What does that mean?"

I did not answer, too tired to do anything but sink to my knees. The boards, crusted with ice, stuck to the bloodied fabric of my dress and the bare skin of my ankles. I did not try to tug free, only stared at the flat edge of the boat as Vakarys pushed us away from the black river rocks. The water bubbled as countless mottled bodies in states of decay pushed close to the boat to shepherd us across.

"Where are the others?" I asked, voice soft, moving my attention to the back of Vakarys's black cowl as she dipped the staff into the water.

"Waiting." A skeletal hand rose, barely more than bone, to gesture to the dark land blossoming into view.

Each time I closed my eyes, it was Ren I could see so clearly now, the image burned into the back of my lids. Resignation to his fate written all over his face. Our vow the final words upon his lips. A hum of agony rumbled in my chest while rage bubbled beneath my skin.

In the quiet of the mist, I thought again of the way my shadows had changed in the throne room. The satisfied smile that had curled across Typhon's lips, superimposed upon the water shepherds at the edge of the boat. Somehow, he had taken my power. Taken it and harnessed it against me. The ring was the key—the ring and the chains.

I could only hope once Ren resurrected he would be able to escape and my power would be enough to stitch him back together from whatever he lost in this new death. And if he could not escape, then it meant devising a plan to sneak into Aethera to find where Typhon was keeping him. We'd spoken enough of his power for me to know that he revived wherever his body was left, which surely meant Typhon would keep him under lock and key.

Slowly, Vakarys turned the boat, sliding the bow toward the rocky shore where Horace and Dimitri waited. I took one step off the boat, then another, stumbling on the rocks before Dimitri caught me, shushing me as I clung to him, the words spilling out of what Typhon had done.

"He will resurrect, and we will find him."

I nodded, extricating myself from his hold, giving Horace a grateful nod as he held me by the elbow.

"Dimitri..." Drystan breathed, footsteps clunky against the shore.

Ren's second-in-command froze, eyes—the same size and shape as my guard's—widening before he rushed forward to fling himself into Drystan's arms.

"Tell me you do not come here for judgment," Dimitri cried, face pressed into his throat. "Tell me you are not bound to these shores."

Drystan cupped the back of his head, eyes glassy before they closed. "I am not."

When Dimitri pulled back, he cupped the demigod's cheeks tenderly. His shoulders rose and fell with heavy breaths, and though grief clung like tar to my heart, there was a small spark of warmth at this reunion.

"It is good to see you, Brother," Dimitri said.

Brothers. Twins. Separated by death and now brought together by ruin. Drystan murmured in kind while they broke apart. Dimitri turned in a swirl of his cloak to press his hand to his heart and dip his chin respectfully.

"*Myhn lathira.*"

Horace repeated the words before gesturing toward the looming castle in the distance, a silent invitation toward home.

"How did you know to wait for me here?" I asked, gazing up into the ruby-flecked gaze of the God of Judgment.

The corners of his mouth hardened, a flicker of pain flashing over his face as he tapped his chest with two fingers. "Ren felt you through your soul bond. It was enough to tell us to be prepared."

Tears burned my eyes, but I nodded. Drystan was close at my back, a hand wrapped protectively around my shoulders.

"Will we be safe here?" he asked, his other falling to his hip where his sword usually rested.

Horace's brows pulled together in confusion. "Of course, you will, friend."

"Trust him," I encouraged, placing a gloved hand over Drystan's, patting when he did not relax. "And if you do not trust him, trust in me."

But he did not relax, even when Dimitri murmured that all would be well. I frowned at the sentiment, unsure if it was the truth. Something was *wrong* as if the world was not as it should be. Those chains...the ring.

"We should not linger here," I said.

Quickly and quietly, we divided. Horace took Dimitri in hand, using his power to move him closer to the palace while I wrapped a hand over Drystan's and did the same.

A shiver skated down my spine as my shadows swallowed us, the reminder of what Ren had sacrificed thrown in my face. I swallowed back the lump in my throat as the castle melted into view when I pushed us through the dark. The high towers and darkened bones, once so horrifying, were now the only place I could call home.

In silence, we walked up the steep stairway into the antechamber, Horace and Dimitri falling back to allow me to enter first. There was a rumbling from the throne room, voices sliding beneath the heavy onyx doors I stopped in front of. One deep breath, then another. Heat pricked at the corners of my eyes, and my knuckles bleached white against my bloody gown.

But I did not want to change. No, let my people see the horror Typhon had wrought.

"Oralia," Drystan murmured. "Wait, we need to discuss—"

"Later," I cut across him, not sparing a glance for my guard as he was held back by his brother.

Later, we would talk. Later, I would tell him all that had transpired from my time in Infernis and apologize for continuing the charade in his presence. The doors groaned, sliding apart with a whisper of my power. and blue flame light poured across my face.

The throne room was not as full as it had been for our soul-bonding ceremony. Perhaps only a dozen or so gods, demigods, and souls gathered around, speaking quietly to one another. Ren's inner circle—*our* inner circle. At once, all turned to us. The familiar faces were a balm on the wounds pulsing through my chest and yet not enough to calm the rising grief.

He will resurrect.

He will return.

I did not hesitate as I strode into the room and tugged off my gloves—nor did I think of Drystan behind me as all dropped to their knees. No, I could only think of the first time I'd been brought through these doors, sure Ren had been my enemy, and had witnessed his people do the same for him.

Each being murmured my title, hands pressing over their hearts, and I took the time to touch each soul in turn while being sure to avoid the living. My fingertips passed over shoulders or brows, a small zing of peace flaring through them as I did.

"What..." Drystan repeated.

Slowly, I turned, surrounded by my subjects, all bowing. I was closest to Sidero—one I counted as a friend above all else and I placed a hand on their shoulder.

"I am *Lathira na Thurath*," I explained with an apology in my gaze for the secrets I'd kept.

There was something like heartbreak in his eyes as Drystan looked me over with an unfamiliarity—as though I was someone new standing before him.

"What...what does that mean?" he eventually managed.

It was Dimitri who stepped forward, encouraging Drystan down on one knee with a hand on his shoulder, head bent low to his brother's ear.

"She is the Queen of Infernis."

CHAPTER

EIGHT

Oralia

Q*ueen..."* Drystan breathed.

I nodded, sagging with the weight of the night, but Sidero stood before I could stumble, placing a hand on my elbow. Their kind face was tense with worry before they turned to catch Thorne's eye. Everyone rose to their feet as Thorne cut through the crowd with his large shoulders. His bright red beard twitched with his frown. Morana, the God of Night, followed close behind. Her ice-blue eyes were intent upon my face, and my stomach churned to realize she did not appear surprised.

The night had told her this day would come.

"May I?" Thorne asked, raising his hands to gesture at the gashes along my throat.

A muscle twitched in my jaw. "Later." I turned, leaning heavier on Sidero than I wanted to take the few steps up the dais so I could look upon Ren's people.

My people.

Our people.

"Typhon has slain our king." The words were hollow, an echo of the grief slinking through my chest. A murmur slithered through the crowd. "Now he keeps Ren locked within Aethera to be held prisoner upon his resurrection."

I took a deep breath, steadying my shaking hands. This was all too soon—too much. Ren should be here. Ren would know what to say, how to rally his people, and how to strengthen Infernis's borders. I was an impostor in his place, merely a placeholder for the god who truly ruled this kingdom.

"I do not expect you to fight...or for those of you who can leave these lands to infiltrate Aethera." My gaze flickered from Horace to Thorne to Morana, to the other gods I barely knew within the room. A tall, willowy god with golden skin and eyes like citrine gems I'd seen only a few times gazed back at me with something like approval in his gaze and flames dancing over his fingertips. "I only prepare you that soon Typhon will be at our door, and we must do what we can to fight and retrieve our king."

Dimitri stepped to the edge of the dais, withdrawing his sword and balancing it in both hands. Morana was the next to follow, the blackness of night curling between her palms, sharpening into a star-tipped spear. Thorne was next with his short dagger and Horace with his scythe I rarely saw. One by one, until Drystan was the last standing, his face struck with horror-laced confusion.

"I will not ask you to fight or pick a side," I murmured only for him.

Sadness crumpled Drystan's face, light catching on the glass of his eyes. He shook his head slowly, taking a step forward. "There is no side but yours."

Dimitri shifted, allowing Drystan space to kneel. The sight of it sent strange empty chord thrumming through my chest as he raised his empty hands.

"You are my sovereign as you are my child, my queen as you are my daughter," he whispered, emotion thick in his voice. "I do not understand how this has happened, and I will need answers. But regardless of how this came about, I will follow you to the ends of this world and beyond. Merely place a sword within my grasp."

His face blurred as I blinked back tears. I wanted to rush into his arms, to have him hold me as he had when I had been merely a child terrified of a storm. Drystan was right—he was the only father I had ever known. I swallowed and nodded once before gesturing with an open palm for all to rise. The sight of so many powerful beings on their knees before me was...*wrong*. I might have been their queen, but I was no match for their power.

The doors swung wide, heavy footsteps rang through the room before Mecrucio and Aelestor skittered around the corner. They were breathless, hair wild and cheeks ruddy. Aelestor's cloak streamed behind him with his speed. Mecrucio's eyes were glassy as both gods closed the distance between us, falling to their knees and pressing their foreheads to my bloody feet.

Mecrucio gasped. Beside him, Aelestor was silent, but his shoulders shook with grief. Slowly, I tugged back on my gloves and crouched, placing one hand on Mecrucio's shoulders, and the other on the back of Aelestor's head, shushing them even as my throat burned. Horace appeared at Mecrucio's side, running a gentle hand through his curls.

"I offer you my life, Your Grace, for you to exact your vengeance upon," Mecrucio murmured, pressing a kiss to my ankle. "I have failed you both."

"I have no need for vengeance against my own," I answered, gripping his shoulder until he looked up. His eyes were bloodshot, face pale. "Why do you say such things?"

The God of Travelers licked his cracked lips, glittering tears pooling at the corners of his eyes before spilling down his cheeks. "Because our king is gone."

"For now," Horace said gently. "He will—"

"*No*," Aelestor cut across him, fingers gripping the bloodied hem of my gown while Mecrucio fumbled for something in his cloak. "You do not understand."

I blinked, a buzz filling my ears as Mecrucio withdrew a familiar black box and the air thinned. His hands shook as he proffered it toward me. It was the same as the one Typhon had received in the throne room. My power shied away from it even as my heart beat in my chest, the thrumming of the absent soul bond moving me closer.

"Tell me what you know," I commanded, the words coming out in a rasp.

Aelestor sobbed. The sound was so pure in its grief, fresh tears dripped down my face.

Mecrucio's throat clicked with a swallow. He held the box higher, but I did not touch it. "Typhon is not keeping Ren within the castle. He...he has—" He cleared his throat.

It was Aelestor who finished for him in halting tones. "Ren was ripped apart, piece by piece, and scattered across this world."

A moan slipped through my lips, and I fell back onto the step, horror creeping around my throat. My magic pulsed, shadows flared in time with the beating of my heart. I shook my head, a negation on my tongue before Mecrucio's eyes caught mine.

"He will not return. His magic requires a complete vessel to resurrect."

Dimitri's face paled. "But his wings—"

The last time Ren had died, his wings had been stripped from him and he had returned.

"His wings are a mark of our kind," Horace explained. "A mark of a timeless god. They were made before this world truly began, and once removed, they cannot be regrown. He can resurrect without them, but he cannot reanimate *from* them. They are outside of our realm and all that grows."

Mecrucio nodded, pushing the box forward, but I did not take it, and after a second he slid it over my knee.

"What is it?" I asked.

The god closed a hand over my forearm, lifting my wrist to place my palm upon the box. There was old magic imbued within this box. It danced across my skin the moment it made contact, calling out to me as kindred. All was silent in the room save for the beating of my heart and the rushing of blood in my ears. With trembling fingertips, I pulled back the lid, bile rising thick in my throat.

Nestled within the black silk lay a heart, perfect in its form, pulsing with a soft and imperceptible rhythm. I made some sort of noise, one I thought only daemoni made, before I closed the lid, shaking so violently Horace reached forward to take it from me.

"How did you get this?" My voice was hoarse.

Aelestor ran a hand over his tear-stained face. "Typhon wanted it sent to you so you might feel some sort of...hope."

Hope. The word curdled in my chest. Aelestor's bloodshot eyes were fixed on my face as he reached out to grip my gloved hands.

"Typhon knew I would want to return to Josette, and he ordered me to bring the box to you. I am sorry, Oralia, so deeply sorry."

His shoulders shook with his renewed grief, fingers falling from mine to the floor. I could only stare at him in mute horror. This was a game to Typhon. He had sent me my mate's heart as a taunt.

My breaths came quicker, magic flaring deep within my chest. Rising to my feet, I took one step away, then another, and another. I could not be here. I could not bear witness to the grief at my feet and comfort this god when I was dying inside. Shadows flared around my shoulders and my neck. I squeezed my eyes shut, taking another stumbling step back, only to find myself beneath the wide yew tree Ren and I would travel to so I could learn my power. My throat gurgled as acid sliced through my chest, the shadows around my shoulders thickening until they were as dark as night, as endless as oblivion.

Ren was gone, scattered across the world like leaves in autumn.

He would not resurrect. He would not stride from beneath this tree with his hands in his pockets and a smile on his lips.

I lay my heart in your hands.

My scream echoed off the glittering mountains as if there were hundreds locked within this grief. It was sticky, like tar, devouring me inch by inch until I could not breathe. I clawed at my chest, my hair. My knees cracked against the stones beneath my feet. I was blind within the dark. Icy fire skittered across my arms, threaded through my fingers, churned through my ribs. My power yawned, flooding my senses, and I found I could not find fear.

The darkness nourishes.

The darkness protects.

The darkness wipes the slate clean.

I spread my arms wide and allowed my power to consume me in the hopes that perhaps I would find my mate on the other side.

CHAPTER
NINE

Renwick

Stars.

So many of them I could not keep count. They twinkled brightly all around me, even beneath my feet.

I ran a hand over my face and moved through this strange space. There was no pain here, no hollow throb within my chest. There was none of the coldness of resurrection. It was also not the strange place I usually found myself in while my soul waited for my body to revive. No bright colors or scent of spices on the air—no long-forgotten god I never spoke of there to share my pain with.

Though it was unfamiliar, I thought I recognized the magic flowing through the air, the hum of power vibrating against my skin. A star shot across the sky to my left, a beacon of light flaring across the dark before dying out. My feet carried me in slow steps toward the dying star as I tapped my chest, searching deep within my power for an echo of the bond.

It was there, but silent, a string hanging limp within eternity.

I could not pluck the cord, nor follow it to Oralia. Instead, it was merely the acknowledgment of our bond, the understanding that should we be reunited, it too would live on.

Memories came back slowly through flashes of pain and bright light. The agony of the arrows piercing my skin. The last breath of my magic pushed out to carry Oralia through the mist along with her guard, who I knew would protect her with his life. Mecrucio and Aelestor would need to stay hidden within Aethera so they could pass information to Oralia and the others.

Her face swam behind my lids, the blood splattered across her cheeks, pale lips drawn back as she screamed my name. But I did not want to carry the horrible memory. Not when so much of my existence was nothing but ice and violence and blood. I would not allow Typhon to destroy this too.

And so, instead, I remembered the look on her face as she'd strode into my rooms, hair wild and skin flushed. Her sapphire dress had clung to the curve of her waist, her bitten lips were pink, and her fingers tangled in front of her skirts.

I want you, Ren, she had said. Her first admission of her feelings for me.

That was the memory I would carry, not her horror as her mate was wrenched limb from limb.

Soft grass appeared beneath me. The sweet scent of it heavy on the air with each step. The night was dark, casting the grass and the forest beyond into shadow. These woods were unlike any I'd seen in millennia—a forest so thick one could not walk in a straight line. I slipped through the trunks, learning their rough texture and trailing my fingers across the soft spines dripping from branches.

I thought perhaps I knew this place from my childhood if one could call it such a thing when time had not yet been created. It was an era of my existence I struggled to quantify as events did not move in a linear fashion but merely overlapped one on top of the other. It was a sense of *being* and an acknowledgment of those around me— gods who had survived after the Great Mothers created the first moment and others who had been lost to us through creation, never to be seen again.

The dense forest lightened as I walked, untouched by thirst or fatigue, as it had been before time. I stepped between two thick trunks, finding a wide clearing with a single fallen tree cast within as if its fellows were in mourning. The bark was rough beneath my palm and dry save for the moss climbing up one side.

Was this to be my existence now: an endless wandering through this forest until I grew mad with grief? I sighed, squatting down to observe the decay rotting through the bark against the grass. Relief swam through my veins.

Decay meant time. I was not beyond it. Though I was somewhere else, I still *was*. Which meant, perhaps, there was a way out.

"I do not know if there is a way out," a voice murmured.

I jolted to my feet. My heartbeat hammered in my veins while I spun toward the voice. My throat clenched and I stumbled toward a woman with long black hair waving around her face, a gentle smile pulling at the corners of her mouth. Silvery wings flared behind her, each flutter sending shimmering light into the sky. She held out her luminous pale arms, fingers spread wide as stars dripped from her palms.

And though I was taller than she, I fell into her embrace as a boy might while she cradled the back of my head tenderly. She made a comforting sound, rocking me from side to side. I gripped her tightly for another heartbeat before pulling back to touch her cheeks and gaze into her eyes—the same size and shape as mine. She did the same, pushing back my hair as she drank me up as greedily as I did her.

"*Maelith*," I breathed.

The smile on her face was sad as she touched the space between my brows.

"Oh, my son...what ruin you and your brother have wrought."

CHAPTER
TEN

Oralia

If I had experienced this feeling before Ren was destroyed, I would have called it pain, agony perhaps. Now I could only observe it with an empty detachment as my power ripped me from the inside out, my cries breaking off and darkness swallowed me. Icy fire tore through my limbs. My bones broke only to mend again. My body was and was not. Pain existed and yet was intangible.

All at once, the pain vanished as I fell to my knees. Wood groaned beneath my weight, warm beneath my palms from the sunlight streaming overhead. Nothing hurt. There was no agony—no exhaustion. But the light was too bright as it played across my clean hands, and when I lifted my head, I had to shield my eyes from the way it rippled across vibrant water.

Before me, a dock extended out over the bright blue sea, where a few large ships were moored. Grand, vast ships, the kind I had read some humans built within their world to traverse the oceans and conquer new lands.

I blinked as if it might change the vision. Slowly, I reached down, dipping my hand into the water. It was warm, like a bath, lapping at my fingers with the waves from the ships. Yet it did not feel real. My body was too light and at the same time so heavy I struggled to rise to my feet. When I turned, the movement was both fast and slow as if time did not behave the same.

The city before me bustled with activity and was filled with bright colors, down to the humans who wove through stalls piled with wares. The mountain above was crammed with building upon building, painted in different designs and hues like a vast field of wildflowers.

Yet, for all the countless humans who rushed past me, not one noticed me. I slid a hand down my gown, only to realize it was not bloodstained. No, in its place was soft white fabric, gathered at each shoulder with bright gold pins before falling to my feet. When I lifted the skirt, it was to find leather straps across my feet, holding thick soles protecting me from the rough wood beneath.

Panic spiked, and my heart thrummed in my chest so hard it echoed in the crooks of my elbows. I fisted the fabric of the dress tighter, my knees threatened to buckle, and I squeezed my eyes shut. If this was a dream, then I could wake. I could force myself to open my eyes.

"Breathe," a deep voice soothed.

When I opened them, it was to find a man beside me, black hair like a waterfall around his shoulders and chest, save for a bright white streak framing the left side of his face. I startled, stepping back, only for him to catch me by the wrist with a scarred hand. His beauty was disarming and yet heartbreaking. Though there was a strange film through which I saw this world, he was clear.

"It takes a moment to settle," he encouraged, thumb running once over the thin skin of my wrist before letting go. "Take a breath."

I shook my head, rubbing my tingling wrist from where he'd held it, and found I could not breathe. He touched my shoulder, encouraging me to turn back toward the boats.

"Count the masts." His scarred hand pointed toward the large sails before us.

My brows furrowed, and though I called to my magic, I could not find it. Yet it was unlike when Typhon had clapped me in chains. I could sense my magic was there, only it could not reach me through this dream. So I took a breath, counting the masts with him as he pointed to each in turn until my breathing slowed.

The man nodded, and his eyes glowed bright through a half-skull mask fitted snugly across the top half of his face. Power rolled off him in waves as ancient and unknown as the magic that had clung to the box with Ren's heart in it, yet it was not the same. This magic felt kindred to mine like Ren's did.

His lips pursed as he caught me assessing him. The scarred left side of his mouth pulled taut from the movement. "It has been a while since one of you graced this world."

I cleared my throat. The slowing beat of my heart picked up speed again. "And what world is that?"

The god shrugged, gesturing with an open palm toward the bright buildings beyond. "This is the city of Yesinda, the capital of the country of Mycelna."

I blinked, following the journey of a woman swathed in white robes, a diaphanous veil over her face held in place by many tinkling chains. Every few feet, she was stopped by another human, appearing to listen intently before dipping the tip of her finger into a small bowl she carried in the palm of her hand and pressing it to their brow.

"There are so many humans..."

He gave a hum of agreement. "This entire world is made up of humans. You are quite far from home."

I whirled on him, pain pricking across my palms as my hands fisted. "Then how do I get home?" When he did not answer, my voice rose in volume. "Who are you?"

The god smiled, and the sight of it sent my heart to aching. It was a smile I thought I had seen on Ren's face—the echo of a millennia of suffering, of coming to understand the meaning of the world through agony and heartache.

"I am the scythe in the hands of my queen. I am not the harvest, but the vessel that carries the grain."

My brows furrowed. "I do not understand."

He shrugged, and with the movement, his mask disappeared, eyes flaring before dimming to a normal brightness. The right was a similar shade of midnight to Ren's, but the left? The left shone a milky white, the scars of his face creeping around his brow into his hairline.

What could have done such damage to a god?

"You have no such god within your world because I am here. We are the cast-offs who fell to the wayside when time began."

Ren had spoken of such things—of gods in other realms who possessed powers beyond our understanding. I'd also been told stories of the gods humans worshipped within their world.

"He never told you?" the god asked with lifted brows.

I licked my lips, throat dry. "Who?"

But I already knew, didn't I? There could only be one *he* this god referred to.

The god before me smiled so sadly at me, it pricked the corners of my eyes. "This is the land Renwick's soul travels to when he dies, called here by the souls of the dead who await my reaping or my queen's judgment."

Grief burned through my throat. "Is...is he here?"

The god shook his head, hair spilling across his chest. "He is not."

Perhaps that meant then that he was not dead...or he was already resurrected. And yet, I knew it could not be true. The pieces of his body were spread far and wide. His heart lay within a box in Infernis. It would take centuries, perhaps even millennia, for those pieces to find their way back together if allowed or for him to regenerate from the heart in the box.

My magic had brought me here for a reason. I could feel it, even if it was merely a dream.

So I cleared my throat, wiping quickly at my cheeks. "He is destroyed."

A soft, warm chuckle curled around my face as a scarred hand covered mine. He placed it in the crook of his arm before guiding me through the crowd.

"He is not destroyed," the god answered. "Merely waiting."

I ground my heels into the dirt, ripping my hand from his arm. "You cannot know that."

We paused to allow a man to pass, a wide plate piled high with fragrant spices balanced upon his head. Nearby, two soldiers ducked from one of the stalls, identical in their features, with closely cropped black hair and silver markings on their skin. The brother snatched a fruit from his sister's grasp, peeling it quickly before stuffing a wedge between his lips. I caught a grumble from the woman in a language I could not understand as she raised her fist in retaliation.

When all was quiet once more, the god sighed. "I know many things. My magic speaks to me as yours does. The fates are even louder in my ears, telling me the truth of my words."

With a shake of my head, I made to turn away from him but his hands closed over my shoulders, and he crouched so we were eye to eye.

"I know what it is to wait, Oralia." My mouth popped open at his knowledge of my name. "I know what it is to feel a bond that has not been sealed, to ache for a mate who is out of reach. For the world around you to fall into chaos and yet you must stand in one place."

I squeezed my eyes shut, blocking the sincerity dripping from each word. "Is that what this world is? One of chaos?"

The god straightened, and I chanced a glance at him as his mismatched eyes roved around us. "Soon, yes, this world will be one of chaos and sickness and pain, proscribed by the fates. But for now, it is merely the beginning of such suffering."

My stomach gave a lurch. My attention caught on a mother swathed in bright pink robes, a baby swaddled against her chest dozing against her shoulder.

"Why?"

He laughed, shaking his head. "You are not asking the right questions. You are running as you always have."

I clenched my teeth, fighting back the flare of anger. He was right, of course. I was allowing myself to worry for people I did not know instead of facing my failures.

"I do not know what to do."

With a noise of understanding, he straightened, moving me forward with a light hand on my arm. We wound our way through the serpentine streets, dipping beneath vines heavy with white frothy flowers and climbing the steep staircase up one side of the mountain. Each step was more dreamlike than the last—the colors a bit too bright, the sounds of the city a touch too loud. I followed the god, frowning when we paused before a door fashioned from jagged rock. As a human might, he grasped the handle and opened it without effort, ushering me inside.

The room was vast with small alcoves filled with stone tables and tiny fragrant fires spiraling smoke toward the high ceiling. In the center of the room, a statue stood as tall as the chamber itself, a heavy shroud obscuring it from view. But we did not pause before the statue as many within the temple did. Instead, we made our way toward one of the alcoves and stopped before one of the stone counters where a wide bowl filled with ash lay.

"Tell me what happened to Ren," he murmured as if he was being mindful of the humans who roved the chamber. Some were outfitted with strange delicate chains around their face and shoulders. The same diaphanous veils hid their faces from view.

I swallowed, the story raw within my throat as I explained Typhon's wrath and the fate that had befallen us. The god's face fell into the perfect expression of compassion as if he too understood such agony.

"I do not know what to do," I repeated, hands spread before me. The dark scars on my wrists caught in the candlelight.

"Can a god be mended?" he asked, a scarred fingertip tracing the bowl of ash.

It was only then I realized his fingers were all tipped with black as if he had dipped them within a vat of ink.

My chest panged, and I swallowed the dread creeping up my throat. "I...I do not know."

His smile was sad as he tilted his head back and forth before pressing his palm into the bowl. "I think you do. Only, you are too afraid to hope."

Could a god be mended? Ren had once hoped he could be reunited with his wings—he wore his heavy cloak to keep him strong so he might take flight again. I had never heard of such a thing, but he was convinced if he reopened the wounds he could be restored.

"Perhaps..." I breathed.

The god nodded, fingers digging into the ash. "Then perhaps, he could be restored if you were to find all the pieces."

I frowned. "He has been scattered far throughout my world. To find him would be like—"

"Finding a golden thread within a haystack. But through your bond, you could find a way."

A shudder rippled through me. "Our bond is brittle now, broken by his destruction. It..." My throat thickened, and I stared, unseeing at the flickering candle before us. I breathed slowly through my nose to calm the rising grief threatening to sweep me out to sea. "It is one-sided."

The god before me looked so sad. I wondered what he had meant by his words before. If he too had suffered the loss of a mate.

"You have a key if you are brave enough to use it," he answered, his voice heavy with pain. Ashes poured from between his fingers as he lifted his hand, but a black heart rested within his scarred palm. "If you are brave enough to take within yourself a piece of him to link you together. Blood of your blood, soul of your soul."

I lay my heart in your hands.

"What do I do?"

"You rise and begin again."

The god tipped his wrist, the heart crumbling into ash to fall back into the bowl. His black-tipped fingers rose to press between my brows.

"Wake up, Oralia."

CHAPTER

ELEVEN

Oralia

I woke to the light of a muted dawn rising over the tops of the Tylith Mountains.

For a few moments, I lay gazing up at the brightening sky. The mist was heavy around my shoulders before I rolled to a seat. I gave my head an experimental shake, trying to quantify the strange feeling thrumming through my bones. My hands flexed, then relaxed, the wounds angry and raw upon my wrists and throat. Somehow, I was here. I was alive.

And yet, I knew what I had seen was more than a simple dream. The god's hand on my arm had been too real. The scents of the city—Yesinda, he called it, in the country of Mycelna—were too clear. My magic had taken my consciousness there for a purpose. Now I had to understand why.

It took me a little longer to make my way to my feet, sluggish from the kratus resin working through my system. But I managed eventually to stand, reaching out a tentative hand to my power, which greeted me with relief before shepherding me home through the in-between.

I appeared in our chambers with a sigh that turned into a strangled groan. Ren was everywhere. His presence dripped from every surface, and each sight was a stab through the heart. A dark cloak thrown over one of the dark-winged chairs, a pair of scuffed boots beside the door, both physical reminders of what I had lost. The air thinned, hands clamped around my throat, and I could no longer find the space I needed to breathe.

My fingers are tangled in front of me, nails digging at my palms. A strange rustling in the room I realized a moment later was the sound of my breath scratching at my throat. Blood flaked off my skin when I twisted my head, and I squeezed my eyes shut as if I could hide from even the scent of him lingering here. My bones filled with lead. My knees weakened with the weight until I staggered, catching myself on one of the chairs and running my fingers over the soft fabric of his cloak.

How could I live and yet feel such agony? No, this feeling was *beyond* agony. It was despair without end, a great yawning ocean I did not know how to swim. Surely, I would die from this. Any moment now the darkness would take hold to send my magic back to the earth. And yet the darkness did not come, my magic did not rise, and his cloak merely bunched beneath my palms as any ordinary piece of clothing.

"Oralia." Sidero's voice was soft. Softer still was their hand pressed between my shoulders, turning me toward their wide chest.

They wrapped me tightly in their embrace, holding me as if it might prevent me from falling to pieces. I clung to them, even going so far as to wrap a hand around their braid as if it might keep me anchored here to this place.

"I wish I had your power...that I could offer you some semblance of the peace you have offered others."

I did not reply. There was no need. Because until Ren was restored, I would never know peace, and Sidero knew it. We did not speak another word as we parted. In the same silence, they guided me into the bathing chamber, offering a hand into the steaming tub. Not even as they helped me cleanse my wounds did we fill the quiet with our usual chatter. The stinging pain of cleansing each cut was a mere wisp of a cloud passing over an endless sky in comparison to the storm raging through my heart.

It was not until the day had fully broken outside the tall windows that I spoke from my seat on the edge of Ren's side of the bed. I pressed my hand to his pillow. His scent here was faint as if he had not slept in days. Timeless gods did not need sleep, though it helped to refresh them in times of great stress, or so Ren had explained. But I touched my pillow only to realize his scent was stronger here as if he'd chosen my side of the bed as I now chose his.

Sidero was puttering around the room, but all I wanted them to do was to sit with me, to breathe here in this empty space.

"Leave it," I said, my voice a bit too harsh as they reached for Ren's cloak.

They froze, hand only a hair's breadth away from the cloak before it fell. I exhaled, shoulders slumping and chin dropping to my chest. I had slept the whole day and night at the base of the mountains, and yet I could sleep for another century.

"Tell me what you need." They drifted toward the bed and covered my hand with theirs. "Give me a task, Oralia."

Their voice broke on the last request, some of their grief cracking the words. I took a deep breath, shook my head to clear it, and squeezed their fingers once.

"Would you please gather Horace, Thorne, Aelestor, Mecrucio, Dimitri, and Drystan if it's not too much trouble?" I traced the seam of the pillowcase with my free hand. "I would like to meet with them in the library."

By the time I dressed and reached the library, everyone was assembled. Horace stood by the mantel with a hand resting on the dark wood as he stared into the flames with Mecrucio beside him. Thorne leaned over one of the tall chairs, speaking quietly to Dimitri, who stood on the other side with a hand wrapped around Drystan's shoulder. But it was Aelestor who stood closest to the door as if waiting for my arrival. Sidero was beside him.

"Where were you?" Aelestor asked the moment I appeared, striding forward to assess the now-healing wounds with gray eyes.

My chin jutted higher. "At the base of the Tylith. I needed some... time."

Something in Aelestor softened at the tight expression on my face. His arms dropped from his chest. But Drystan stepped between us, full brows furrowed. He paid no attention to the God of Storms at his back, who huffed quietly about how we were *in the middle of something,* as Drystan tentatively brushed the hair back from my cheek. I knew the action was strange for him, regardless of fact that the power to turn the living to ash only lived in my hands. For two and a half centuries, this sort of affection had been forbidden.

"*Burning Suns*, Oralia, I was so worried," he breathed, resting his hands on my shoulders.

For a moment, a muscle in his jaw ticked, and though I wanted to collapse within myself, I did not. Instead, I nodded once, moving into his embrace with a sigh.

"You are queen," he murmured as if I alone could hear.

I nodded against his chest. "I am."

Drystan's sigh swirled the hair around my face and he drew back. "When you left Aethera the first time, was it of your own free will? Did you know of Renwick?"

Confusion played across his features, heavy brows drawing together. In his eyes—a demigod pushing a millennium, I now realized, if Dimitri was his brother—I was still a child of five he would sling up onto his shoulders. My time in Infernis for him had been merely a blink of an eye and yet also an eternity.

"No, I was not taken of my own free will. But throughout my time here, Ren and I were drawn to each other. Our magic is...kindred."

My throat burned. I cleared it, squeezing my eyes shut as if it might stop the images rolling through my mind. A clearing. Asphodel flowers. The first time Ren said my name.

Drystan did not look angry, nor did he look concerned. Instead, there was merely a heavy sort of pain lingering in the corners of his eyes. Perhaps it was regret that I had not trusted him enough to keep my secret.

"Kindred," he repeated. "And so Renwick is..."

"He is my mate. We soul-bonded a little over a week ago."

A slight flush crept through his cheeks, eyes taking on a glassy quality before he sniffed. "I would have liked to see that."

I did my best to give him a small smile. "I would have liked you there."

Finally, I pulled away, squeezed his fabric-covered shoulder once, and stepped around him toward Ren's inner circle. They all looked haggard as if the last few days had been agonizing—and *stars,* they probably had. I was unsure what would happen to Infernis if both Ren and I were gone.

But it was to Mecrucio and Aelestor I looked, holding each of their gazes for a long moment before I spoke the words I'd heard Ren say countless times.

"Tell me what you know."

CHAPTER

TWELVE

Oralia

"Typhon has found a weapon," Aelestor said at once.

My chin dropped, and Drystan huffed a humorless laugh. From the way Typhon had somehow twisted my shadows, I'd assumed as much.

"You are unsurprised?" Mecrucio asked, brows ticking up.

Pursing my lips, I nodded, gesturing between myself and Drystan. "I believe we received a firsthand demonstration of the weapon."

"According to the gossip of the soldiers, it is something ancient," Aelestor offered. "Though none save Hollis know exactly where it is from. Some believe Typhon has contacted the gods on Iapetos, while others think he slipped through the veil of the realms and into the human world."

Each was as unlikely as the next. Iapetos was the island most of the timeless gods had fled to when Daeymon—Ren and Typhon's father—had shut Asteria up into the first kratus tree. It was said to be impossible to reach unless the gods granted you favor, much like Infernis.

Though now, of course, Typhon had found a way through. Perhaps he had done the same with Iapetos.

"What is its purpose within this war?" When neither answered, I pressed on. "What is the purpose of this weapon?"

"To take Infernis," Aelestor murmured. "He has said if you will not be swayed, your death will allow him to put another in your place."

I shook my head, but Dimitri's huff rumbled through the room. "But such a thing takes time, centuries. He cannot know how and who Oralia's magic will manifest into when she reincarnates."

Aelestor's face paled, a greenish sheen dancing across his cheeks. When he swayed, I reached out to steady him with a hand on his shoulder.

"The weapon…it draws magic to itself. He believes it now has had a taste for hers. Should she die, it will call her magic to it, and he can use the weapon to place it in another body."

Drystan scoffed. "Lies."

"It is not a lie." Horace's arms lowered to his sides, and he exchanged a look with Thorne. "Daeymon was obsessed with creating such a weapon. He spent centuries working on a way to take another's power. It was how the first daemoni were made."

Nausea curled in my gut, and now I understood why Aelestor looked so sick.

Thorne nodded, tugging at the end of his beard in a nervous sort of way with a distant expression on his face. "Before he died, there were whispers he was close to finding a way. When Asteria was imprisoned and my mother and the other timeless gods left, I believe they stole most of his work in fear of what it might do in his hands."

I thought again of the ring Typhon had slipped on his finger and the dark metal chains that cut into my wrists. "And now it has been returned."

Aelestor nodded.

Mecrucio, silent through this exchange, cleared his throat. "We also know Typhon has found a way through the mist, though only a select few of his highest-ranking generals know the route. But he boasts of his ability to enter Infernis now, as if he is taunting you and Ren. And he brags of having allies '*beyond our borders,*' allies who have provided him power which '*transcends our understanding.*'"

With a frown, I turned toward Thorne, who oversaw our own soldiers and borders. He nodded, though his gaze was still distant with the past.

"Patrols of our border have been increased, Your Grace, and in the last day, many souls from Rathyra have approached asking to enlist into our ranks to better serve. I feel confident we will be able to protect our borders from any Aetheran who seeks to make their way through."

Drystan let out a small huff. "A single soldier, yes, but what about an army?"

Thorne frowned, but I had to agree with Drystan. Our ranks were perhaps two thousand strong, but Typhon's? Typhon had an army twice the size, perhaps more, all spread out through the world.

"We will prepare, Your Grace. We will be ready," Thorne answered.

"That is all we can do for now," I agreed before turning to Horace, steeling myself with a deep breath. "What of Ren's resurrection?"

He knew what I meant—what I could not bear to say aloud: could Ren resurrect with the pieces of himself strewn across the world? Horace crossed his arms over his chest, dipping his chin in thought. His ruby eyes danced across my face before falling again to the blue flames in the hearth.

"With time, the pieces would find their way back together if unencumbered, and he would revive. There is also a chance a new body would grow from his heart. But the process would take time, Oralia. Time we don't have."

Acid pooled in my gut. "How long?"

Slowly, his attention moved back to me, and for a moment, I was reminded that before me stood a timeless god, the same as Ren and Morana. Horace might not have wings as Ren and Typhon did, but his power manifested in other ways, like the brightness in his irises—the same as the scarred god I'd seen in my dreams.

"Centuries, perhaps longer. A millennium."

The corners of my eyes burned at the idea of so much time without Ren, time we did not have. "So we find the pieces."

"You might be strong enough—" Horace started.

"We find the pieces," I cut across him, raising a hand. I did not want to hear how I might be strong enough to get us through this war without him.

Aelestor ran a hand over his face before drawing back his copper curls into a twist at his nape. "But how? It would be like..."

His voice trailed off, and I nodded, repeating the words of the scarred god. "Like finding a golden thread in a haystack."

The God of Storms gave a hum of agreement, and around the room, they all shifted uncomfortably. The scarred god had spoken of how there was a way for our bond to be resealed—if I was brave enough to use it.

Though I had slept for so long, weariness curled around my shoulders, tangling with the threads of grief that lived in the space where our soul bond used to live. I pressed my hand to my chest as if it might stanch the invisible wound bleeding out.

"So for now, who returns to Aethera?" I gestured between Aelestor and Mecrucio.

Both froze.

"One of you must return, if not both. We need information, and Typhon must believe he has spies within Infernis."

It was Aelestor who moved first, gesturing toward Mecrucio. "He would be better suited to return. Typhon knows of my loyalty to Josette."

Josette, his human mate who resided within Rathyra, her memories only recently restored after drinking from the waters of forgetting—the Athal. It was the reason Aelestor had turned spy all those centuries ago: so he might have a chance to be in her presence, to build some new bond with the shell of what she had once been.

"And what of your loyalty to Infernis? To me?" The words were strange on my tongue. Yet, I knew these were the questions Ren would ask...so I asked them for him.

Aelestor blanched as if I'd slapped him. He took one step closer, spreading his hands wide and staring down at them as if he might find something there to offer me. "You have given me something I never hoped to receive, Oralia. You are the reason Josette remembers me, *loves* me. It is a mercy and a gift I can never even begin to repay. And beyond that?" He shook his head, laughing bitterly. "It does not serve me to betray you. I want Josette and nothing else. My loyalty lies with you, with Ren and Infernis. Without Infernis..."

He trailed off, eyes turning glassy. Without Infernis, there would be no reaching Josette. And who was to say what Typhon would do to those gentle souls if he were to somehow control these lands?

We stared at each other, a silent understanding passing between us. Aelestor would not offer me the flowery language of loyalty. He

74

would not fall to his knees to offer me his sword as the rest had when I'd arrived back covered in blood. But what he did offer was under-standing—the understanding which comes from being willing to sacrifice everything for the one you love.

I gave him one short nod and turned to Mecrucio. "Then it is you who will return to Aethera and Typhon. Find out all you can, delay what you can, and report back."

Mecrucio's expression darkened uncharacteristically, but he fell to his knees and pressed his hand to his heart. "I am yours to com-mand, Your Grace."

I managed a small smile, gesturing for him to rise. "Keep yourself safe."

The darkness in his features evaporated in the wake of the charm-ing smile he usually wore. "And you, *myhn lathira.*"

Without another word, he nodded to those in the room, lingering for a moment longer on Horace before he left in a swirl of his dark blue cloak.

In the silence, Drystan cleared his throat. "Who will you take with you to find these parts of Renwick?"

Some tight knot within me loosened at his question. It was some-thing I'd been considering for the last few hours. Sidero and Dimitri could not leave the boundary of Infernis, as they were souls. I could not take Horace or Thorne. They would need to care for the souls and prepare our borders in my absence.

"You and Aelestor," I answered, looking between them.

Aelestor ran a hand through his copper curls, worry tight in his expression. I knew he was thinking of the mistakes he'd made, the storm he'd created which had almost cost Caston his life, the count-less years of taking his anger out on me for the hand he'd been dealt.

Yet I trusted this god. We had reached an understanding within our short time in Infernis.

"Do you accept?"

Drystan murmured his acceptance immediately, but Aelestor's throat bobbed with a swallow. He dropped his hand before bowing his head once, placing a palm over his heart. "I will follow you to the ends of this world, *myhn lathira*."

Horace stood, a shimmer of white mist slithering around his palms before a familiar black box appeared, pressing it into my hands. "Go, rest, and we will speak more tomorrow. The ascension begins, and we will need your assistance in Ren's place."

The ascension... I held back a frown, a bubble of anxiety broke through the heavy weight in my chest.

Horace smiled gently. "I will guide you, Oralia, I promise."

With a nod, I allowed myself to be steered from the room by Sidero, Drystan following behind. But it was alone that I entered Ren's and my chambers and placed the black box on his bedside before crawling beneath the dark blue sheets. The muted light of day flared out the window as I stared at the box until I flipped it open.

Ren's heart was as perfect as if it had only recently been ripped from his chest, dark red and glistening in the drab afternoon glow of the mist. Each passing breath was another beat of Ren's heart, a reminder that somewhere his magic lived.

The heart was the key, but I must be brave. The scarred god had spoken of his intuition, guided by his magic, and how *the fates* spoke in his ear, though I did not understand the term. Slowly, I pushed myself up onto an elbow as the last of the light died from the window, the hearth in the room flaring to life with bright blue flames.

When I closed my eyes, I saw Ren standing beneath the Tylith

Mountains, cloak swirling around his feet, black waves of his hair caught in the wind. There was the sensation of his hand on my face, fingertips over my eyelids, thumb stroking my cheek. His was voice deep and low in my ear.

It is your fear you feel. The fear amplifies, the fear multiplies, and it is the fear you are a slave to...You are more powerful than you know.

With trembling hands, I lifted Ren's heart, cupping it reverently in my palms, and the action reminded me again of our vows as we bonded our souls. The tang of pomegranate, the way his eyes shone with love and relief at our union. My power, working through him, stitching together the lost pieces of himself while he mended the pieces of my broken heart.

Slowly, I brought my hands to my lips, iron splashing across my tongue.

I ate his heart.

And welcomed this small piece of him into my soul.

CHAPTER
THIRTEEN

Renwick

Unreal to stand face-to-face with my mother after so many millennia apart.

To gaze upon her wings and see them twitch, flare, and punctuate each word she spoke was like a dream. I could remember the innate movement, as instinctual as breathing—how it felt to stretch my wings wide and take to the air, to be *free*. And yet we were not free, here in this dark forest seated side by side on the fallen trunk of a tree, my hands wrapped in hers.

How much time had passed outside this place? Did she know how long she had been trapped here within this realm? I was afraid to ask—afraid to startle her with the thousands of years that had spanned since our last meeting. The final night when we'd taken to the skies, and she'd spoken of ruin, of mending the rift between myself and my brother was millennia ago.

Asteria had been dragged from her bed and locked up within the trunk of a tree by the god she had tried to convince me to protect from another who claimed to be our father. Typhon had loved her, or so I'd believed, and she had loved him fiercely as if he were her own.

"She has grown strong, your mate," my mother observed, thumb brushing like a whisper over my knuckles.

I could not help but smile. Oralia's face, furrowed in concentration, filled my mind—her shadows, darker than my own, spilling over her shoulders and flooding the air from her fingertips.

"I must find a way to return." I glanced down at our hands before letting hers go.

Asteria squeezed my fingers once before rising to her feet with a flare of her wings and extended a palm out to me. "Come."

We stepped through the trees, following a winding river covered in large boulders and mossy rocks. My legs burned from the steep climb up a towering mountain, capped with snow and fraught with icy wind, which could have lasted hours or minutes. And as we traveled, I could not help but wonder what it was I would lose when I eventually resurrected.

I could not accept that this was my existence now. I would return. I would find a way. But *stars*, what would I be when I woke? Would I be merely a hollow shell of who I had been? I feared all the love I cradled deep within my soul would leach from me with the resurrection until I was a cruel and icy thing—worse than even when Oralia and I first met.

She had told me she'd seen moments of warmth flare within me in those early days. Moments where she thought she saw the god who could instill such fervor and love within his inner circle, who would be worth fighting for. It had been her touch slowly working on me through the weeks, beginning with the first brush of her palm against my face within the throne room. Her desperate attempt to destroy *the Under King* in hope of release.

Eventually, Asteria and I descended the mountain, trekking through tall grasses and waving fields of reeds, ducking beneath the heavy branches of a willow tree.

"Do you know where you are?" she asked, releasing my hand.

It was dark beneath the tree, quiet and peaceful. I took a deep breath, reaching out with my magic, but I could find nothing that whispered of this place. Only the tree, the breeze, and somewhere farther the rushing of a stream.

"I do not," I answered.

"This is the in-between."

My brows furrowed. The in-between was the darkness in which we traveled when shadow-walking, the twilight space between sleeping and waking. In all of my existence, I had never known it to be anything other than the brief moment where the world bent to connect two places. "I have never seen this before."

Asteria nodded, circling the wide trunk of the tree. "You move too fast within this space to see it for what it is. For you, it is merely the road you travel to get to your next destination. A physical body cannot exist for long within this plane. But this is where I have resided since your father and brother shut me up in that tree thousands of years ago. Not my body, but my mind, my *magic*."

So she did know how much time had passed.

"No one lives here, save me and the occasional visitor. It took years to attune myself to arrivals...Even longer to learn how to see them, to interact with them, and to watch the passing of time and wait."

Slowly, she appeared on the other side of the trunk, a sad smile tugging down the corners of her mouth. Her fingertips grazed over my cheekbone, drawing back my hair from my face to tuck it behind my ear the way she'd done when I was young and time was merely an idea in the Great Mothers's minds.

"When your mate was small and fevered with the daemoni bite, I found her consciousness here on the bank of a river, shivering. I gathered her up and sent her back into the world, shepherding her mind and magic into her body and giving her the strength to continue on." A knowing look crossed her face, and she shook her head. "No, I did not know then what she would be to you. Then I only saw a child who had suffered so much, who I saw myself within."

My heart twisted with longing. "You taught her the song of creation."

Asteria's smile widened, her nod one of pride. "I did, and, my, did she create."

I reached out to place a hand on the thick branch of the tree, the moss damp beneath my fingertips. "You are saying there is a way out."

"I am saying there is a way to connect, to perhaps speak, to learn."

We could not break free from this prison, but perhaps we could be retrieved. And I knew then it was Oralia who could find the way out.

I did not believe in the old ways. I did not believe in the fatefulness of magic or the rightness of the universe. I believed in Oralia, in her power and her strength. And I believed she would find a way.

"Why did I come here instead of the human realm?"

Asteria knew of my travels to the human world and how the souls of the humans called out to me, begging for salvation or release. There were so many more souls there than in my own world, so many it overwhelmed me, pulling my waiting magic toward them while my body resurrected.

"I do not know, Son. Your magic is what takes you to that place. It should have guided you there."

The memory of those chains—my father's chains—seared across my lids. They had taken my power from me, reduced me to merely a shell of myself, and then Typhon had delivered the killing blow. Perhaps that was why I had not gone to my usual place, why I hovered within the in-between, unable to revive—there had been no magic to shepherd me.

My heart clenched within my chest, and I dipped my head, pressing a hand over my sternum. Another thrum of pain, then another. I grunted, reaching out to steady myself as the air knocked from my lungs, as power zinged through my skull. Was this the final death? My magic returning to the earth? This was not my body, merely my soul and magic taking form here in this place. Yet it *hurt*.

My chest gave a steady beat, harder and firmer than before. My magic pulsed, sighed, before settling with ease into my veins. I could not help but search for the bond, and found it sharp within my senses. Flaring with magic and heat and light, zinging out of the darkness and through the world to *her*.

"*Stars*," I breathed, gazing up at my mother in wonder. "She has already begun."

CHAPTER
FOURTEEN

Oralia

A buzzing filled the air.

My fingers flexed, covered in dark blood. They looked like the hands of the scarred god. Gore dripped from my chin onto my chest, and I stared unseeing through the tall window out into the thick mist clinging to the grounds of our kingdom. The air skittered through my lungs as I breathed, the buzzing in the air settling in my chest with each beating of my heart, a strange echo of it in my ears.

No, not an echo.

His heart beat alongside my own.

This was more tangible than it had been within the soul bond. And when I followed the line of the connection within my power, it spiderwebbed out in many different directions, bright silver paths I hoped would lead me to him.

"I will find you," I said into the dark. "I will make this right."

I did not know how long I sat there, relishing the feel of his magic skittering through my veins. But I savored the growing bond between us, even as I mourned the one lonely thread I could not follow fading into nothingness. Eventually, my head fell onto his pillow, and I turned, breathing in the scent of him and allowing myself a moment to imagine Ren was here. He had only stepped away but would soon return to drag me into his arms and bury his face in my hair.

Eshara, *I am yours*, he would say.

As I fell into a fitful sleep, it was not only blood staining his pillow, not merely the gore coating my lips, but the grief I could no longer contain.

The souls assembled had not needed anything other than a witness to their evolution. I had not needed to say a word or touch them. Instead, as one, they bowed their heads, hands pressed over their hearts, and melted into white balls of light—giving in to their magic and its need to return to the world. Their power had been so bright I'd shielded my eyes against the glare as they shot into the sky, leaving streaks of darkness in their wake.

Magical reincarnation was different in our world depending on who the soul was. Humans contained little magic, and therefore, their souls needed a place to rest before they could give themselves back to the earth to begin again. Demigods were much the same though, their magic was a little stronger. When they died, any true power they had returned to the earth to start again in someone new while their human souls lingered in Infernis. Gods, however, were fully magical—it ran through our blood, it was what made up our souls. When we died, no hint of our consciousness remained when our magic returned to the earth to start again in someone else. There was nothing to shepherd into Infernis or beyond.

The entirety of the ascension ritual was conducted in silence. Bright white streams of light burst into the sky, leaving in its wake a sort of calm which could not touch me. Horace and I stood for a long moment, observing the space where the souls had once been before I found my courage.

"I believe there is a way to find him."

Horace turned toward me slowly, those bright red eyes assessing. When I did not continue, he dipped his chin. "I am listening."

"There is a new...*connection* between us," I began carefully, eyes trained to the bare space of grass. "A connection that splits out in seven directions like silver threads I might follow."

The faint beating of Ren's heart in my chest intensified for a moment as if confirming the truth of my words. On my tongue lay the memory of the taste of his blood, the feeling of his power growing inside.

He frowned. "How was this connection forged?"

"I took his heart within myself," I whispered hoarsely.

With wide eyes, I turned to face Horace, expecting the same wild fear to be reflected in his gaze. But he only nodded solemnly, running a hand down his face before resting it over his chest.

"I have seen many things in my existence, Oralia. I have seen the creation of time, witnessed the first death of this world. My soul is outside of this reality. It is why you can touch me and Morana with your bare hands and we do not die. My body does not adhere to the laws of this realm as yours does." He leaned down until we were eye to eye. "And neither does Ren's. I trust in your power, I trust in your magic, and most importantly, I trust in the bond you forged with him."

My throat clicked with a swallow, and I blinked rapidly to clear the haze of my vision. One of his heavy hands closed over my shoulder, squeezing gently.

"You must prepare yourself that more facets of your magic will begin to appear. Not only from the training you have done with Ren and Morana but from this new bond."

"More facets of my magic..." I repeated, tangling my fingers together.

He hummed. "You possess more than merely life and death, Oralia, and I can sense your magic waking even now. More than likely it will feel much like you are once again going through prime. We must prepare for when your new magic arrives."

Stars. My prime had come so long ago. I barely remembered those years when my magic had fully manifested. It was a volatile time for gods when emotions ran high and their power might burst from them without warning. To go through it again now with powers I could not fathom...

"It is not a guarantee," he murmured. "But for now, you have forged a way forward. We have much to do, and if Typhon is intent on your death, we must do what we can to keep you safe through this next journey."

I nodded and, without another word, drew the shadows around us to meet the rest of the inner circle at the steps of the palace.

I could not blame Aelestor for his incredulity even if I lacked the patience for it.

Drystan was busy strapping daggers to every available part of his body within the leathers and baldric Dimitri had lent him. He had already done the same for me. The dagger Ren gifted me was heavy at my hip. Others were strapped to my thigh and beneath the sleeves of my tunic. I'd left behind the gowns and dresses in favor of fighting leathers, complete with a black cloak and cowl that could cover my face. My hands were covered in the soft black gloves Sidero had made before I ever left Infernis if I learned I could not pull back the power of death from my hands.

Now, we would be traveling into a part of the world where a single touch could destroy everything. I would not risk such a thing, nor be the cause of such suffering.

"You will be quick." It was not a question as Dimitri checked over the pack Drystan carried before handing another to Aelestor.

"I do not know," Thorne rumbled. "I hear Severa is lovely this time of year. Perhaps our queen would like a bit of sightseeing."

The towering god winked at me, and though I found I could not form a smile, I did my best to give him a sound of acknowledgment. Thorne had already sat the three of us down this morning before the ascension to discuss what would happen in the event we were attacked, but the reality was once we left the kingdom, we were on our own. If I was incapacitated or killed, it meant more than Aelestor and Drystan having a long journey home.

Who knew what range Typhon's weapon had.

We would travel to the closest string first, hopefully retrieve the piece of Ren without issue, and return to Infernis, where Thorne would hold on to it for safekeeping before moving to the next. Over and over until we had all the pieces of him. I tried not to think of the fact that now I held one part of him inside myself—the most vital part—and what it meant for his resurrection.

"Are you both ready?" I asked, beckoning Aelestor closer.

Drystan's *yes* was soft while his gloved hand closed over my arm.

Aelestor's mouth was set into a firm line, one hand closing over mine while the other gripped the pommel of his sword. "I have already given my goodbyes to Josette."

I nodded, taking one last look at Horace, Thorne, and Sidero, the last of whom gave me a small, confident smile.

"Do not rush," they encouraged. "Keep your heads down and your eyes open."

Dimitri huffed his agreement, the corners of his eyes tight with worry. The three of us nodded our understanding before I took a deep breath. I could do this. I had to—there was no other choice. So I closed my eyes, reaching out for the strange silver thread, plucking at the one closest. I did not need to open my eyes to know shadows had blossomed over my shoulders, slithering out across my chest to wind around the two men beside me. Drystan tensed, but he did not speak as I focused on our destination, gritting my teeth with determination before I stepped through the shadows.

Bright sunlight bled across my lids before I blinked. A rolling field of green lay before me, dotted with flowers and trees, some of which I recognized from their silver branches and black leaves as kratus. The scent of cooking meat was heavy in the air, mixed with smoke and the stench of humans. Aelestor was the first to release, spinning with precision and half-drawing his sword. Drystan followed, flanking my other side.

The human settlement behind us reminded me a bit of Rathyra, our own city of souls, with its cramped houses and narrow walkways. We were right at the edge of the town, nestled beside what appeared to be a well, the scent of fresh water bright against the other thicker scents.

"What now, Oralia?" Drystan breathed.

Humans meandered farther off through what appeared to be a busier street. Gripping the edges of my cowl, I drew it over my head. The two of them followed suit.

"Now we find our king."

CHAPTER

FIFTEEN

Oralia

We traveled through the serpentine streets, coverings pulled over our faces. My power pricked, tapping at the back of my skull. The feeling reminded me of Horace's warning that soon new powers might manifest. Even now, the intuition was stronger like a voice warning me to stay vigilant.

The silver thread curved toward the north on the opposite end of the village. I was disappointed to find I could not shadow-walk us to the exact location, merely an approximation of it. Drystan and Aelestor followed a pace or two behind as we slipped through the streets, crowds thickening while we journeyed deeper into the village.

My throat clenched with nausea and I fought the urge to press the fabric tighter to my nose. The stench of decay was everywhere, mixing with the smell of sickness and unwashed bodies, and beneath it all was the ever-present scent of *despair.* Instead, I bit the inside of my lips, parting them enough to allow a small bit of air to slip through my teeth, only to find the scent heavy on my tongue, and my stomach spasmed.

From what we could gather given the direction the thread had pulled, the village was on the edge of the Aetheran border. All my life, there had been stories of it and I'd seen the offerings they sent each tithe. There was always talk of the hospitality and generosity of its inhabitants—how the residents enjoyed many benefits from being so close to the kingdom. How was it then that they lived in such squalor? The humans we passed appeared gaunt with heavy circles beneath their eyes and bones protuberant in their faces as if trying to break free of their skin.

The deeper we traveled, the more attention we caught. At first, it was merely passing glances as we skirted around human men, shoulders rounded with their burdens on their backs or hands clutching curved swords, but as we crossed into a square heavy with foot traffic, silence fell. Activity froze at our arrival from the mouth of one of the alleys. The area appeared to be some sort of trading post with crude benches set up as display tables—nothing like the bright stalls swathed in fabric I'd seen in Mycelna with the scarred god in the human realm.

"*Great Mothers,*" Aelestor swore as each human turned toward us, scowls heavy on their faces.

Drystan stepped closer to my side. His arm pressed against my back, where he no doubt had his hand closed over his sword.

"You are not welcome here," a man called. His face was smeared with dirt as if he'd been digging through a field, hands caked with it, earth blending into his pale skin.

Beside him another man stepped forward, dark brown skin dotted with blood from an animal he had been butchering. In his hand, he weighed a heavy knife, bloodshot blue eyes narrowed upon my party. "We have nothing to give. Not to *you*."

My brows furrowed, and I reached for my cowl. Aelestor grabbed my wrist, but I shook him off, drawing back my hood so I could properly look at the men.

"And who is it you believe we are?" I asked, crossing my gloved hands in front of me.

My magic danced across my shoulders, though my shadows did not flare. The rhythm of my heart was steady but heavier with the weight of Ren on my chest.

The humans looked at one another, incredulous at my question. But the two who had appointed themselves as spokespeople took a step closer. Aelestor jerked, but it was my turn to place a hand on his arm.

"Do not play dumb," the first man spat. "We have nothing for your king. You lot were here two days ago, drained us dry, and that was after your bloody tithe took most of what we had anyway."

Two days.

I frowned, taking a closer look at the stalls within the square. They were meager offerings: half a basket of grain, a handful of tiny fish. The animal the second man was butchering was so small I was surprised he was using such a large knife.

"We are not Aetheran."

A rumble slithered through the crowd, and my magic gave a warning pulse.

The second man shook his head, ran a hand over his face, and smeared the blood. "We have heard that before. You will receive no hospitality from us."

"We do not look for hospitality," Aelestor retorted. "Something was taken from us."

I cursed under my breath, resisting the urge to press my fingers to my temples. The rumble through the crowd grew tumultuous, humans jostling through the square, and the small bubble of space around us grew smaller.

"Something taken from you?" the first man cried, thick brows raising in mock concern. "You believe we have stolen from *the Golden King?*"

Our negation was drowned in the outrage echoing off the short walls. And though the three of us shouted our explanation, it was lost as the humans surged forward, faces twisted with fury. Something small sailed through the sky, and on instinct, my shadows coiled up, sending it flying behind us before it could find its mark. But the humans did not appear stunned by witnessing such power. It only spurred them forward.

We had made a grave mistake.

Thunder rumbled overhead, and I did not need Drystan's hand on my elbow urging me to turn and run from the crowd. A roar sounded at our back, the stomping of feet deafening in our ears as lightning cracked across the sky, rain falling heavy upon our shoulders.

"I do not know if a storm will help us," Drystan grit through his teeth, steadying himself with a hand on a wall as we skidded around a corner, only to find a group of humans advancing toward us, armed with wooden stakes and metal pots.

We turned and catapulted down a narrow passage to a blessedly vacant side street. The rain lightened, though the thunder roared and lightning continued to crackle. My shadows flared at my shoulders, and I allowed them to pool out behind us, a *thwack* sounding against my constructed shield as a crude wooden spear clacked to the ground at our heels.

"Take this right," I panted, rushing forward to lead the group. The silver thread pulsed, and we ducked beneath low awnings, careening over a cart, one of its wheels cracked in half.

We slipped in the mud as we turned the corner, only to find a rude mob. Each human held a makeshift weapon, and though I did not fear for my life, not without kratus resin, I would not become a prisoner when so much was at stake. Their numbers made them powerful, even against two gods well into prime and a demigod who carried the scent of fading favor from Typhon.

And yet my heartbeat did not pound. My magic curled over my shoulders, shadows twining over my wrists. The slice of metal rang through the air as Drystan unsheathed his sword, the black blade glinting in the bright noon sun. Our shoulders hit the wood at our back as the humans pressed closer, hungry looks glinting in their eyes at their prey cornered.

"Try not to—" Drystan began.

"Kill them?" Aelestor interrupted. "What do you propose we do instead? Dance with them?"

The scent of desperation rolled off the crowd in waves. Though I understood their despair, I could not find the compassion I desperately needed to control my power. I took a deep breath, steadying myself as I pressed my shadows forward, creating a barrier around us.

"It will not hold long," I growled over their argument. "Find us a way out."

Immediately, Aelestor spun, metal splintering through wood, drowned by the angry shouts on the other side of the barrier. Sweat trickled down my temple, and I grit my teeth. This power was strong—stronger now than it had been even a week ago—and though I had done much to learn control, finesse was a ways off. The shadows fought me with each breath I took, wanting to expand, to contract, to snap back and splinter like the wood at my back. And there was another beneath the pool of darkness like fire and ice and ash waiting to wake.

Closer than the unknown power was something else roiling beneath my skin. Something thirsty for blood that would be unrepentant if I destroyed all these humans with my next breath.

A hand wrapped around my waist, tugging me backward and through the narrow hole Aelestor had created. The fabric of my cloak tore on the splinters as I jerked through, tumbling into a darkened room, the stench of decay heavy in the air.

"Stairs," Aelestor called, loud enough over the din of humans approaching.

I pushed my power forward, shoulders rising to my ears with the effort as Drystan guided me backward, my heel catching on the lip of the threshold.

"Drop them when I close the door," he instructed, hand closing over the wooden handle.

But my shadows fell before the final word. A great wail echoed from the street, muffled only slightly through the wood as Drystan tugged the door closed and slammed the rusted metal latch into place.

"Oralia!" Aelestor cried, voice swallowed by the dark.

Slowly, Drystan and I shuffled down the stairs, blinking to force our eyes to adjust to the pitch black. The scent of wood was heavier here, and I barely made out Aelestor's mass of copper curls from where he stood before a pile rising to the ceiling.

The silver thread throbbed in my chest. "What is it?"

With a tentative hand, I reached out to feel what lay in front of us.

Rough bark crumbled beneath my fingertips, magic recoiling with a single touch. Kratus wood. Piles and piles of it, stashed within this human cellar, unbeknownst to the inhabitants within the city.

The room brightened until I could make out the black wood piled high against the roughhewn wall, little more than clods of earth. And toward the top, a flash of pale white within the wood, only a mere sliver.

"This must be from the forest nearby," Aelestor said. "Perhaps this is where Typhon holds the excess until they have need of it."

Fists pounded on the door above, cries and grunts of frustration slipping through the cracks.

"He is here," I murmured, sliding my hands over the wood to look for a strong enough hold.

Drystan moved closer to the stairs, sword drawn. "Work quickly."

"Help me up." I tugged my gloves tighter over my hands and reached high to curl my fingers over the logs to find purchase.

Aelestor's hands closed around my waist, steadying me as I created a foothold, pulling myself higher up the stack. It swayed, a few logs from the top tumbling around us as I climbed. My heart thundered in my chest, shadows spooling to cover us as more wood fell, splintering at Aelestor's and Drystan's feet. There—it was there—unseated by my climbing.

Fingertips hanging over the edge, pale skin with half-moon nails, covered in blood and grime.

Ren's arm.

CHAPTER
SIXTEEN

Oralia

The door above us splintered, cracking with the first blow of a knife.

Carefully, I wrapped Ren's arm in my tattered cloak, cradling it tight to my chest while Drystan and Aelestor closed in around me. Power hummed through my veins, a spark of recognition in my magic and the small sliver of Ren's I possessed prickling at the back of my neck.

"Do you want me...?" Drystan asked, his voice barely audible over the din at the top of the stairs.

I shook my head, extending an elbow toward him as Aelestor took my hand. The door shattered above, raining down bits of broken wood over our heads. But I took a deep breath, shadows twining around our bodies, even as feet thundered down the stairs. Something shimmered in the light streaming through the door, streaking through the darkness of my power, a slicing pain rippled through my shoulder.

A step. Then another. Darkness ate away the cacophony of out-rage before the dim light of Infernis pooled around us. The mist curled over my face, stroking my cheeks, before I stumbled.

"*Ow,*" I grunted, gritting my teeth as I stared down into the sharp-ened wooden stake protruding from my shoulder before clattering to the stones.

Only the tip had been coated in kratus resin—barely enough to make an impact. But Drystan swiped it from the ground as Horace appeared a few steps higher toward the palace in a swirl of white mist. I pressed a hand to the shallow wound, a little blood dripping through my fingers as I cradled the piece of Ren with my injured arm.

"This is too dangerous," Aelestor muttered, steadying me.

I raised a brow at the God of Storms. What were our options other than hiding for the remainder of eternity while Ren regenerated on his own? But I did not respond to his complaint, I merely nodded at Horace as he descended the stairs. Sidero and Thorne pushed through the doors above, panic in their expressions.

"Please keep this safe," I said as they approached, proffering the wrapped bundle to Thorne.

All three pairs of eyes widened as Thorne cradled it in his wide arms. I wondered if they could sense Ren's power as I could—if Thorne recognized the small piece of his king he now carried. But he nodded, tucking it under his arm before reaching out toward my wound.

Taking a few steps back, I shook my head. "I am fine. I am in no danger of dying."

But it was Drystan who made a small noise of impatience, brush-ing past Thorne and knocking my hand aside. "*Burning Suns,* you treat her as if her word is law."

Thorne huffed a laugh. "She is queen, friend."

"She is stubborn." A muscle ticked in Drystan's jaw while he pressed on the wound, shooting me a look when I jerked back.

I hissed through my teeth when he squeezed harder to expel the resin. "And she is *right here.*"

Sidero came to my side, offering Drystan a small cloth to press against the wound. "Tell us what happened."

My attention wandered to the bundle in Thorne's arms, skin itching with anxiety. Drystan tugged on the sleeve of my tunic, exposing the wound to the air and mist, dabbing at the coin-sized gash.

"Humans—" I started.

"Madness. That is what happened," Aelestor cut across me.

I grit my teeth, exhaling through my nose. Drystan mirrored the action, gray eyes flashing toward the redhead.

"And why did the madness happen?" Horace rumbled in question.

"Humans are unpredictable," Aelestor countered.

Drystan and I laughed bitterly while the other three stared between us.

"Aethera has been stealing from their stores, and you all but accused them of stealing from Aethera. I believe their reaction was absolutely predictable." The last word feathered out into another hiss of pain before it melted into relief, blood trickling onto the cloth with the last of the resin.

"Come, let us get inside, and we can discuss further." Horace extended an arm in assistance.

My strength was already returning, the gash knitting into a red mark that would fade into nothing within another few minutes. I followed them up the stairs, weariness hanging around my shoulders with my shadows.

With a sigh, I scrubbed my hand over my face. "There is not much to discuss other than Aelestor is no longer allowed to speak on these trips."

What if there is no reviving him?

The words circled my mind, over and over until I pressed my fingers to my ears, dipping my head to my knees to block out the blue light of the candles lit throughout the room. Bathwater lapped at my skin, the heat biting like many-headed snakes and fear like venom swirling through my veins. With each movement, my muscles bunched. Each moment that existed as if Ren was not ripped from this world was a gash across my heart.

What was the point of running a bath? Of brushing out my hair? Each simple act was another stone upon my chest until I was unsure if I could even stand again. Even drying myself off and slipping between the sheets was an insurmountable task.

Pain sliced through my temples where my nails dug in. And yet I could not help but ask the question. What if Ren was already gone? I could travel to the ends of the world, gather each and every piece, and then what? Could I risk not only my own life but Drystan and Aelestor's? And what if my absence was opening another door to let Typhon in?

My stomach roiled as acid climbed up my throat. I swallowed, and the dry click echoed through the room. Instead, I tried to think of what Ren would do in my place if our roles were somehow reversed. The corner of my mouth twitched at the thought of the carnage that would lay in his wake as he razed the entire world. I knew he would stop at nothing to get me back, and he would never experience a single moment of doubt.

With a heave, I rose from the tub. The movements were mechanical as I dried myself off, ignoring my usual sleeping gowns in favor of pulling one of Ren's soft black tunics over my head. Gathering up his discarded cloak, I carried it with me, pressing the fabric to my nose as I slipped between the sheets. I breathed in the scent of him as if it was a life source.

There was no world for me in which he did not live. But I had to go on. Infernis needed us—needed me in the absence of an *us*. Yet all I wanted to do was sink through the ground and follow my mate, whether it was to release my magic back into the world or into another realm like the human one of Mycelna. After today, however, I was done with humans for a long while.

Tonight had been long with endless discussion of the horrors in the human village. Irritation had crackled beneath my skin each time Horace or Dimitri pointed out what could have been done differently, measures which could have helped us to avoid such a mess. How could they truly understand the threat a mob of humans could pose? A single human was nothing, but hundreds?

A giant could be felled by a hundred humans. I'd read tales of it.

I gazed unseeingly at the window. The pitch-black night pressed in through the open drapes, all at once a suffocation and a comfort. In many ways, it reminded me of the first time my power had taken over when the darkness had swallowed me and stars had popped into existence. Ren's mother had been there, waiting for me with words of comfort and reassurance, of strength. I thought I could use such a thing right now.

Sleep came on slowly, and when it did, it was with tangled

memories and visions of Ren. His face swam before me, lips on my cheeks, my forehead, my hair. Words I could not remember whispered in confidence.

And when I woke, it was to a wet pillow and my hands clenched around Ren's cloak.

CHAPTER

SEVENTEEN

Renwick

Time passed, and yet, it did not.

I could not say if it was minutes or days that Asteria and I wandered the forest around the willow tree. We talked as we had thousands of years ago, and she asked me gentle questions about Oralia, our bond, our journey from distrust to devotion, and everything in-between.

All the while, there was a humming within my chest. If I listened carefully, I thought it sounded much like Oralia's voice as she grew the trees in Rathyra and the grasses in Infernis. The sound of creation was swimming through my veins. I missed her, but the sentiment was too simple for the bone-aching need I had for my mate.

The humming became louder like fingers plucking on a silver string. We were crossing a narrow creek, the clear water rushing over dark river stones, glittering in the dim moonlight, when something shifted in my peripheral vision. A figure with waving hair stepped carefully through the trees.

"Oralia," I breathed.

But as I made to move forward, Asteria cautioned me with a hand on my elbow. "It is merely her consciousness on the edge of dreams. You must be gentle."

I took a deep breath, quelling the urge to rush her into my arms, smother her in kisses, and never let her go. Instead, I took a careful step, then another. Oralia's attention was fixed instead on the high snow-topped mountain in the distance. I placed my hand on her arm, breath catching in my throat at the feel of her beneath my palm and the curl of her hair around my wrist.

"*Eshara...*" The word was soft, barely more than a breath, and she turned with the slow dance-like movement of dreamers, dark green eyes distant.

She stared at me in wonder, brows furrowed as her gaze flicked across my features. But the look was dazed, merely an approximation of truly seeing. I cupped her face in my hands regardless. The burn of grief was so hot in my throat I could not speak. Oralia smiled in the same strange fashion as if she could not truly understand what she saw.

"Ren," she murmured in the same tone she often used in our bed as she drifted off in my arms.

The corners of her lips dipped down into a frown, and I leaned forward, pressing a kiss to one side. She sighed, falling into the touch, hands featherlight as they skated up my arms.

"What if there is no reviving you?" The question was whisper quiet, barely a hum of vibration, but it carried such weight the words were stones dropped into my pockets.

And so I kissed her cheeks, her temples, the furrow between her brows until it smoothed, allowing her to trace the planes of my face with her fingertips even as her eyes turned glassy.

"You will find a way," I answered, catching a tear with my lips before it could fall.

Her mouth pursed, face crumpling, and I shushed her with soft sounds. Horror was a heavy shawl wrapping around us while I enfolded her in my arms, tucking her head beneath my chin as she wept into my chest. I stroked her hair, pressing my mouth to her hair before dipping my lips closer to her ear.

"It is you I believe in, *eshara*. You are who I light a candle to, as humans do for the gods they worship. You are who I lay my offerings before. And you have already accomplished so much, my heart. I can feel the bond between us as I could not before, stronger now than even when we were parted by mist and magic."

Oralia drew back enough to look up into my face, fingertips trembling as they traced the outline of my mouth, her other hand pressed to her chest. "Your heart."

I nodded, even though I was unsure as to what she meant, but I pressed my lips to hers. "You have my heart. I have laid it in your hands."

A tremor racked through her body, a whimper of distress echoing in the space between us.

"Let her go, Son," Asteria instructed, agony heavy in her tone.

My hands flexed around my wife's shoulders as she clung to me for the first time with a strength I had not known she would possess here.

"No." Oralia shook her head, clutching herself tighter, her voice breaking with each word. "No, no, do not leave me. Don't leave me, Ren. *Please don't leave.*"

Pain sliced through my chest—through whatever remnant I had of my soul. She scrambled closer, arms winding around my neck. Her face was pressed to the skin of my throat. It was like when I'd carried her out of Isthil, and she'd wept for the things she had lost. The press of our skin had been oxygen in her lungs, feeding the fire of desperation. And it was the same now.

"I will not leave you," I soothed, voice raw and heat pricking the corners of my eyes. "I will come when you call. Soothe when you are hurt. Protect you when you are in need. I will never leave you, *eshara.*"

Her form flickered in my arms even as her arms tightened around my neck. She repeated my name again and again, falling from her lips like hail from the sky, each one louder than the next, a desperate plea to not be abandoned. I held her tightly, trying to pierce her cries with words of comfort, of love, and yet I could not reach her.

"*Ren!*" she screamed.

And then she disappeared.

My knees hit the damp grass, fingers clenching around air. And for the first time since I arrived in this place, the grief of all we had lost crashed over me in a wave, and I wept into my empty hands.

CHAPTER
EIGHTEEN

Oralia

W hat if he cannot be revived?"

The bitter air burned my lungs. My face was raw from the icy wind slapping across my cheeks. But I did not stop to look at Aelestor, who pushed through the high snow beside me, hands tucked into his sides and his cloak drawn tightly around his face. The question he'd spoken aloud burned deeper than the ice forming on my brows and lashes.

We had gathered before dawn to leave Infernis at my insistence. The mess of two days ago in the human village burned in all our minds, leaving behind worry at what we would find now. Aelestor had not been seen much in the day we rested, preferring to spend his time in Rathyra with Josette while I kept mainly to my and Ren's rooms or spoke with the others in the parlor attached to our chambers.

"He can," I answered, pushing the words out even as they stuck to my tongue.

We stumbled through another snowbank, visibility so low I was unsure whether we were at the peak of a mountain or traveling through a valley. All I knew was the bitter cold and the ice eating its way through my chest until warmth was barely a distant memory. Each step felt like a hundred. Each breath through my lungs was so painful I was unsure if I could take another. And it was not the snow or the cold, but the paralyzing fear now spoken aloud.

The question had not left me no matter how long I tried. When I slept, they curled through my mind, though after the first night, I had not dreamed again of Ren. Only long, narrow halls with no end, lightning streaking across the sky to pierce me through the heart, and a long fall through distant worlds to land on a boat that almost over-turned. A voice spoke in my ear of trust and prophecy and strands of thread on a loom slithering through time and space over and over in an endless cycle until I woke with a gasp, clutching my chest.

"Are you sure?" Aelestor rasped, catching himself before he fell face-first into a deep trench.

That was the problem. I was not. Had I not spent the last two nights worried over the same matter? But I could not speak my heart aloud. To do so would be to admit defeat, that perhaps what we were doing was a fool's errand, and risk him refusing to go any further.

So I pressed my gloved hand to my chest over the place where Ren's power now lay. "I trust our magic"—my foot slipped on ice and Drystan's hand shot out to steady me before I tumbled—"and our bond. If he cannot die then he can be revived."

Drystan's grip did not waiver as we met a high, icy wall of smooth gray stones, marked with time and grit from the wind. Each step was more treacherous than the last. The snow was blindingly white—so thick I could barely see my hand before my face.

The magic I spoke of tugged within me, guiding me to the right up the path leading to what had to be the side of the mountain. It was the only sensation I welcomed now: the reminder that within me a piece of Ren still lived.

"So how will we revive him?" Aelestor pressed.

"Aelestor..." Drystan warned.

I did not respond. But Aelestor did not relent, his voice clear at my shoulder as if he were the echo of my own worried consciousness.

"I do not mean any disrespect, Oralia. However, I must ask the questions others are too afraid to. You do not have his heart any longer—it lives inside of you."

The words were needle pricks to my brain, each spot bleeding until panic lanced through each breath. What would I do if we gathered all the pieces of him? We would have all save one.

"How could you possibly—"

"Enough," I snapped, turning so quickly my feet slipped, and I steadied myself with a hand on the sheet of rock beside us.

Aelestor skidded to a stop, gray eyes wide beneath the icy cowl covering his nose and mouth.

I tugged down the cowl covering my nose and mouth. "You do not trust me."

He shook his head. "It is not a matter of tru—"

I stepped closer, looking up into the face of a god I'd once believed was my tormentor. Now he was my conscience, speaking the fears aloud I could not put voice to. Part of me understood and was grateful for his counsel—another time, I would have welcomed it. But not now, not when we were trudging up the side of a mountain in a blizzard.

"If you do not believe in the success of this mission, then your presence is not needed." My voice was smooth, only the barest hint of tremble in the back of my throat. It was the voice I thought a queen might use. "I have no wish to drag you across this world kicking and screaming like a petulant god well before prime."

Drystan gave a gruff sound of agreement, swallowed mostly by the howling wind. The cowl around Aelestor's mouth shifted, small icicles breaking off and falling at our feet, but whatever he would have said next was drowned by an ear-piercing screech, like nails on porcelain. The three of us started, hands flying to our frozen weapons as small dagger-like shards of ice rained down upon us. My power flared outward on instinct, shielding us from the worst of the shrapnel.

"We need to move," Drystan called over the tumult.

I spun, slipping on the rocks before charging ahead and around the corner. Whatever my magic led me to was close, the silver thread within my soul humming as it had before. The path inclined, wind whipped around my face, and the sound of my name was drowned by an ear-shattering wail beside my head.

Only a moment—it was all the time I had to throw up my shadows before an icy swipe caught the skin of my cheek. It did not tear my flesh, but the impact sent me tumbling backward into Aelestor. Scrambling within my cloak, my frozen hands fumbled with the dagger, but a heavy weight shunted me to the side. I fell with a sickening crack of my head against the ground.

Someone screamed my name.

The world spun, shouts dying in the storm raining ice and snow upon us. Unsteadily, I pushed back to my feet, looking around for the others and shaking my head.

Aelestor was on his back, copper hair spilling out from his cowl, a strange, four-legged creature pinning him to the ground as big as he was. Drystan stood over them, hacking at the monster with his short sword for all the good it was doing them both. It was strange—with each blow Drystan dealt, chunks of ice flew from the body, and thick legs pushed against Aelestor each time he bucked.

I slid forward, darkness shooting out and dragging the creature off him. Another screech filled my ears, the sound crackling and sparking inside my head until my shadows faltered from the pain and the world went silent. The storm raged, and Drystan's mouth moved. The covering flapped around his face, and yet I could not hear.

The creature smashed against the opposite wall, falling onto its strange, pointed feet. The bulbous head rocked from side to side. It staggered, swaying, and I realized its face was covered in a thick layer of ice, as was the rest of its body. As if it had built these layers upon itself like armor, leaving only the sharp pincers around its mouth and feet free.

Aelestor shot to his feet, flipped the dagger in his hand, and drew his fist in to protect his chest. His clothes were tattered from the attack. There was no fending this creature off with blades, not with the sheet of ice protecting it. It would continue to attack until it met whatever its goal might be. Perhaps we were close to its nest, and it sought to drive us off the mountainside. Great Mothers only knew how far the drop was to the bottom. We would survive it, but it would take us time—time I was not sure we had.

The silver thread pulsed within my chest, a reminder of the mission we were on. This creature stood between us and my mate. It crouched and sprang forward with an agility surprising for its size. The three of us rushed it, and I forced my power to wrap around its limbs, holding it in place as Drystan and Aelestor hacked through the ice. Sweat froze across my hairline. My skin was tight and chapped in the bitter wind.

Drystan grabbed his short sword in both hands, thrusting downward, but the blade glanced off the thick ice, barely an inch chipping off in its wake. Frustration pounded in my temples, the heat of it burning through my veins. I was tired of the delay, ready for the bed I would fall into, to clutch Ren's pillow to my face, and fall into an endless sleep.

Heat flared, similar to the warmth I would feel as I used my magic to grow life, but sharper. A knife tip instead of a paintbrush. Power tapped at the back of my head, and I knew it wanted me to listen, to focus.

Fear is not your enemy here. The words were merely a distant memory, a reminder that my power was an extension of myself. I should not fear it, nor fight it. As the creature thrashed against the shadow bonds, I slowly relaxed the hold I had on my magic, gritting my teeth against the onslaught of heat as it flared across my fingertips, the sides of my neck, and the center of my ribs.

And then my shadows exploded into ropes of flame and the creature died, its screams vibrating through my bones.

CHAPTER

NINETEEN

Oralia

Ringing buzzed through the world, rattling my skull.

The skeletal body of the creature crumbled to ash between the three of us, the armor of ice melting away and refreezing beneath our feet. But I could not spare a glance for the monstrous, segmented remains before me—my attention was glued to my hands, inconspicuous beneath the black gloves.

Fire.

A power I'd never known I possessed now coursed beneath my skin, tangling with the dark web of death and bright golden life. Drystan and Aelestor stared with wide eyes. Their ragged breathing filtered through the ringing in my ears, and I realized how vital it was, my growing power. Vital in a way I had feared when Horace had first spoken of it growing.

A gash bled on Drystan's cheek, knitting itself together, dark blood freezing. He was a demigod, far more fragile than Aelestor and me. Did I have the power to bestow favor as Typhon and Ren did—to strengthen his body and magic? From the gash on his face, the favor he'd been bestowed in Aethera was waning, if not gone.

"Are you injured?" I asked, voice tinny in my ears.

Drystan shook his head, swiping at the now-healed wound with the back of his hand. "That *suns-cursed* monster only landed one blow. And you?"

I shook my head as well, turning my attention to Aelestor. But he was gazing at me with unreadable gray eyes.

"Oralia..." His tone was soft, barely audible behind the dimming ring, and it was clear he wanted to continue our argument from before.

But I had no more space for it, not as the silver thread connecting me to Ren hummed, pulling me higher up the mountain. So instead, I turned on tired legs. This new magic was a drain on my energy as the shadows had been when I first learned them. If Aelestor spoke, his words were too quiet for my healing ears.

Drystan fell into step but did not comment, only offered me a shoulder as we traversed slick, rounded boulders. I was as grateful for his support as I was that he did not try to ask about this new power, what it meant, or where we were going. The questions would come later, I knew, after the danger had passed for the moment and we were tucked back inside the safety of the castle. But for now, he was my silent companion as always, offering me peace while Aelestor offered questions I could not shake even within the quiet of my mind.

"Here," I said, reaching out to touch the small opening in the rock.

There was barely enough light streaming through the opening to illuminate the small cavern. Deadly stalactites of ice hung from the ceiling, walls as shiny as the rock outside. But the center of the cavern was odd, strange shards gathered within a circle in the middle.

"It is like a nest..." Drystan muttered, stepping closer to look inside.

"*Stars,*" I cursed, peering over the edge.

It was a nest, with hundreds of egg-like ovals nestled inside, a thin layer of ice protecting them from prey. The tiny, wiggling embryos were nothing more than dark smudges beneath.

"I'd hate to be here when they hatched." Drystan's voice was louder than before. The last of my hearing repaired as he squatted to inspect them further.

Somewhere in this cavern, a piece of Ren was waiting for me, and though I searched within the ice-covered nest, nothing jumped out. Not the tip of a boot, or fingertips, or an elbow. I sighed, rose to my feet, and slowly walked the perimeter of the cave. My hands slid over the walls. Aelestor stood within the entrance, attention fixed on me, but I ignored him, stopping before a dark slice of rock.

"Here," I breathed, the jagged chunk of ice opaquer than the rest and bulbous as though someone had patched it.

I unhooked the knife from my belt, flipped it, and hammered at the ice with the hilt. I did not trust this new magic of mine with such a precise task, not with a piece of Ren on the other side. Frustration bubbled through me as I slammed the handle over and over. Tiny shards fell to my feet while making no headway.

"Let me." Aelestor's voice was soft as he placed a hand on my shoulder, gently moving me to the side.

With a swing, his broadsword cracked through the ice more effi- ciently than I could have, the entire plate of glass falling with a crash before him. But he did not reach in—merely stepped away, allowing me to move forward and reach with tentative hands to grasp at the piece of Ren they'd left behind.

"I do trust you," Aelestor murmured, offering me a small square of fabric he'd tucked into his belt.

I wrapped the leg, grimacing at the crusted blood, the slow-healing break. "You have a strange way of showing it."

Aelestor huffed. "I ask these questions because I fear you have not asked them of yourself. Because I am afraid you have not stopped to consider each side."

Cradling the piece of Ren in my arms, I turned to Aelestor. His hair was wild from the wind, his face was raw like mine and Drystan's, but his gaze was sincere. He wore similar look I'd seen him wear when discussing Josette, his mate, and her recovering memories.

"I think of nothing *but* those questions. Each night I fall asleep wondering if I have done the right thing—if I am endangering my people instead of saving them. And the only answer I get when I reach deep is to trust my magic." I clutched the bundle tighter to my chest. "If our roles were reversed, Ren would be here as well."

Aelestor laughed, shaking his head. "If the roles were reversed, this whole world would be nothing but shadow and ash."

My lips twitched, and I nodded, offering my elbow while Drystan's hand covered my shoulder. "Wherever Ren is, I have no doubt he has made his displeasure known." I pulled the shadows around us before we took the step toward home.

"Oralia..." Drystan's voice was unobtrusive behind me as I stared at the two pieces of Ren laid out on Thorne's work table.

Strange to see these pieces laid in such a way as if they were broken remnants of a statue laid waste and not my mate. When I touched them, there was some lingering residue of his magic, but it was merely the echo of what once was. The promise that perhaps there might be again, but nothing more now.

Thorne stood opposite with his wide hands curled around the stone table that had once held Caston on the edge of death. He was gazing upon the pieces with a strange mix of fear and wonder, no doubt considering the same question: how would we resurrect him?

"Yes." The word was not a question, more an acknowledgment that Drystan had spoken. My shoulders hung heavy, rounding forward until I was in danger of sliding to the floor. I'd hoped to feel some sort of...triumph as we gathered these pieces of Ren, but there was only the climb of dread through my throat, threatening to pour out my mouth.

"We need to discuss what happened," he said, choosing his words.

Thorne's attention flicked up to us, auburn brows tugging together into a line. "What happened, Your Grace?"

The title rankled. It was Ren's title, not mine, and I had not had enough time within Infernis to adapt. Even now, I had the urge to look around the room to see who Thorne spoke to.

My hands opened and closed before me, the same scalding heat thrumming through my veins. I'd been unable to push it back as I could with my other powers, that merely waited beneath the surface. This power was strange like a limb I had not known I possessed or a stranger that had attached itself to my back. A part of me, but unknown. I explained what happened on the mountain—how the heat had built inside of me like a pyre and how my shadows turned into ropes of flames. But I spoke each word to the pieces of my mate, afraid of what I would see when I looked at Thorne.

I had not known I'd burned Aelestor and Drystan. In the moment my magic had changed their skin had blistered—even Aelestor's. It was Drystan who filled in those blanks, who explained that when the fire had manifested it burned like its own monster—he'd seen strange shapes within the flames.

"*Stars,*" Thorne cursed.

I swallowed back the nerves as I looked at him.

Slowly, he circled the table, stopping before me to press a hand to his heart, his head bowing. "We are blessed by the universe to have such power on our side. It is a *gift*, Oralia. A gift."

Biting the inside of my cheek, I nodded. "It feels untamed like a wild creature within me."

"Your shadows were the same, were they not? Before you and Ren trained, before Morana assisted, I heard you say many times that they felt as if they had a mind of their own and you feared them."

With a frown, I looked back at the table. Of course, the entire kingdom had heard the way Ren and I argued within the grounds, stomping around the kingdom on each other's heels, desperate for the last word.

"Are there any here within Infernis who have such a power?" Drystan asked when I did not respond, lost within the memory of Ren.

Thorne pursed his lips, the corners of his eyes tightening.

"What is it?" I pressed when he did not respond. "Are there none here?"

With a shake of his head, Thorne ran a hand down his beard. "There is but he is...strange. Zayne holds a seat within Ren's inner circle and has for millennia as a child of a timeless god, the same as I. But he is reclusive like Morana, preferring to spend his time within the maze rather than the castle."

The maze. It was a strange creation of nature between Rathyra and Pyralis I'd looked at often, though never explored. Odd that a god would prefer to spend his time within, but I gave a small noise of acknowledgment.

In the morning, I would find Zayne and ask him about his power to see if he could offer me any sort of insight into my own. But for now, my footsteps were heavy as I climbed the stairs, unable to find the energy even to gather the shadows to bring me to our chambers. And I was sure I was asleep before my head even hit Ren's pillow, a vision of his face already swimming through my mind.

CHAPTER
TWENTY

Renwick

Had it been days or hours? Weeks or centuries? I could not tell as we wandered through the in-between. Each time I closed my eyes, I saw Oralia, her face contorted with grief, her cries echoing through my ears. It was not the memory I wanted to hold of my mate, and yet it was what burned the brightest when we stopped to rest, when my mother stretched her wings and took to the skies for brief flights, leaving me stranded on the ground. I had not known such a sight could hurt so much.

A tall mountain loomed beside us, its jagged black peak visible from our vantage point. I groaned, frustration itching through my veins as Asteria perched beneath a gnarled tree, its bark black in the ever-present night.

"What is the point of this wandering?" The words slipped through my clenched teeth, nails biting into my palms.

Asteria looked at me sadly, hands clasped around her knees, gray robe untouched by the miles we had traveled, the wild woods we traversed. Time was different here. I could feel it with each breath I took, though I could not understand the disparity. But we moved through space strangely, one vista melting into the next like space folding upon itself.

"I know you wish me to tell you there is some reasoning to my wandering," she murmured, reaching out to stroke the trunk beside her. "But I have none."

"Then why do we walk? Where are we going?" My tone was sharp, much too sharp.

Her expression only melted into one of a sad sort of acceptance. "I have walked this realm for millennia, Son, and it is for no other purpose than to stave off the sorrow that creeps in when I rest. To run from the madness lingering like a shadow from so much time alone."

The fire of my frustration blazed into an inferno. Typhon had done this, a co-conspirator with our father, and had subjected my mother to this...*torment.* I roared, turning my fury on the tree before us. I slammed my fists into its sharp bark, screaming as the wood splintered beneath my hands, as pain blossomed across my knuckles.

Oralia flashed behind my lids, her frightened face another gash within my heart. I roared again. Each blow did nothing to stem the raging tide. The pain, instead, increased, multiplied, until I was heaving in the night, my screams echoing off the mountainside.

"Quiet," Asteria soothed, brushing back the hair from my face as I knelt before the destroyed tree with my skin throbbing.

My breath whistled through my lungs, and I looked down at my hands, brows furrowed. It was not blood dripping from my knuckles, but an odd, shimmering substance.

"A kratus tree..."

My mother gave a noise of agreement, reaching forward to sift the pieces of wood and leaves through her hands. "Yes, it was."

Power unfurled through my veins with my heightening senses. I took a deep inhale, then another. Strange, it was as if I could smell the mist of Infernis—the mist that I hoped was clinging to Infernis in my absence. And when I turned, I thought someone had been speaking, there was a flicker of light within the mountains.

The Tylith Mountains.

"Mother..." I breathed, rising to my feet.

Asteria turned, frowning and following my line of sight. "What is it?"

With a shaking hand, I pointed at the mountains, at the caves carved into the sides, the strange shimmering liquid dripping from the deep cuts within my hands onto the ground that now turned bright green beneath my feet. "Do you see?"

But my mother only shook her head, stepping closer to examine the wounds. The luminescent fluid smeared across her palms as she pulled a few splinters free and stiffened, breathing deep. "What is that?"

My heart gave an unsteady lurch. "It is the mist I created to separate Infernis from Aethera." I spun her, pointing again to the light within the mountains. "And those are the Tylith Mountains, where souls go to face their deepest fears."

Her jaw slackened, hands flying to cover her mouth. "How have you done this?"

I tugged her hands from her face, looking at the silver smeared across our skin. "This must be my blood, only I do not recognize it."

"But this is not your body. It cannot be blood," Asteria murmured, turning over my hands and observing the slow-healing wounds before closing her eyes and breathing deep. Her connection to this place was strong after millennia trapped here, and I knew she'd found ways of communing for brief moments with the waking world, though only through those who dreamed or were fevered, as Oralia had been as a girl. "It is the essence of your magic, I believe. The purest form of your power."

That essence had created a rift within the in-between, a window into the waking world through which we walked as phantoms. I did not stop to think, only grabbed up a shard of wood and ran toward where I knew the castle would be. The landscape blurred as if I was caught in a gauzy curtain, the outline of the elm tree Oralia and I would sit beneath fading in and out of focus. A silver thread tugged through my chest, calling out. I ran faster, the flapping of Asteria's wings at my back as she followed my progress.

I skittered to a stop, breaths heaving, as there before me a god with waving sunset hair walked toward the Athal. The water of the river was gentle, merely a bubbling, and my magic told me this was not truly Oralia, only her dreaming form I had seen before.

"*Eshara*," I called softly as I would with one who walked while they slept.

Oralia stopped with the slowness of dreamers, turning with a dazed look on her face, a smile tipping up her lips. Cautiously, I approached, my hands now covered in the dried magic, and tugged her from the shores.

"I do not want..." her voice trailed off, attention wandering back to the river.

She did not want to remember. Pain sliced through my heart. Suffering was plain upon her face, the dark circles beneath her eyes and the heavy way her shoulders hung. I brushed back the hair from her cheeks, tilting her face up to mine.

"I do not blame you," I answered, pressing a kiss to the space between her brows.

Awareness prickled at the back of my neck. She did not appear to truly hear me, as if the veil between us fluttered, filling her ears. I took a step back, her hands falling back to her sides when I let go. Perhaps...

"I am sorry, love." The words were low as I brought the jagged piece of wood to my palms, slashing open the skin so magic poured between my fingertips.

Closing the distance, I pressed my hands to her face, the shimmering magic smearing across her freckles before I closed my mouth over hers. At first, her lips were slow, a mere approximation of a kiss. But as the seconds lengthened, a whimper slipped between us, her mouth firming and her fingers scrambling across my back and clutching me tighter.

"*Ren*," she cried, drawing back with clear eyes before they filled with tears.

I stroked her cheek, the blood wet on her face, before kissing her again. "I do not know how long we have."

She frowned, clutching me tighter, pressing her forehead to my chest. "This is a dream."

I shushed her, my hands closing over her shoulders to push her back. "No, this is the space between dreams, the moment between sleeping and waking."

Oralia shook her head, fingertips gliding over my jaw greedily, unable to tear her gaze from my face as I was hers. "I do not understand."

"It does not matter right now. Tell me what is happening."

My arms closed around her shoulders, unable to endure even a sliver of space between us. Her breaths came out jagged, and she fought the tears threatening as she told me in fits and bursts of Typhon and his plan, my heart sent to Infernis as a taunt. How she'd taken it into herself and strengthened our bond.

"My brilliant mate." I kissed her hair, holding her tighter while she continued. Her story was a waterfall, unable to be contained: the threads of the bond between us, how she was following them to find the pieces of me, the plan she had to resurrect me from this realm.

But already her voice was slowing, the dreamlike quality taking over. I gripped the wood tighter in my grip before a hand covered my wrist.

"It might not be safe," Asteria cautioned. "Her mind needs rest."

Oralia blinked up at my mother with a dazed sort of warmth, murmuring her name with reverence. Asteria leaned forward, brushing a kiss across her brow.

"Keep going, little corvus," she said to my mate before stepping back. "You are on the right path."

I nodded, pressing another kiss to Oralia's cheek. Her body grew limp in my arms.

"Ren..." Oralia's voice was distant, fingers falling from my tunic.

"I love you," I called as her body faded with the deepening mist, only catching the faint echo of her returning the sentiment.

She was finding the pieces, pulling me back together. I turned to look up at Asteria, her fingers twisted with worry in her robes as she gazed at the place where Oralia had stood, motherly affection and concern plain on her pale face. I would return to the world, and I would take my revenge—I was sure of it.

But what of my mother?

CHAPTER
TWENTY-ONE

Oralia

I woke with a gasp, shooting upright in bed.

My hands clawed at my chest, the pounding of my heart sickening beneath my ribs. The room was dark. Only small threads of morning light slipped through the heavy curtains. Every time I blinked, I saw Ren's face and felt his mouth on mine.

I am sorry, love, he'd said.

Real. It had been so real. The way it had standing beneath the baking sun on the docks of the human realm with the scarred god. Yet it could not have been real. Ren was gone, his magic waiting in some space beyond us for a body to return to. My mind was merely grasping for comfort, tired from our journey and the battle we'd fought.

But for a moment, right before I'd woken, I'd hoped. But the hope shattered with the realization that it was merely a dream. A sob slipped through my lips. I fisted the sheets, bowing forward until the fabric muffled my scream.

I wanted Ren—no, I *needed* him. It did not matter how much power lay within me or how the others believed we might win this war without him. I could not do this without him. Each breath hurt as I gasped for air, allowing the pain to leach from my body like poison from a wound.

As the light brightened in the room with the rays of dawn spilling through the cracks in the curtain, I quieted. The tears dried in tracks across my cheeks and left in their wake merely a hollow numbness.

My brilliant mate. Ren's voice was a mere memory in my ears. *I love you.*

The memory was enough to pull me from our bed and usher me out into the grounds below.

The maze stood sentinel between Rathyra and Pyralis, forming from the branches of a great tree growing on its side, gnarled and strengthened by time.

"Have you spoken with him before?" I asked Sidero, who had kept me company once I'd eventually made my way out of bed.

When Sidero had arrived with a tray of food, it was a relief to settle near the window in the sitting room and watch Infernis out the window. We'd spoken of mindless things, from the weather to what I would wear, and for a moment, I could pretend it was any other morning. I could pretend Ren was down with Horace and Dimitri seeing to the souls, and soon, he would crash through the door, throw his baldric to the floor, and tug me into his arms.

Eshara, he would purr before his mouth would cover mine.

"I have not spoken with Zayne," Sidero answered, breaking

through my reverie. They were gazing at the entrance of the maze with its monstrous walls made of tangled branches and rotted leaves.

I rolled my lips together, wringing my fingers in front of my gown before releasing them. My gloves were tucked into one of my pockets, and I savored the feel of the mist on my palms, the fabric of my skirts beneath my hands. The maze itself was unknown as most did not venture through it. There had been a purpose long ago, but it was rarely used now. Even Thorne had difficulty recalling the last time Horace had sent a soul there. I got the impression it was similar to the caves within the Tylith mountains where souls went to face their fears.

"Would you like me to go with you?" Sidero offered, gesturing toward the looming archway.

Shaking my head, I managed a small smile for my friend. Already my magic was prickling at the back of my neck, speaking to me without words. "No, thank you."

They nodded, squeezing my arm before they placed a palm over their heart. "I will find you before dinner, yes?"

"Of course," I answered. Aelestor, Drystan, and I had decided to leave the next morning. I'd begrudgingly agreed to wait a day to gather supplies, as this piece felt farther than the others and... stranger. Though I could not have quantified what made me feel so.

They had all insisted upon dinner that evening, convincing me it was best for the morale of our people to see a bit of normalcy within the kingdom. I did not know if I would be able to stomach a single bite at the table—the table where I'd first realized the growing desire between Ren and me.

My first step through the entrance of my maze shot a shiver down my spine, shadows instinctively sliding over my shoulders like a shield. Over the threshold, the world went quiet. Morning light dimmed until it could have been twilight. The scent of earth and decay overpowered any other sense until I was choking.

I turned right at an intersection before pausing, a sense of *wrongness* curling my gut and dewing on the back of my neck until I backtracked and took the opposite path. Relief washed away the discomfort as I took another left, traveling deeper into the maze, passing through courtyards of perfect circles, some bare and others with pits deeper than I could see or sense. Each wrong turn I took was another wave of sickness, pushing me toward...*somewhere*.

Ahead there was break in the maze. The center, I was sure of it. Seated in the middle, legs dangling over another pit, sat a god.

He did not appear surprised to see me as I stepped from one of the many paths and tugged on my gloves. With a languid confidence, he pushed to his feet, hand covering his heart. This was the god I'd spotted only a few times within the castle: once at my coronation, and another when our inner circle had first sworn fealty to me before I'd left the kingdom, and then the morning I'd arrived back in Infernis.

Citrine eyes stared back at me, and I could have sworn I saw them flare with power the way Horace's did. Some recognition sparked in his gaze. His heavy black brows furrowed as his hand dropped, head tilting to the side. The skin across my face prickled with his inspection, and I took a step forward, offering my hand.

"Oralia."

His lips flattened into a suppressed smile, and he nodded as if to say, *Yes, of course I know who you are.* Skin rasped against the fabric of my glove, but it was not the callouses of warriors but scars—deep burns crisscrossing over his palms.

"Are you Zayne?"

The god gave another small smile, dipped his head in confirmation, and patted two fingers to his chest. I frowned, wondering why he did not speak, but he guided me toward the pit with the hand he held. My heartbeat thundered in my ears, and I dug my heels into the soft earth.

"No...*no*." I was ashamed at the break in my voice even as my body shook.

But he shushed me in soft, crooning noises, let go, and settled himself on the edge as before. With one scarred hand, he gestured to the darkness below his feet, and the other patted the ground beside him. Magic tapped at my consciousness, like a hand on the back of my neck pushing me forward until I tentatively settled at the edge, feet tucked to my side instead of dangling off into the abyss.

I was not sure I liked this new form of my power if it wanted me to sit at the edge of a vast chasm.

Zayne did not comment on my trepidation, only giving another hum in the back of his throat. I blew out a breath, carefully peering over the edge before jerking back when my head swam and the world tilted.

"How can you stand it?" I asked, gesturing toward the pit.

With pursed lips, he tilted his head from side to side and pointed at the dark beneath his feet before settling his hand again behind him on the ground. All right. I could not say it was the most helpful response, and I was starting to understand what Thorne meant. Zayne did not appear inclined to speak, though every few minutes, he gestured toward the pit as if to remind me it was there.

I worried the edge of one of my gloves, trying my best not to look over the edge. "Thorne said you are a God of Fire..."

Zayne frowned, the deep golden skin of his cheeks drawing down.

One hand rose, fingers curling into a relaxed fist before opening once more. A single flame danced across his palms, and he tilted his hand, sliding it to each fingertip before holding it out to me. When I did nothing, he sat forward, offering his palm a little more firmly.

I shook my head. "I do not understand."

He sighed heavily, and my cheeks heated at his obvious disappointment. But then, he tapped two fingers to his chest before reaching forward to do the same motion over my heart and then offered me the flame.

Was he saying we were the same?

"That is why I am here," I said, leaning away from the fire before it caught my hair. "I need you to teach me. I cannot control it."

With a nod, he offered me his hand once more before slowly reaching for mine. I stiffened when he carefully took my wrist, vanishing the flame to tug off my black glove. There was an odd sort of reverence in the way he handled it, laying it on the ground between us before summoning the flame once more.

"It is not safe," I murmured as he maneuvered my hand palm up before me by gently twisting my wrist.

Zayne only smiled before placing his fingertips barely a breadth from mine, flame dancing across his scarred flesh, and blew gently as one might upon an ember. Warmth tingled across my fingers, magic unfurling beneath my skin, prickling as it might in a lightning storm. He did not appear concerned when nothing happened, only smiled encouragingly, and squeezed my arm. I frowned but did not move as he took a deep breath, slowly exhaled, and then tapped two fingers to my chest.

I copied the movement. Nodding, he breathed again, a hum of satisfaction low in his throat when I mirrored it. We breathed, slow and steady, and each exhale unwound another tendril of tension from my shoulders. My power sighed in relief before the unfamiliar heat sizzled beneath my palm, and with one final exhale, Zayne blew gently across the flame.

The fire danced across my fingers.

I wondered again how he'd come to attain the scars on his hands since this fire did not burn. It only lingered for a moment on my palm before sputtering and winking out with the breeze. Zayne chuckled, nodding again in approval before vanishing his own and picking up my glove. With careful movements, he wiped the dirt from the fabric before offering it to me, chin dipped respectfully.

"Will you teach me?"

The smile slipped from his lips, eyes tightening before he gestured again to my now-covered hand.

"I need someone to teach me like before with my shadows."

Zayne blew out a breath, lips curled down in distaste as he gazed into the pit. His mouth tensed and relaxed, throat working with a swallow. The longer I observed him, the more power I could sense as if it was unfurling from him in waves. His magic was vast with power as deep as the pit below us. Eventually, he nodded, pushed to his feet, and wiped his hands on his trousers before offering me assistance.

But he did not let my hand go, only guided me slowly into the maze, winding a dizzying path with confident steps. Sometimes, he hummed, and I thought the sound was familiar, some echo of the song Asteria had taught me when I was young before my own song of creation had taken form when prime began. Yet nothing grew or changed as we walked, it was merely comfort in the quiet.

"Are you taking me somewhere to train?" I asked, squinting at the light ahead. Perhaps it was another courtyard, easier to maneuver through without a pit.

We stepped across the threshold, and I blinked in the afternoon light, the mist slithering around my shoulders and cheeks. Far off, the grasses of Pyralis waved in the breeze and the soft tinkle of laughter and clanking of metalwork from Rathyra filtered through the air. Gently, two fingers tapped my shoulder. A hand squeezed mine, and I turned back to him.

"I thought..." My voice trailed off as he bowed his head with a hand pressed to his heart.

He tapped his chest twice, then my own, gesturing to the maze, and I thought I understood.

"When I return?" I clarified.

Zayne nodded, dipped his chin low, and ambled over the threshold, the darkness swallowing him whole.

CHAPTER
TWENTY-TWO

Oralia

T his one feels...odd," I muttered, adjusting the baldric I'd strapped across my chest.

After the attack on the mountainside, Drystan and the rest of the inner circle—save Mecrucio, who we'd sent back to Aethera to spy— had agreed that from this point forward I would be outfitted with more weapons than Ren's dagger. Though I had little experience wielding it, Ren's spare axe was affixed to my chest, along with a few short knives. The cloak around my shoulders was heavy enough to keep in the warmth wherever it was we went next.

"The baldric?" Drystan asked, gesturing to the strap I was adjusting.

"No..." My gaze drifted across Thorne's workshop, where the pieces of Ren were stashed away. Each table and counter gleamed with meticulous cleaning, and I spied the blades of a few knives where they were tucked beneath his workbench.

"The next piece?" Aelestor guessed, shifting his own weaponry, running his thumb across a particularly deadly-looking short sword before sheathing it.

I nodded, dropping my hands when I realized my adjustments were becoming more anxiety-induced than necessary. "It is farther, and yet, it calls to me more than every other as if it is begging to be found."

Both froze.

"Are you worried?" Drystan asked.

I drew up the hood of my cloak, offering them each an arm. "I am no more worried than I was for the others."

Neither hesitated to grab hold, which softened me a bit. I was expecting Aelestor to question me, to suggest we bring others— Thorne perhaps—but he only searched my face and nodded. Something had changed between us since our time on the mountain. I knew he'd respected me before, but some final wall I had not known remained had fallen. I trusted him to speak his mind, and knew I could count on him in moments of uncertainty.

The silver thread within me hummed and tugged. I frowned, unease clawing through my gut as the shadows flared from my chest, enveloping us. Aelestor and Drystan relaxed in the hold of my magic, finally comfortable after enough time traveling this way. As one, we stepped through the darkness, and for a moment, I thought I saw a shimmer of someone standing within the dark of the in-between. No, not one but two: a man and a woman with great silver wings. But they were gone in the next breath, wiped away by the shadows as they dissipated.

I blinked as sulfur stung my eyes and burned my nose. For a moment, I was frozen in the dark, thinking we were still shadow-walking before my eyes slowly adjusted. Ahead, lay a gnarled tree, spider-like branches reaching out in all directions and dipping into an eerily calm pitch-black lake. The ground squelched beneath my feet as I shifted my weight, and farther off, a bubbling noise emanated from a collection of rocks.

"*Stars,*" Aelestor cursed, voice dropping to a whisper. "Where are we?"

Neither of us responded, and I heard more than saw the two of them withdraw their swords. The axe was heavy in my hand as I pulled it from its sheath, but a shimmer of warmth trickled up my arm as if Ren was here with me in this place.

"Tread carefully," I cautioned, taking a small step forward.

With each step, the ground suctioned our feet until we were panting, tugging at our limbs as though the ground would rather keep us as its prisoner. The navy sky deepened to near black. Heavy mist droplets fell over our faces and slicked through our hair. My eyes stung as sweat rolled down my forehead, and I wiped it away hastily with a corner of my cloak.

The tang of something cloying and sweet danced across my tongue, my limbs all at once heavy and light. Each step was more difficult than the last, and a strange haze crept into my thoughts. Was I dreaming? Had we not left for the next piece of Ren yet?

When we had walked about a mile, I stopped, frowning at the tree. "We have not moved."

Drystan panted, hands on his knees before straightening. "*Burning Suns*, it cannot be the same."

"It is," Aelestor wheezed, stumbling as he dragged one foot from the spongy ground. "And the same lake beneath it."

"Is this real?" I murmured, running a hand over my hair, tugging at the strands, and trying to quantify the pain zinging up my scalp.

Aelestor's hand closed over my shoulder, squeezing hard enough

I hissed. "It is real, but there is a strange magic here, Oralia. Can you feel it?"

I could. The magic was heavy in the air. Awareness prickled on the back of my neck. I whirled, axe thrust forward, a cry slipping through my teeth, only to stumble back a step when my blade was mere inches from Drystan's throat, the tree still in front of me. Again, there was the tap of power, now on my temple, and when I turned to find it, it was to see I was standing in the same place.

"Something is wrong..." I breathed with my heart racing in my chest.

A *zing* rent the air like an arrow flying through the sky. My shadows threaded up to meet it, only to find nothing above. I shifted my weight, but my feet would not move. Pulling, I glanced down, a bubble of panic rising through my throat as black tar slithered up my boots and around my calves. The handle of the axe slipped in my sweaty palm as I tugged fruitlessly on my feet.

But when I lifted my head to ask for help, Drystan and Aelestor were gone.

In their place stood Ren, resplendent in his black finery from our soul-bonding ceremony, obsidian crown gleaming upon his head. He smiled, but the smile was wrong, too cold for his face. This was the smile he'd managed when we first met, one of bitterness and grief. I blinked, and the fine clothing was gone, replaced by his tunic and leathers, cloak slithering across the ground.

"*Ren*," I whimpered, arms splayed wide to keep my balance.

Another blink and he was spattered in blood, horror dripping from his cheeks. Another blink and his ceremonial clothes returned, but there was no smile for me anymore, merely a cold calculation in his gaze. Disgust slithered across his face, and he took a step closer.

The scent of him was odd in my nose, and it took me a moment to realize it was the absence of mine on his skin.

"Was it you?" he asked, fine tunic disappearing in another heartbeat, axe gleaming in his hand. "Did you betray me?"

"What?" I shook my head, but Ren caught my chin, grip so tight pain flared across my face.

"Was this your plan all along? To lure me into Aethera so my brother could destroy me?" Cold, so cold, the voice of a god who had lost so much.

A god who had nothing left to lose.

My heart drummed in my ears, and I tried to shake my head again but was stopped by his punishing grip. Sunlight hurt my eyes, and the cloying scent of wildflowers was overwhelming until I could no longer catch his scent at all. Was that what he believed? That my love for him had been nothing but a charade, a game in a war of kings?

A fissure cracked within my chest. "Of course, not. I am yours: your mate, your *eshar*—"

His hand closed over my throat, squeezing until the words cut off with a gasp. A small bone in my neck cracked, hot pain spreading out from my spine to my head, and the world tilted. Ren's eyes glittered in the bright light of the sun, moon-pale skin flushed with anger. My fingers scrambled over his wrists as I fought for small sips of air.

"You are nothing to me," Ren growled. "Nothing at all."

My arms grew limp, my head spun with a lack of oxygen, and I did not fight as his hand tightened. Instead, I used the last of my energy to raise my own, cupping his cheek as I'd done on our first meeting. When I'd believed I could destroy him in a single touch.

How wrong I'd been.

The hand on my throat jerked, grip loosening until I wheezed in a deep lungful of air. Something warm splashed across my face, and we both looked down at the arrow protruding from his chest, dark unearthly metal snapping out to hold it in place while a chain tugged Ren back a step. Ice hardened in his eyes even as he faltered, another arrow blasting through his arm and drawing it wide.

I dropped with him. My throat was raw. The scream was merely an approximation of a wounded animal as my hands slipped over the metal. Blood pooled between us. Another arrow and yet his face did not change. Not even when his arms splayed wide and a golden sword gleamed in the morning light. I wrapped my arms around his chest, my cheek pressed to his, and closed my eyes tight, waiting for the final blow.

We would not be separated, not this time.

But the strike never came. I tipped forward, mud shooting up my nose when Ren vanished, sun winking out in a blink. Feminine laughter curled through my ears, dancing the line between bone-chilling and kind. Coughing, I pushed to my knees, wiping a hand over my face to clear the mud from my eyes.

Not real. It was not real. An illusion, a trick. But *not real.* And yet the crack in my chest did not ease. The panic skittering down my chest did not wane.

"Not real, not real, not real," I repeated. My hands tremored as I pressed my palms together.

"The dramatics, my goodness," someone mused, a strange clicking noise accompanying the words, like the tread of heels of marble but...different.

A shadow fell over the mud. I clambered onto my backside, feet locked into place. The woman was unassuming in stature, olive skin clean with the barest hint of rose upon her cheeks. She would have

139

been beautiful if it hadn't been for the hardness in her features, the tight set of her mouth, and the strange decorative band dipping between her brows.

She took a step forward, clicking with the sway of her hips, when I realized the ornate embellishment around her chest was not metal, but *bones*. Whether they were god, demigod, or human I could not tell, but they clattered with each step. Similar, smaller bones blackened with time decorated her brow.

"You are an interesting creature," she mused, the edge of her dark gown tattered as it dragged through the mud. My fingers scrambled over my baldric, only to find it empty. The woman clucked her tongue, violet eyes flashing as she shook her head. "Your first mistake was bringing weapons into my land." She paused, pursing her lips. "Well, it was the *second* mistake. The first mistake was coming here at all."

"We meant no offense. We are not here for you," I gritted through my teeth. My pulse raced in my throat.

A soft, delighted laugh filled the space between us before black-tipped fingers shot out to wrap around my chin. "Such a political answer, though I should expect nothing less from a queen." She patted my cheek. "I know what you are here for, child. I allowed the sunlight soldiers to leave alive, after all. In fact, I am a bit put out it took you so long."

Heat rushed through me, and my power shot forward, shadows rippling out to wrap around her throat, but she only laughed again, slicing her hand through the darkness as if it were mist.

"Where was this fight a moment ago when your king had his hands wrapped around your throat?" She leaned forward, and her lips brushed my ear. "Or do you like that sort of thing, Oralia Solis?"

I lunged, only to find my hands trapped within the mud, rooted into place. A growl slipped through my lips, my shadows flinging forward before heat sparked. My gaze narrowed, and I allowed the fire to catch, ropes of flame wrapping around her waist, her throat, and her wrists. "I will send your magic back to the earth before you utter that name again."

Another tinkling laugh. Black-tipped hands clapped in delight before she inspected the fire. "Careful, sweetling, or I might start to like you."

My flames winked out as the ground beneath me bubbled like tar. But I did not fight it. I only stared in fury while it climbed my legs. The heavy beat of the kettledrum inside my chest vibrated through my ribs, loud enough I wondered if she could hear it. We stared at one another, her violet gaze flicking over my face before they widened in surprise.

"Oh, I do like you." The god, for she had to be one, leaned forward again, drawing in a deep breath. "You smell like the night and the day. Like a cavern where a heart might lay. Like you have drowned in blood and been born again."

I cringed away as her claw-like hands gripped my chin once more, the wet heat of her tongue slid up my face to catch the tears staining my skin.

"Once so starved and now you cannot feast. Once so full and now you have broken piece by piece."

Nails bit, pain slicing over my cheeks, and I gasped, kratus resin stinging through the shallow cuts. But her tongue soothed the wounds, lapping at the blood with a hum.

"Yes, you will do quite nicely," she murmured. The pressure around my legs and hands disappeared, the stinging across my cheek evaporating in the next moment. The woman's lips covered mine in a passionless kiss. "I think I will keep you."

With a bright smile, she pushed to her feet turning to face my companions who appeared suddenly behind her. The back of her dress clicked with the movement, bleached vertebrae lined her spine, sliding down the back of the gown to give the illusion of a tail.

Drystan turned, eyes wild when they rested on me. His cheeks gleamed in the dim light from tears on his face. The sigh of relief he gave was as tangible as it was visceral.

"You're safe," he groaned before falling to his knees, and weeping into his palms.

Behind him, Aelestor was screaming, reaching for something he could not see. He tore at his hair, bowing forward as Josette's name fell from his lips. After a few long moments, his cries quieted even while his shoulders shook. I could not move, my knees too weak, but I nodded at Drystan.

"I am," I murmured, though I was not sure if it was true with how volatile this unknown god appeared to be.

My voice shook Aelestor from his trance. Slowly, he turned, ruddy-faced and looking between Drystan and me before his eyes fell on the god between us.

She spread her arms wide, darkness dripping from her arms like shadowy wings.

"Hello, boys."

CHAPTER
TWENTY-THREE

Oralia

Aelestor and Drystan drew their swords in one heartbeat, and in the next, the weapons clattered to the ground at the god's feet. She laughed lightly and turned to kneel beside me once more, pushing the sweaty hair from my face. There was no mud on my hands or caked on my face. The blood I'd thought sprayed across my cheeks was absent, along with the scent of Ren.

None of it had been real. I was sure of it. Then why did I tremble? Why, when I closed my eyes, did I see his distrustful face staring back at me?

"Do not touch her," Drystan growled, darting forward to grab his sword.

The god allowed it, a smile tugging at her full lips while her claws dragged across my scalp. His blade appeared at her throat, but she merely tapped the edge, skittering her fingers across it like the keys of an instrument.

"I have what you are looking for, darling," she crooned in my direction, wrapping a hand around my arm, and with a strength that far surpassed her stature, she dragged me to my feet.

Drystan and Aelestor rushed forward, but she maneuvered me effortlessly between her and them, providing a barrier they would not dare to break.

"Come, children," she called, slithering an arm around my waist to guide me forward.

My knees shook as she guided us over the boggy terrain, and for the first time, it changed. Dark swamp spread out in all directions. Water rose around our ankles. Tangles of vines threatened each step. Yet this god did not pause as we waded into the water toward the towering tree, wide branches dipping down into the water. She only hummed under her breath, occasionally looking back to catch my eye or else reaching for my hand to brace me.

"Young gods are so...*vital*," she mused. "Watching you and *myhn latska cahdren* here was the most excitement I have had in years."

My brows pulled together. "It was not real..."

The words were more for me than for her. But she shushed me, brushing back the hair clinging to my cheeks before reaching back to gather my heavy cloak where it dragged in the waist-high water. The gnarled tree grew larger as we approached, and out of the corner of my eye, I caught her checking over one shoulder to ensure Aelestor and Drystan were following.

"Of course, it was not real," she answered, voice honey-sweet. "You do not know who I am, do you, sweetling?"

Aelestor mumbled under his breath, pulling a tinkling laugh from the god. But it was Drystan who answered in a hollow tone, raising his sword higher to avoid the water.

"Dreams."

The god hummed again, gripping my hand when I slipped on the murky silt as we climbed onto the opposite shore. "Close, demigod." But she did not release her grip, only tugged me forward toward the gargantuan trunk.

I remembered the horror washing through my veins, the strange thickness on my tongue, and heaviness in my chest. How the image of Ren had flickered with each blink. The words he had spoken, putting voice to my deepest fears. Even now, I could not shake it. The memory lingered on my skin like a grimy film.

"Nightmares," I breathed.

The god crooned, patting my hand once. "Very good, sweetling."

"*Stars*," Aelestor grunted. "Just what we need."

But I could only stare at her, the delicate slope of her nose, her hair braided over her crown which caught the faint unearthly light of this place in shades of auburn. Her power was different than mine and Aelestor's, different even than Thorne's. She reminded me more of Morana.

We did not stop before the tree as I assumed. Instead, she halted our progress in the shallow edge of the water lapping at our ankles.

"You are timeless..." My words were soft. I feared this god and all she could do—the power roiling beneath her skin. She had made me see my greatest fears without even realizing her magic was working on me. It must have been the prickle I'd felt on the back of my neck, but her power had taken hold the moment we arrived on these shores.

Something like sorrow crossed her features, lips downturned into the approximation of a frown. The look was so soft it changed her entire countenance, breathtaking beauty shining through for an instant before it winked out like a flame.

But she did not respond, only extended one hand out to the side, clicking her tongue twice. Muck bubbled, and a great groan rumbled beneath our feet. Aelestor and Drystan slid closer to my side, staring at our new companion with tight eyes.

"When you endanger her, you endanger this entire world," Aelestor warned, his hand gripping tightly around the hilt of his weapon.

The god grinned, white teeth catching in the dark. "I can see why your Josette likes you. Protective"—she winked at him—"possessive, even of your queen. But lower your sword, Lord Thyella. I mean your queen no harm. Not anymore."

Behind her, the mud bubbled higher, a sickening, rumbling suction vibrating through the ground. I blinked, and a creature dragged itself from the mud, wide haunches twisting to free itself, heavy front feet flaring wide to balance. On four legs, it ambled in our direction, clumps of earth slapping to the ground with each step. A tail flicked, exposing a razor-sharp talon slicing through the air with a whistle.

The god crooned, clicked her tongue again, and wiggled her fingers. "Come, Hezanah."

Her grip tightened on my wrist as I stumbled back. The monster's head was large, higher than even Drystan's and Aelestor's height, with slits for eyes, glowing yellow in the dark. Something protruded from its flattened muzzle, wrapped in dark cloth untouched by the muck dripping from its body.

No...this creature was *made* of the muck and mud and earth.

The monster—Hezanah, the god had called it—chuffed and dropped the bundle at her feet with a splash before nuzzling her open palm.

"Good boy," she praised and leaned forward to press her forehead to the creature's huge muzzle, nearly the size of her head. "Listen for me. I will call when we need you."

Aelestor spluttered while Drystan shook his head. I had not realized they'd shifted to place themselves between me and the creature. My chest ached, and I rubbed at it with my free hand before drawing him back before the god noticed.

"What is it?" I asked. For the first time, I realized the silver thread within my chest was humming again. Only through its reappearance had I realized its absence.

The god scooped up the bundle carefully as one might a child before passing it into my arms. She ran her fingertips across my forehead, and each touch sent a shiver down my spine, discomfort roiling in my gut.

"You know, I wondered what it was connected to, that thread," she mused, reaching out in the space between me and the bundle and twisting her wrist.

When she tugged, I gasped, the feeling echoed in my sternum.

She had been the one pulling on the connection, somehow able to see it when others could not.

"How can you..." I started, unable to finish.

Ice-cold hands cupped my face, and I frowned, fighting the urge to cringe. This time, she did not smile. The strange, wild amusement melted from her expression the way sleep melted from one's shoulders.

"I am Samarah, the God of Nightmares. My power rests within the in-between, the space between dreams, the moment between sleeping and waking."

Something prickled on the back of my neck at her words, a memory as insubstantial as the mist flickering through my mind: Ren's face, close to mine, his midnight eyes earnest in their expression.

This is the space between dreams, the moment between sleeping and waking.

Before I could question further, she reached out, tugged Drystan closer, and placed his hand on my shoulder and doing the same with Aelestor. "Come, children, we should be off. I will help you carry the load."

Power slithered across my wrist where she held me, and my shadows flared of their own accord. My brows furrowed. "Where is it you want us to go?"

Samarah blinked. "Infernis, of course. I want to see what my nephew has done with the kingdom since I last saw it."

"Nephew?" Aelestor huffed with incredulity.

The God of Nightmares rolled her eyes. "You lot are *slow.*"

"Ren..." I breathed. "Ren is your nephew."

She shrugged. "It is a human term I found I quite like. If anything, he was a son, though before time began it is strange to try to recall his birth. But I remember I was the one to pull him from Asteria's womb. I watched him grow and guided him with the others. I mourned him when we left, mourned him when Typhon plucked off his wings like a child with an insect. Horrible thing, to be stripped of one's wings. It is the easiest way to subdue a timeless god, you know." Her magic vibrated against me, my shadows widening in reaction to engulf us. "Enough chatter, darling."

The three of us exchanged a tense look before I blew out a breath and pulled the shadows around our group. Shadow-walking Aelestor, Drystan, and myself was a skill I'd been taught before I left Infernis for Aethera, a preparatory measure Ren had insisted I learn. But to shadow-walk four of us was too much. Her power strengthened my own, slotting into the fraying gaps

We stepped in unison, the darkness swallowing all light and sound. There, again, I thought I caught sight of a pair standing close to the end of the dark, staring, waiting, but for what I did not know.

I felt more than saw Samarah raise a hand as if she was greeting them before the shadows melted and Infernis appeared. She gave a hum of approval, gazing up at the bones of the castle, and reached out to stroke the closest. The same soft look fell over her face.

Footsteps clattered over the stairs before Horace reached us, ruby eyes wide as he looked over our group before he froze.

"*Maelith*," he breathed.

And as the old word registered in my mind, I realized who it was standing beside me. A bright smile broke across her face.

"Miss me?"

CHAPTER

TWENTY-FOUR

Renwick

ho was that?" I breathed, surging toward the small space
of grass Oralia had passed through.

"Ren," Asteria called, her tone a warning.

"*Who was that?*" The words came out as a growl as sweat broke
out on the back of my neck.

It had been only a moment, barely enough for me to make out
their features alongside my mate, but they had raised their hand in
greeting to us. They had *seen* us. And if they could see us, then perhaps it meant they could help us.

"It was Samarah." Hands closed over my upper arms, the flare of
her wings halting my progress. "Only Samarah."

I froze, cursing under my breath, while my hands clenched
around empty air. Samarah, the God of Nightmares, one of the
Great Mothers who had made the world. She had disappeared millennia ago along with the others who had left due to my father's
madness.

"I thought she would be in Iapetos," I murmured, relaxing in my mother's hold.

Asteria gave a soft laugh. "Of course, she was not. Samarah was never one to follow the herd."

Yet she'd abandoned us—abandoned me—when I needed her most. I could have used her terrifying power on the battlefield. Her ability to bend reality to her will and fill her enemies with their greatest fear was incomparable. It was as tangible as my and Oralia's shadows and ten times more terrifying.

I stared at the place where they'd stood for less than a heartbeat. It was Oralia I'd been focused on until Samarah had raised a hand—the fighting leathers she'd worn, my axe strapped to her chest, the haunted look in her dark green eyes.

"I need to get to her."

"To Samarah?" Asteria clarified.

Shaking my head, I turned toward the direction of the castle in Infernis, though here, it was merely another shadowy mountain in the distance. "Oralia. I need to get to her."

It was more or less the same thing I'd been saying for however long I'd been trapped here. But now Samarah had thrown her name into the fire. She was unpredictable at best and dangerous at worst. If Oralia had crossed paths with her, then that meant...

That meant she'd shown my mate her greatest fear.

It was enough to make the strongest of us go mad. My blood ran cold at the thought of what she was having to endure, trapped within the confines of her mind. I knew better than most what a horrifying place her thoughts could be, how she could retreat within herself. Now, she would add this extra stone to her back to weigh her down when she already had so much to bear.

I closed my hand over the shard of kratus bark, slicing through my skin with the point I'd sharpened. At once, the mist filled my lungs. The scent of asphodel flowers and mist were heavy on my tongue. A hum of voices reached my ears, and I blinked, the castle appearing in place of the darkened mountain.

Samarah stood beside Oralia, a possessive arm around her waist. But it was my mate I observed, the firmness of her mouth, her shoulders scrunched up to her ears. The God of Nightmares had never been understanding of boundaries, not with one foot in the in-between.

In the in-between.

Violet eyes flicked up to meet mine, and a slender auburn brow raised. Silvery magic dripped between my fingers as we stared at one another through the space between Horace and Aelestor. Dimitri's heavy steps thundered down the staircase, attention fixed upon Samarah.

Oralia looked up at me, mouth popping open in surprise. She jerked, restrained by the arm around her waist. Samarah leaned forward, lips brushing her ear, whispering something before Dimitri stepped forward, a blade held to the God of Nightmares's throat.

Stars, Samarah considered such a thing foreplay.

Oralia's gaze did not leave mine, but something flickered there, a shadow crossing over her pupils. The surprise on her face turned to wariness, the hope to anguish, until she crumpled, shoulders rounding in on themselves. Samarah frowned, releasing her as the others stepped forward. I watched helplessly as my mate was crowded, trembling hands rising up to cover her eyes, fingers pressing into her ears.

"Get back," I yelled, voice swallowed by the wind. "Get away from her!"

Samarah's gaze caught mine, and I saw an expression on her face I had not seen often: concern. She crouched, covering Oralia but not touching her, speaking in a low tone to the others, who backed away slowly.

My feet were heavy on the ground, the power drying on my palms, but I pushed through the deepening mist. I needed to get to her, to release the pressure on her soul.

"Bring her to me," I growled at Samarah.

Her lips parted and fear tangled with the worry on her features.

"You owe me this." I slipped between Dimitri and Horace.

They jumped, sucking in a sharp breath, but I was reaching for Oralia, ready to pull her into my arms.

Before they vanished in a sudden gust of wind.

CHAPTER
TWENTY-FIVE

Oralia

W as this your plan all along?"

Hands wrapped around my throat, squeezing. A sharp pain sliced through my belly. I clutched the axe now protruding from my womb.

"You are nothing to me."

Blood filled my mouth. I choked on my scream.

"Nothing at all."

Hands closed over my shoulders. A voice called my name, murky through the blood now pouring from my ears. And then I jolted awake, tumbling into arms winding around my shoulders, pressing my face into waving auburn hair.

"Merely a dream, sweetling," Samarah crooned. "Breathe for me."

The scream I'd been choking on echoed through the room. My fingers clutched the bones circling her waist. She shushed me, razor-sharp nails scraping over my scalp, rocking me as a mother might. I pushed and scrambled away from her.

"I did not betray him," I muttered, panic smearing the words together.

"No, you did not," the God of Nightmares answered, brushing the wetness from my cheeks, ignoring my recoil. "What you saw was not him, only your fear—the thing your subconscious dreads above all else."

Shaking my head, I ran a hand over my face and through my tangled hair before tugging down the hem of Ren's tunic. Samarah's violet eyes shone in the dark, delicate brows drawing together before she placed a hand on my shoulder.

"Do not," I breathed, shaking off her touch.

But she only clucked her tongue and tugged me again into her arms with overwhelming strength, shushing me when I struggled.

"The broken pieces of you fear what you have lost, but that does not mean you do not need them." She rocked slowly, passing a hand up and down my back. "What I showed you was not real, sweetling. It is a reflection of *you*, not him."

I knew she was right. Drystan had been subjected to a similar vision, but it had been me, not Ren. He'd been weeping over the image of my body strung up with chains, the blood pouring from my throat and wrists. And in his vision, I'd jolted to consciousness only to choke on my own blood and die before his eyes.

Aelestor's vision had been one of Josette drinking from the Athal. He'd spoken of it in halting tones, refusing to say more before he'd raced off to Rathyra to no doubt assuage his fears. I was jealous of them for that comfort. Drystan could pull me into his arms as a father might and comfort himself it was all a dream. Aelestor could do the same with Josette.

But I could not. Ren was lost to me and the only thing left behind was the memory of his face, the accusations like a bruise upon my mind. The bond I had come to rely on was silent, no reassurance of his love or contentment—merely a rhythm of his magic like a heartbeat.

Slowly, I forced myself to relax into her hold, tears drying into tracks across my cheeks. "Do you regret it?"

"Using my power on you?" Samarah's voice was soft beside my ear, the strange earthy scent of her coating my tongue.

I nodded into her throat, tracing the slope of a bleached white rib where it lined her chest. She sighed, gathering my hair from my shoulders, nails scratching across my neck, forcing a shiver down my spine.

"No, I do not. I do not regret using my power to protect myself, even if the cost is high. Even if I cannot weigh the damage."

Her voice was different here in this room, lacking its strange, lilting quality of riddles and hysteria. I wondered if this was who she truly was or if it was merely a means with which to subdue. Samarah had staked some sort of a claim on me. Even on the steps of the castle, when I'd been sure I'd seen Ren standing feet away from us with silvery liquid dripping from his hands, she had not allowed anyone to get close to me when I snapped and began wailing. Embarrassment twisted through my stomach at the memory—how weak I'd appeared. What a wonder that these gods viewed me as their queen when I was merely a shivering, quaking fawn succumbing to fear.

It was only I could not quantify what it was I'd seen before me. Ren had been dressed in a black tunic and trousers, the same as I'd seen him in my dreams. The expression on his face was one of concern, love bleeding from his eyes like the silvery substance from his hand. Samarah had seen him too, I was certain. She'd whispered something to me, but I'd been unable to hear her over the pounding of my heart. And all I could think was that I could not bear to see the moment when his face hardened, the moment the accusations would begin again.

Samarah had been the one to guide me to my rooms with a hand on my waist, all but growling at Sidero when they attempted to follow. It was Drystan she had allowed in to check on me, some sort of brittle trust threaded between them.

"Lie back," Samarah murmured, pushing on my shoulders until I followed her instruction.

I fought her, negation slipping from my lips even as she caught my wrists, shushing me while she pressed my head onto Ren's pillow. The quiet, liquid language of the timeless gods slithered through the dark. Only a few words stood out to me, and they confused me further. *Harm. Good. Guide. Breathe.*

With gentle movements, she drew the covers up my chest before closing my lids with the slight pressure of her fingers. But it did not remind me of the motions of a mother—this was more like the actions of a human undertaker—of one preparing a body for burial. The scent of earth swirled closer, hair tickling my cheek.

"Take a breath, sweetling."

"What are you doing?" My mouth tensed, and I held my breath.

But fingers smoothed the space between my brows, sliding across my lips. My mind swam, a strange heaviness falling across my limbs. I was breathing deeply, gulping in her scent tinged with a pungent sweetness like rot. Shaking my head, I slapped against her chest, but Samarah only gripped my wrists, pressing them against the mattress.

"I am keeping my promise, *latska lathira*. Because it is to them I am loyal above all else."

I was too far gone to understand her words. I wandered through a thick wood at twilight. Stars twinkled overhead. The simple gown I wore was soft against my skin, dark in the night. A hand wrapped around mine, squeezing tightly, before violet eyes flicked toward me and away as Samarah guided me over a shallow brook.

My heart hammered in my ears with each step. I swallowed, unsticking my dry tongue from the roof of my mouth. This was not a dream, or it did not feel like one. Her hand was too solid against my own, the air too crisp on my skin, the ground too soft beneath my bare feet. I was *too awake.*

"You are awake," Samarah answered, voice clear as a bell. "Sleeping with your eyes wide open."

That sounded quite a bit like I was asleep. I ducked beneath a low branch, steadying myself with a hand on the trunk of another as we descended a winding path. "Where am I?"

"You are here and you are there. You are in the space between, one foot in dreams and the other in waking. Your body remains in your bed, but your mind is gone." She pushed another wide bough out of our way, the woods thinning to sparse trees.

"The in-between," I murmured.

Samarah gave a small noise of confirmation, patting the back of my hand. But she did not speak again as we rounded a bend, a large clearing sprawling ahead at the base of the mountain. I first caught sight of a pair of wide, silver wings, shimmering in the faint moonlight. Asteria's long black hair rippled down her back, wings flaring with each step she took, following the progress of the man pacing.

I had barely stepped into the clearing when Ren raced forward, but I skittered back, a soft cry slipping through my lips. My stomach turned to stone and acid roared up my throat. Soon, the sun would shine, the arrow would fly, and his hands would wrap around my neck.

"Please, *please*," I cried, hands held in front of me as if I could stop the nightmare before it began. "I promise, I did not betray you. I would never betray you."

Gently, Ren's hands wrapped around my wrists. I cringed away, but he only pressed a kiss to my upturned palm, tugging me into the circle of his embrace.

"You would never betray me, *eshara*," he murmured, velvet tone a balm against the stinging wounds.

"You went too far, Samarah," Asteria chided over Ren's shoulder, but I could barely register the words or the admonishing look she was giving the God of Nightmares before they kissed lightly on the mouth.

I stiffened in Ren's arms, bracing myself for the dream to change, for these clothes to melt into his ceremonial garb. For the dark to seep into the corners of my eyes, and the world to bleed out its oxygen. Hands slid up and down my back before winding around my nape. Stars burst behind my lids as I squeezed my eyes shut, childishly believing if I could not see him, then the torture would not start.

"Whatever you saw, it was not real," Ren breathed.

But unlike the words Samarah had spoken, these trickled through my consciousness, sliding into the cracks broken within my soul.

His lips brushed against my lids, fingers slid over my jaw. "You are mine, Oralia. Until the end of time—after, even. Nothing could tear us apart."

When his lips covered mine, I did not fight the kiss. Ren breathed new life into my chest, and I moaned, wrapping my arms around his neck. His tongue swept into my mouth, demanding in its fervor.

There, within his kiss, was the taste of truth, old magic sliding between our lips, wrapping around our hearts.

The murmurs of Asteria and Samarah melted away as they left the clearing. The flapping of wings as they gave us privacy was a faint song in my ears, drowned out by the beating of my heart. No...*our hearts*. Beating as one within my chest, the silver thread I had not been able to follow humming between us.

Leading me here—to him.

CHAPTER
TWENTY-SIX

Renwick

It did not matter that this was not Oralia's true body in my arms. Her physical being was deep within the castle, nestled in our marriage bed, out of reach. This was her essence, her magic, her *soul*, here in my embrace, and I could not ask for anything greater in this moment.

She gave a soft little moan as I forced her mouth wider, taking control of the kiss and deepening it while I guided her to the ground. My body came alight with magic, skittering over my skin and settling deep in my belly. I could not touch enough of her. My hands ran over the planes of her face, sliding through the waves of her hair. The gown she wore in this realm was nondescript, merely a shift of fabric gathered at the waist and shoulders, like the clothing of old.

"Ren, please," Oralia breathed against me, greedy fingers tugging at the laces of my tunic, diving beneath to caress my skin.

"I know, *eshara,*" I hummed, pressing a kiss to the curve of her jaw, nipping at the skin beneath her ear. My cock throbbed at the knowledge of her aching the same as I, this insubstantial body reacted the same as the one scattered across the world would.

I seated myself between her knees, gazing down at her kiss-stung face. Her dark green eyes were wild. A shimmer of the panic from only moments ago lingered in the corners. Her chest heaved with each breath. Her fingers curled around the front of my tunic. Slowly, I dragged the skirts of her gown higher, exposing the smooth skin of her thighs and the constellation of freckles across her hips.

"I would never betray you." Her words were deep in her throat as if the need to say them outweighed the need between her thighs. "I did not come to Infernis to destroy you. My allegiance is to you, to our people. I swear it."

Sitting back on my heels, I allowed her to get the words out despite the urge to cover her lips with mine. Instead, I curled my hands around her knees, soothing with gentle touches, attention trained on her face. And when she finished, I cupped her cheek in my hand, thumb brushing over her lower lip.

"I know you would never do such a thing, Oralia."

She frowned, pushing up onto her elbows. "But how could you know? How could you not wonder?"

I smoothed the hair back from her shoulder, fingertips sliding across her throat. "Because I saw the blood spilling from your skin as you tried to get to me. Because I felt your anguish here"—I touched my chest—"in our bond. And because I know the most important thing of all: you feel the same as I do for you."

Blood blossomed through her cheeks, eyes turning glassy. "And what is that?"

Wrapping a hand around her nape, I dragged her to me, lips separated by mere moments. "That you are *everything* to me."

Oralia surged forward, fingers tugging my hair, cementing her chest to mine. I groaned, my fabric covered cock finding the scorching apex of her thighs, and I could not resist the urge to thrust once against her heat, steadying her by the hip. The words unlocked some primal need inside my mate, her breaths heavy across my face as she kissed my cheeks, my brow, my throat. Delicate fingers tugged at the hem of my tunic, pulled it from my trousers, and cast it aside.

This was more than satiating a need for her. This was speaking with our bodies what our lips could not. The endless hunger, the scorching desire, the longing I could not bear even as one moment bled into the next. I trusted her with everything—she could take *everything* and I would be whole because I was already hers.

Reverently, I unclipped the fastenings at her shoulders, humming with appreciation as the fabric pooled at her waist. With the hand on her nape, I pulled away to gaze hungrily at her breasts, the rosy peaks of her nipples tightening under my attention.

"*Kalimayah*," I breathed, slipping into the old language.

And she was beautiful—heartbreakingly so. The ancient word encompassed what the common tongue could not: the ethereal quality of her beauty, the wonder I experienced when I gazed at her. I lifted her wrist to my mouth, kissing the black scars across her skin, worshipping the marks which had forged a horrifying connection to my kingdom as I worshipped the power she had so fervently feared and now conquered. But Oralia was already reaching for the placket of my trousers, hand diving within the fabric to caress my aching cock, leaking with need for her.

"Do not make me wait." Her voice was stern, commanding, only the barest shiver of desire breaking the firmness.

"I would make you beg if I could, merely to hear the sweetest need falling from your lips," I countered, allowing her to draw me forward.

My hand replaced hers, and I groaned as I slid the head of my cock through her wetness. Her back arched, and I guided her down again on the thick grass, heavy with the scent of rain that would never fall in the in-between. Oralia's knees opened while I braced myself beside her head, nestling the tip within her heat.

Strange how even here, her power could thread through mine. I shivered, a moan falling from my lips as I sheathed myself deep. Her answering noise of relief mirrored mine, dragging my face to hers. Slowly, I rocked my hips, savoring the squeeze around my cock, how with each drag she fluttered around me, already so close to the edge.

"I know you have been aching for me, *eshara*," I murmured against her skin, dipping low to capture the tip of one nipple between my teeth.

She gave a whimper, nails scratching across my scalp, holding me to her.

"But did you know here, in this realm where all is provided, where I do not need food or rest or shelter, there is one thing I need?"

Slipping my hand between us, I circled her clit with two fingers. Oralia's cry was music to my ears, a balm on my aching soul. Tiny broken pieces of me, marred by the violence that had been wrought, knitted themselves together. Though my chest lightened, a weight on my shoulders grew. Our magic tangled around us, shadows and light and surprising, sparkling embers—a cocoon of power shutting out the world.

"W-what is it you need?" she cried, lids fluttering.

"You. You against me, your sweetness on my tongue, your cunt on my cock. Your body is the only place that has ever felt like home."

I grinned, leaning back to churn my hips, slipping my fingers onto either side of her clit. A movement behind me rustled in the wind, the sound barely audible over the moans sliding between us, and though I wanted to turn, I was too enraptured by the sight of me disappearing into her slick heat.

Oralia's eyes popped open, lips parting in surprise before her brows knitted, and her cunt squeezed around me. She rose onto one hand, reaching with the other behind my back. A shiver ran down my spine, pleasure coiling tight.

"That's it," I praised, kissing the sparkling wetness spilling across her cheeks. "Just like that."

Her moan echoed off the mountain, sliding through my sternum to wrap around the space where my heart would be if it was not in her chest. And her pleasure drew mine with it until her name was falling from my lips, my hips jerking erratically, chasing her over the edge until I was spilling deep within her womb.

"Ren," Oralia panted, hand sliding over my shoulder again, eyes fixed behind me. "*Stars,* Ren. Can you not feel them?"

My brows furrowed, but I was not ready to be parted from her, so I drew back enough to read her face easier, the wonder in her eyes baffling. And with the movement, there was another rustle behind me. It was heavy, the weight, unfamiliar but not forgotten. The magic around us slowly dissipated, the last of the embers of her new power winking out into the dark.

"What is it?" I asked, sliding out of her with a sigh, wishing I could nestle myself within her and never let go.

Tucking myself back inside my trousers, I looked down between us, pleasure churning in my chest at the sight of silvery magic leaking from her swollen cunt. But she only drew her legs together, pushing up onto her knees to reach behind me.

Her hand caressed the curve of...*something*. The touch sent a shiver down my spine, heat flaring within my cock until I was ready to flip her over and drive into her again. It could not be what I thought—what I hoped. I could not allow myself to believe it, even if it was only temporary here within this realm.

But then she drew back, eyes bright with unshed tears, cupping my face in her hands.

"Your wings."

CHAPTER
TWENTY-SEVEN

Oralia

I had not wondered why Ren did not have his wings in the in-between. He had appeared before me whole except for those long-mourned parts of him he was never sure he'd be reunited with. But as we'd joined and our magic had tangled around us, I thought I understood. Even here in this realm, Ren held onto those broken pieces of himself. In a world where he needed for nothing, his soul was not truly whole.

They had been insubstantial at first, merely shadows flowing behind his back, shivering with each breath he took. But as our pleasure had reached a fever pitch, as magic had shimmered around us, his wings had taken form. Wisps of shadow made real, tangible, until I could reach out to stroke my finger over the junction where black muscle faded into pale skin.

Ren's hair slid forward to cover his face, chin dipped toward his chest. With each breath he took, his wings shuddered, flexed, responded. His hands, spread wide across his thighs, tensed, then relaxed, as if waiting for a killing blow. I scooted closer, pressing my bare chest to his, to drag my palm over the bend, wrapping my fingers around the silver-tipped talon at the top of the wing.

"They are beautiful, Ren," I breathed.

Different than Typhon's feathered white wings, Ren's were pitch black, thin skin like a membrane stretched out across four narrow bones. Dragging my fingertips over them, I tried to learn the texture—to understand the strange shimmer in the weak light of twilight. In many ways, it reminded me faintly of the souls as they ascended, their shimmering light swallowed by the mist and the dark.

"*Eshara*," he rumbled, darting out to grip me by the hips.

"Do you not want to see them?" I asked, resting my chin on his shoulder while I continued to explore.

My fingers drifted to the meeting point on his back that had once been merely gnarled scars. Tears glazed across my vision, heat dancing up my face to see him as he should have been. I could only hope he would be the same in our world soon.

Ren gave another muffled groan, and I pulled back, brows furrowed. "Does it hurt?"

Breath ghosted across my face, his chest heaving before his fingers dug deeper into my flesh. A flush painted his cheeks, his midnight eyes going black. Between us, his cock strained against the fabric of his breeches where he'd haphazardly put himself away. Yet he did not respond, only stared at me, lips parted. Slowly, I reached out, dragging one finger across the edge of his wing, and his lids fluttered, a moan slipping through his lips.

"Ren..."

His mouth covered mine before I could ask again as he dragged me onto his lap and speared me onto the head of his cock. My hand wrapped around the bend of his wing, and he moaned, bucking up into me, fingers tangling in the back of my hair to expose my throat.

"You ask me if it hurts, *myhn lathira?*" Ren rasped, holding me steady against his punishing rhythm.

My belly clenched, heat spiraling down my spine until embers burned across my skin.

"To have you wrap your hand around a part of me I have not had in three centuries, a piece of me you have never known, and yet restored to me with a mere breath...it is bittersweet *agony*, Oralia."

Teeth clamped down upon my shoulder, and I cried out, holding myself steady with my grip on his shoulders. This was its own kind of worship. A ferocity Ren could not control. His entire existence was loss—his soul had been broken down piece by piece until he did not know his own reflection in the mirror. And now suddenly, in this place, he was whole again.

I fluttered around his cock, release there, right on the edge. But Ren did not slow his pace, only laving at the bite on my neck. Both hands wrapped around my waist, bouncing me on his lap. All I could do was let go, allowing my mate to use me to his own ends and unleash this part of him he had not relinquished. And when he did, I exploded around him, his name a scream ripping through the air.

I was boneless in his grip as Ren moaned into the curve of my throat, hips stuttering. I leaned forward, sliding two fingers across the wide expanse of one black wing, and Ren cried out, hot pulses of his cock dragging a smaller, gentler orgasm from me. We sat in the quiet for a few long moments, foreheads pressed together, breathing in each other's air.

"Do you want to see them?" I asked again, sliding carefully off him.

Ren's fingers dove between my legs, gathering up his seed to press back inside of me, though, of course, it did not matter here in this realm. He cupped my sex possessively. He did not speak for a long time while I ran my fingers through his messy hair, dragging in deep pulls of his scent as if it was the only air I breathed.

"No," he breathed. "I cannot bear it."

With a shake of his head, he pushed to his feet, wings flaring behind him. He stumbled slightly with the overcorrection, and I braced him with a grip on his forearm.

"Why not?"

Ren took a deep breath, wincing as his wings responded, before running a hand through his hair. "Because this place is not real. This is not my real body, nor yours. It is more than dreams yet less than waking. And I know when you revive me, it will not be to this body and these wings."

Closing the space between us, I cupped his face in my hands, stroking across the sharp planes of his cheekbones. "I vow to you, I will do everything in my power to return them, to completely restore you."

He gripped my wrists, leaning into the touch. "Tell me instead what is happening, what is left, and what you plan to do."

There was not much to report, only the things he could parse out from his own observations and the confirmation that Samarah had housed a piece of him within her land. There were three more pieces of him scattered, four if I included his wings on display within Typhon's palace. He asked about my power, the fire he'd seen dancing with the light and shadows, and gave me a strange sort of smile when I told him of my meeting with Zayne.

"He is exactly what you need, *eshara*." Ren tucked my hair behind my ears and pressed a kiss between my brows before sliding the fabric of my gown up my shoulders.

I clung to him, a strange pulling sensation beginning in my belly. "Please do not make me go."

"We must go, sweetling," Samarah called in her singsong voice, appearing through the trees arm in arm with Asteria.

The latter's face was reddened, eyes bright and glassy. But Samarah turned with a smile, pressing kisses to her cheeks before reaching out to me.

"Dawn grows near and you must rest," she continued. "Say good-bye to your mate."

Ren's lips brushed my temples, knuckles tilting my chin up to cover his mouth with mine. "You are on the right path. Trust in your magic."

The vision of him faded, along with the woods at the base of a tall mountain. So did the pleasant ache between my thighs, the evidence of him smeared across my sex. I traveled through strange cities, speaking to strange people with a darkness roiling at my back. Bright sunlight streamed across my face, fading into bitter dark. Someone spoke in a language I did not know, and yet, I understood they spoke to me of danger. In their hands lay a pomegranate, withered and molded with time. I chased Ren through a crowded, serpentine street, darting between humans and demigods, calling out for him until I was unsure if our time in the in-between had been anything more than a dream.

But when I woke hours later to the soft light of dawn sliding through the mist and the sounds of Sidero and Samarah arguing outside my room, I stumbled into the bathing chamber to find a bright red bite where my neck met my shoulder.

Ren's mark. A reminder that he was waiting for me to bring him home.

CHAPTER
TWENTY-EIGHT

Oralia

The maze stood ominous within the thick mist swirling through the entrance like a portal to another realm. I wiped my hands on the skirt of my gown before tugging on the soft black gloves. Samarah, being a timeless god, needed no protection against my touch—something I'd realized after our struggle the night before. This morning she'd entered my rooms on a breeze, Sidero at her side. Another tentative truce formed between her and my friends.

It appeared all one needed to do to endear Samarah to them was threaten her.

Both had offered to walk with me through the grounds, but I'd declined. I took another deep breath, sliding my fingers over the fading bite at my throat, before stepping into the dark. The path was not long, and in merely a few turns, I found Zayne seated again at the edge of a wide pit with a small journal in one hand and a charcoal writing stick in the other.

"Is this a bad time?" I asked softly, not wanting to startle him.

Zayne lifted his head slowly, a smile breaking across his face. With quick, easy movements he closed the book and placed it to the side along with the writing stick before rising to his feet. The god was taller than I remembered, though I'd been so baffled at the time perhaps I had not noticed. In my memory, we stood at the same height, but in reality, he towered over me, pressing a hand to his heart and dipping his chin. His thick hair was shorter than most other gods kept it, curling around his ears and sliding across his burnished golden-brown cheekbones with the movement.

"Have you been well?" The question was a bit awkward as I realized once again Zayne had yet to speak to me.

But the god gave me a grin, nodding once before extending out a hand. I placed my gloved palm in his before he gestured to me with his other in a way I assumed asked the same question.

"I do not know if I can truly answer that," I murmured while he guided me around the pit and toward another path.

Zayne turned his head, a thick brow raised, and I blew out a breath. "I am weary, and we have only recently begun. I worry I will not survive what I must to win this war...to return Ren to this world. And I fear more and more there is a betrayer in our midst—that someone we trust has Typhon's ear."

A hum rumbled in his throat, and I wondered what it meant. Whether it was an agreement or merely a noise of understanding. But he patted the back of my hand, squeezing once while we traversed the labyrinth.

Tomorrow, we would set off for the next piece of Ren. My stomach churned with acid at the thought. Samarah had insisted on joining, so our little band of three had expanded to four. I did not know how the others felt about her presence, but personally, I was undecided. She was undeniably powerful but unknown. I was not sure if we could trust her not to slaughter us or whoever was in our path.

Zayne stopped before a wide wall covered in rotted vines, twisted together like a pit of snakes. With another squeeze, he dropped my hand before catching my gaze to ensure I was paying attention. Another hum slithered through the space—the same melody I'd heard the last time we were together—before he pressed two fingertips upon the vines.

The wall burst into flames.

I gasped, stumbling back, but his hand shot out to hold me in place, fingers tight around my wrist. With careful tugs, he drew me forward, lifting the arm he held toward the flames.

Scalding heat licked at the back of my neck, not from the fire but from embarrassment. Zayne gave another noise of encouragement, tilting his head toward the wall of fire before I pressed my hand against it. The flames shimmered, licking at the fabric of my glove as if desperate to touch my skin. Curling around my wrists and forearms, a tickling warmth slithered into my veins.

When I pulled my hand away, the flames lingered, flickering in the cool mist before I frowned. My magic pricked, and I exhaled, the fire catching once more to slither between my fingers. Zayne nodded, citrine eyes alight with what I hoped was pride, before he gestured back to the wall.

The fire was out, and the wall stood as it had before, untouched by the inferno.

I removed my gloves before I spread my fingers across the vines, sending the same trickling warmth forward, breathing slowly, imagining the flames with each exhale. Surprisingly, as I focused on my task, the vines did not die beneath my fingers, and I wondered if this was the trick to pulling back the death magic from my palms. It took longer than I hoped for the wall to catch and the fire to illuminate the narrow passage. But I smiled when it did, some piece inside of me locking into place.

It was not control I needed but surrender.

And then Zayne gestured, swiping his hand across the wall in a way that made me think he was asking me to put it out. I frowned, pressing my palm against the fire, only for it to burn brighter. Panic skittered up my spine, and I gave him a worried glance, but his face was merely set in solemn contemplation.

He patted my shoulder and shushed me with comforting sounds. I had to put the fire out. But the only thing coming to mind was rain, how if the skies opened it would put the blazing pyre out with ease. Aelestor's power was what was needed, not mine.

One drop fell.

I looked around us, wondering if Aelestor was close, but we were alone. Something new shivered through my chest—infant magic waking for the first time.

Another drop.

The skies opened, and water fell in sheets, snuffing out the flames, and soaking my hair to my face, my clothes to my bones. We stared, wide-eyed, at each other.

"Perhaps I *am* going through prime once more," I murmured.

Zayne huffed a laugh, giving a small shake of his shoulders that made me think he was remembering his own prime. This was much like when my full magic had first manifested. I had wished for rain, and my magic slithering through my skin had listened. I couldn't wait to tell Aelestor. The rain fell in a steady rhythm, cooling the last of the heat from the fire until we stood soaking wet within the maze with Zayne's face tipped up toward the sky.

I wondered what it was about this place that called to him. Why would he choose to spend most of his existence alone rather than with the rest of the kingdom? Surely, he had friends or companions. I'd seen him in the inner circle meetings, though no one had spoken to him save Ren or Morana. Even Thorne was unacquainted with him.

But as Zayne drank in the storm, I thought I understood how, with a power as volatile as the one living within him, being alone might feel safer. Had I not felt the same about my own? The scars marring his palms, like the ones on my wrists, were evidence of that danger.

"Did the fire burn you...when you were young?" I asked, wiping water from my eyes. I took a deep breath, drawing my magic back, imagining it coiling within my chest like a serpent in its nest.

Zayne drew his chin down, all the wonder dripping from his face with the last of the storm as it ebbed away. Fire sparked on his fingertips, warmth wrapping around us to dry the worst of the water before he offered me his arm. It took me a moment to understand he wanted to guide me somewhere else. I assumed he was navigating us back toward Infernis but we stopped within a tiny alcove so dark it might have been midnight beyond.

He gestured, tugging me forward in encouragement to cross the threshold. I swallowed thickly, hesitating only a moment. The darkness swallowed. I could feel more than see Zayne beside me, the shallow echo of his breaths within the alcove deafening.

A single spark flared.

But the fire did not come from him. A small boy stood before us, thick hair brushing his shoulders. Green grass swayed beneath his tiny boots. Though I could see nothing beyond him, I could sense he was alone. The first spark danced across his hands, but his brows drew tight in confusion, little shoulders trembling in fear. I jerked, wanting to comfort him, only for Zayne to wrap a hand around my forearm.

"Mama!" the boy cried, terror zinging through his voice.

The spark within his palm grew brighter, white hot, flaring with each panicked breath he took.

"*Mama!*" he screamed in terror and pain as the fire spread across his palms and up his arms, licking at the skin bubbling and blackening in the heat.

My ears rang with his horrified cries, one blending into the next until it was a single agonizing wail.

The image blurred, and a sob wrenched through my throat. He was so alone in his fear, screaming out for his mother while his power consumed him...It was rare powers manifested in childhood, and I knew the fear all too well. Long, agonizing minutes later, a woman ran into view, blonde hair shimmering behind her before she scooped him into her arms. Water cascaded over his blackened arms, but it was too late to soothe.

Zayne guided me out of the alcove, but I did not take my eyes off the boy until the darkness blotted them from sight.

"You did not speak again, did you?"

He shrugged, gesturing for me to follow. But his shoulders were stiff with the memory and sweat gleamed on the back of his neck. It was easy to understand why he would not speak again. To a young god who screamed for help, for his cries not to be answered would be horrifying. For his magic to turn on him must have been scarier. Yet he communed with his magic, controlled it, and mastered it while refusing to live with others.

The weak afternoon light spilled across my face as we crossed the threshold of the maze, and I wondered if he would join me for a meal if I asked him. I feared he would agree because I was *lathira* and not because he truly wanted to. So instead, I smiled at him, squeezing his shoulder once.

"Thank you for teaching me today."

He frowned, shaking his head before tapping my chest, saying without words that I had taught myself. But he had been there with me in the maze, encouraging me when I faltered and staring in wonder with me as the rain fell. I gave him a nod, deciding not to push him, and wandered back to the castle to find Horace in preparation for tomorrow.

At the steps, I turned back to the maze, catching sight of two figures at the entrance. A small sliver of warmth crawled through my chest as Zayne stepped into Samarah's embrace.

And then tears burned as the God of Nightmares rocked the God of Fire in her arms as if he were merely a child once more.

CHAPTER

TWENTY-NINE

Oralia

W hat news do you have for me?"

Mecrucio stared with tired eyes, fingers tracing a vein of the dark marble beneath his hand. The plate in front of him sat mostly untouched, and Horace frowned beside him, though the God of Travelers and Thieves would not meet his eye.

"Typhon is building an army for battle. He has called all his outlying troops home," Mecrucio answered, voice slow, so unlike the teasing tone I was used to.

"How many?" My stomach twisted. I did not know the answer myself and being left in the dark by Typhon for so many years rankled.

Drystan shifted to my right, exchanging a look with his twin before turning to me. "If he calls all battalions back to Aethera, he will have close to six thousand...give or take."

Thorne cursed under his breath. I knew from our conversations that we had barely over two thousand soldiers, but we were spread thin to protect all the anticipated entry points through the mist. How could we ever hope to win such a battle against an army so large?

"We have the mist on our side," Aelestor said slowly as if he could read my thoughts. "The magic of Infernis will help us."

"Ren creating the mist was the only thing that saved us last time," Thorne muttered, draining his goblet.

Dimitri huffed his agreement. "Typhon would have razed Infernis and taken it by the throat."

My own throat clenched at the thought. No matter that these dormant powers were beginning to make themselves known, only Ren stood a chance against the Golden King. And each moment we spent searching for him was another soldier who returned to Aethera, another nail within our coffin.

"What are his plans for Oralia?" Drystan asked, cutting through the grumbling around the table.

Jaws snapped shut at the question and wary eyes turned toward our spy.

Mecrucio's solemn face grew gaunt as he peered back at all around the table. "He has given up hope of swaying Oralia's loyalty back to Aethera."

"Well, at least one thing has gotten through his thick skull," Thorne mused, leaning onto the two back legs of his chair.

"What is his plan for me instead?" I pressed, ignoring Thorne in favor of Mecrucio.

The latter fixed me with a gaze I could not understand. "To destroy you and everything you hold dear. He is confident now in the capability of his weapon. In killing you, he believes he can take your power and bestow it on another to rule in his stead."

Thorne's chair thudded back to the ground. Around me, all gave voice to their incredulity, their belief I would not be destroyed. But I held Mecrucio's stare, understanding it was regret lingering on the edges of his expression. Typhon would try to destroy me, steal my magic, and give it to another.

"You have seen this happen with your own eyes?"

Mecrucio rolled his lips together before he nodded. "I have, Your Grace. He has successfully used his father's ring to take another's magic. The ring is imbued with kratus resin from Asteria's tree and Daeymon's blood that carries creation. The combination has constructed the perfect means with which to take another's power."

"And you have seen this for yourself?" Thorne rumbled.

Mecrucio ran a hand over his curls, gripping at the back of his head. "There was a demigod in court with a small bit of fire magic. Typhon killed the girl and wielded her flames before bestowing them on Hollis."

Curses slithered throughout the room, but I only had eyes for Mecrucio. "He would not be so stupid as to give my magic to another. If he wants Infernis, he will keep it for himself."

"He has said he has promised the power to another, Your Grace. He has a willing god who will take over the throne of Infernis." His voice was dead, emotionless with the shock of whatever he had witnessed.

Aelestor gave an approximation of a growl. "Who is it?"

A pit opened in my stomach. I could not voice the fear aloud, but I wondered more and more if it was someone close. Someone we mistakenly trusted.

"He would not say. But he spoke of Oralia's death being the beginning of *a new age*, a golden one." Mecrucio turned toward me, eyes full of pleading. "Stop this mission to retrieve the pieces of Ren, Your Grace. I fear what might happen if you leave these lands, what trap he might have lying in wait."

Shaking my head, I lifted my hand to stop him. "I will not be cowed by the threats of a madman."

But Mecrucio's face filled with horror. His eyes shone in the light as he stood from his place at the table and lowered to his knees beside my chair, taking my gloved hand in his and squeezing once.

"You do not understand, Oralia," he breathed, so soft it was as if he spoke only for my ears. "He does not care how long it takes. He will destroy you."

I gave him a soft, sad smile. In the last few weeks, my magic had grown to a fever pitch. Even now, it was humming like a song I used to make the grass outside the palace grow. I lifted my gloved hand to cup his cheek, mirroring his whisper.

"Not if I destroy him first."

The light of the sun was so bright it burned my eyes. Ten times what it had been in Aethera, twenty times how it shone in Infernis. I drew the cowl higher over my face, glancing at Drystan and Aelestor, who did the same. Samarah had not bothered with a cloak or cowl, and her gown of bones clicked in the breeze.

"Could you be any more conspicuous?" Aelestor muttered.

Samarah's auburn hair—left down today—shone bright red in the sunlight when she shrugged. "I could, if you like."

"Let us hold off for now," I said, stepping forward, only for my feet to sink into the ground.

My heart hammered in my chest for a moment. My mind flicked back to the swamplands before dry sand shifted beneath my boot, wind stirred up, and stung my eyes. The silver thread in my chest thrummed, and I did not know if it was in response to my proximity or the deepening bond since my time in the in-between. Last night, I'd dreamed of Ren and been sure there had been a moment when it had been real and I had been in the in-between with him. He'd held me in his arms and pressed a kiss to my lips before ushering me into the beyond where he could not follow.

It made me feel a little less alone, even if he could not be here with me in this realm.

There was a collection of ramshackle huts before us. I was not sure if I could even call it a village. Weathered wood groaned, tattered fabric door hangings flapped in bouts of wind, and rusted metal roofs sizzled in the sun. This was by no means a pleasant existence, and the toll was obvious upon the faces we passed. Each human was weathered with deep lines upon their faces and skin darkened by the sun.

Millennia ago, humans had slipped through the veil between our world and theirs, mostly by accident. A few had returned home but many more stayed, wandering this world to find a better life than the one they led in their own. Or so the stories said. Humans worshipped us because of all we offered: salvation, comfort, guidance.

I could not find a worshipper among the suffering here.

"How do they get their water?" I breathed as we passed a low-roofed hut. The man lying on the packed dirt floor was barely more than a husk.

"Aethera provides them their supply," Drystan answered, but he did not sound convinced.

Samarah chuckled. "You children are so gullible with your tall tales."

We ducked beneath the hangings strung between two slightly taller shacks, tattered laundry drying in the bleaching light. There was nothing but the scent of heat, the dry sand, and something mineral, like rock. Even from the safety of my cowl, my skin ached with the burn of the sun.

"Aethera's reach is not so far," Aelestor murmured, touching the short sword concealed in his cloak when a grizzled man stared for a moment too long before striding off. Strange, but the human did not even notice Samarah beside us.

She gave a noise of agreement, scratching her nails across a crumbling stone. "This is the Western Reaches, sweetling. Here nothing grows, nothing thrives, and nothing survives."

"Except for these last few mortals," Aelestor added.

Odd to see them in agreement on something.

The silver thread tugged, and I picked up my pace, uninterested in the conversation. But Drystan pressed on, asking for clarification. I swiped a hand over my forehead, wiping it on my cloak before pointing to the offshoot of what appeared to be the main path through the tiny village.

"The Western Reaches were said to be rich with resources—" Drystan started.

"Said to be," Samarah cut across him. "And they were, once, before Typhon and *Ardren* Daeymon drained these lands dry within the first centuries of the humans settling."

"*Ardren* Daeymon?" I questioned over the beat of my pulse. Sweat trickled down the back of my neck, forcing a shiver.

She nodded, violet eyes flaring. "Yes, Ren and Typhon's father Daeymon."

The silver thread shifted, and a pang echoed through my gut. I barely heard Samarah's answer before changing course. The sand slowed my feet as I ran, and I was grateful for the compact dirt of the main road. My three companions followed. Though I lost them in my haste when I skidded around a corner and shouldered my way through a weathered door splintering into pieces.

My shadows wrapped around a man holding a bundle tight to his chest, my thick ropes of night squeezing his throat. He dropped it, fingers scrambling around my power as if he might pull it off. My knife glinted in the sun pouring through the slats in the roof as I pressed it to where his neck met his shoulder. Someone shifted in the room, and I did not need to look at them before my shadows sliced through the air toward them, a gurgling cry echoing through my skull.

The blood on the air made my mouth water, my stomach clenched with the need to destroy. I recognized these men from my time in Aethera. They had sat around Typhon's table, drank his wine, and exacted his horrible orders.

The man I held before me turned a strange shade of red, deepening to a purple.

"Where are you taking this piece of Ren?" I gritted through my teeth.

"Oralia," a voice called.

But I did not pay it any mind. I pressed the blade high beneath the demigod's chin, a glimmer of blood dripping onto the dark metal.

"Shadows?" I murmured. "Or fire, demigod?"

"*Oralia*," a familiar voice snapped and I froze. "Let him go."

The heel of my boot scraped against the dirt floor as I turned, lips parting on a silent gasp. The demigod behind me fell to the floor with a *thud*, sucking a lungful of air. But I could only stare at the god before me, rose-gold skin darkened by the sun, wary gaze so different from his usual expression.

His shoulders lowered a fraction, and I realized he was missing his usual gilded armor. He was dressed much like the man behind me—much like the party I traveled with, who now burst through the door behind him. But Caston did not turn to look at them, even when Samarah withdrew a deadly curved blade, from where I could not imagine, to hold at his throat. He merely narrowed his gaze.

"Where is your heart, Sister?"

CHAPTER
THIRTY

Oralia

hom do you serve?" Aelestor snarled, his blade pressing into Caston's belly on his other side.

The Prince of Aethera did not tense at the threats, merely raised his hands in surrender, attention fixed on me. A groan slid through the room and the guard whose belly I'd slashed curled in on himself.

"We need to get Khale to a healer," Caston said to me as Aelestor removed weapon after weapon from his baldric. "Please, Oralia."

I turned toward the man in question bleeding out across the dirt floor. Something white caught my eye as he curled tighter in on himself, hands pressing his innards back into the wound. "Where were you taking this piece of Ren?"

Caston knew I was not talking to the one dying on the ground. His sigh was heavy with grief he would carry for the man as he lowered to his knees. "To you. Oralia, *please*. I am not above begging."

When I looked, his eyes were wide, flicking between me and the man, Khale, in the dirt. I did not know why I waited, why this man's suffering did not move me. But I searched Caston's face, recalling his time spent in Infernis and the friendships he had formed.

It was Drystan who cut through my contemplation, whose hands wrapped around my upper arms, leveling me with a stern gaze. He said nothing, but his look was quelling. For a moment, I was a young girl scolded within the orchards. This man on the ground used to be his brother in arms, as the god at his back used to be one of his commanders.

Where is your heart, Sister? Caston had asked, and the truth was...I did not know.

So I tried to find it again. I knelt beside the dying man, turning him onto his back to better assess the wound. My shadows had sliced cleanly through his stomach, forcing blood up through his esophagus to trickle out of the corner of his mouth. I had done this without question and without hesitation, and yet, I could not find the twisting confusion I'd had the first time I'd taken a man's life.

Magic tapped on the corner of my attention. If there was one thing I'd learned since I first left Aethera, it was to bend an ear to the power churning within me growing more expansive with each day.

"Show me," I commanded my magic.

My palms tingled, a shimmering gold light seeping from beneath the edge of my gloves. Slowly, I removed them, pressing my hands over his wound.

"Oralia, please, take him to Thorne. Do not kill—"

I took a deep breath, allowing my power to flow through me as I had in the maze, surrendering to it. A hum floated up my throat, the melody familiar yet different to the song I sang to grow the crops and bolster the trees. This was haunting, and even with the light trickling through my veins, tangling with my power of life. Shadows hung heavy around my shoulders like a shroud.

The skin beneath my hand tensed, the magic pulling, knitting, until merely a gash remained. Khale gave a soft exhale, shoulders relaxing not in death but relief, as his head thumped to the ground. I stared in shock at the healed wound and drew back my gloved hands before skittering away as if burned.

Caston bolted forward and slid across the dirt to pull Khale into his arms, the other man following as they checked over his wounds. A lock of hair fell across Caston's brow as he looked up, freckles bright against his flushed skin.

"You healed him..."

I pulled my gloves back over my hands, flexing my fingers. The tingling warmth was gone as if it had never been and a tiredness was left in its wake.

"Oralia," Caston pushed.

I nodded, throat clicking with a dry swallow as I stood. "It appears so."

He blew out a breath, head heavy before he reached out to grasp my hand, kissing the back of it before pressing his forehead to my gloved knuckles. "Hail the Queen of Infernis."

My stomach twisted, and I shook my head. "You do not mean that."

The demigod I'd held at knifepoint followed beside him, dropped to his knees, and reached for my other hand, pressing his lips and then forehead to my knuckles.

"Hail the Queen of Infernis," the demigod repeated, though there was wariness in his gaze.

Movement rustled behind me, and I looked over my shoulder to see Samarah kneeling beside me, lips pressed to the hem of my dusty cloak. Aelestor and Drystan on either side.

"Hail the Queen of Infernis," they said together.

"The keeper of all the power of the universe," Samarah finished, violet eyes flashing up to mine. "The one who carries our fate in the palm of her hand."

Samarah rose first, cradling my face, and pressed her forehead to mine. She breathed deep as if she could scent the magic roiling within me. "Do not fear it, *latska lathira*."

But it was not the power I feared. No, as they rose to their feet and Caston used his cloak to prop up Khale's head, it was the regret I could not find in my heart. I had not spared an ounce of compassion for the men I saw as my enemies. And I knew I would have gladly killed them all and slept easily after.

"Tell me what has happened," I said to Caston as he rose, running a hand over his tired face.

"You almost killed him." The words were not harsh, but there was a question there. He was assessing in his gaze as if I was a stranger.

Ice crept through my belly, crawling up my throat to curl around my lips. "I was wrapped in unearthly chains and forced to watch my mate be strung up the same. Forced to watch them wrench him limb from limb and then learn he was scattered across the world. I have faced things you could not fathom in order to retrieve him—to revive him." Stepping closer, I lifted my chin. "You have no idea the things I would do if it means returning Ren to this realm. Now *tell me what has happened.*"

Caston stared at me for a long moment before he turned to the demigod beside him, nodding. "Gather the others."

"Aelestor, join him," I instructed, tipping my head toward the demigod.

I hated that I did not trust my adopted brother, that I was too wounded to welcome him with open arms and not expect Aetheran soldiers to stream into the room with their weapons raised. Samarah gave a hum of approval and settled herself at my left side. Caston's attention flicked between us, but I did not offer introductions. After a moment, he cleared his throat.

"Typhon sent me to retrieve my soldiers stationed here and bring them back to Aethera. On the way, he gave me another task, one he entrusted to few within his circle." His throat bobbed with a swallow, disgust twisting his features. "I endured two days of...questioning... to see where my loyalties lay before he gave me the task."

Acid burned the back of my tongue at the thought of what sort of questioning would have been enough to prove his loyalty. Typhon's own son, his *heir*. And yet it had been the same before. He had readily shot an arrow through his child's chest in an attempt to pull me from Infernis and then place the blame on Ren.

Typhon's games knew no end.

"Others had been sent before me, I knew, but their identities were not shared. However, Typhon sent you Ren's heart. He knows you are gathering the pieces, intent on resurrecting him. No one can tell him how you have found the pieces so easily, but it drives him mad. He is restless, *dangerous*." Caston stepped forward. "I received a message from Typhon only days ago. He bade me move the piece he'd given me—to hide it elsewhere."

"You were moving this piece?" I asked, gesturing to the bundle Drystan lifted from the ground.

Caston shook his head. He took another breath, shoulders rounding, and the door was suddenly occupied. The demigod and Aelestor stood side by side, twenty-some-odd humans and demigods in similar traveling cloaks and leathers behind them. Caston extended an arm out, and a statuesque woman shouldered her way through the crowd, shrugging a pack off her shoulders and into his grasp.

"No, I was tasked with another, told to hide it on my journey in a remote cave to the southwest and then gather my troops to return home. The area is infested with daemoni." He offered me the pack, nodding toward the soldier behind me. "Khale is my second-in-command and was given the piece in your hands."

I weighed the pack. It was not as heavy as I expected, yet not particularly light. But I understood what Caston was saying: within this pack was another piece of Ren. Two more pieces here in this place. And the men I'd nearly killed had gone against the orders of Typhon to bring Caston the piece instead.

These men was not my enemy, yet I had almost slaughtered him like an animal.

"But why...why did he bring it here and not to its intended hiding spot?"

A grimace turned down the corners of Caston's mouth. But it was the woman who spoke, not Caston.

"Because we are not loyal to a king who sits idly on a throne and moves lives like a player on a game board." Her reddish-brown skin flushed when her green-flecked eyes met mine. "And we trust our prince's intuition, his magic. Many of us have seen him through his prime. You and your king saved the prince, offered him shelter, and Typhon slaughtered you for it."

They knew then... Somehow word had reached this far of what had taken place. Caston's hand covered the pack, drawing my attention back to him.

"It is you I swear my allegiance to, Oralia, not him."

I closed my eyes, shaking my head. "But he is your father."

A knuckle touched my chin. "And you are my sister. I was too young to see the horror creeping through those halls, and by the time I did, I was sent away. It was foolish of me to believe you were anything more than a prisoner." His breath caught, eyes glittering in the sunlight streaming through the cracks in the boards. "I stood by while you were tortured, while your mate was destroyed, and I will not stand silent any longer. Let me serve you, Oralia."

I licked my lips, pushing away the memories of aching knees upon marble while acidic pain tore through my bones. The countless healers who had attempted to strip me of my dark magic—the agony, the fear. Typhon's gilded cage I had called home.

Caston took another deep breath, the next words sounding less like a statement and more like a vow:

"I could do nothing to stop his terror then, but I can do something to stop it now."

CHAPTER
THIRTY-ONE

Renwick

O h, Son," Asteria crooned, attention fixed on my wings. I squeezed my eyes shut against her understanding gaze. "Do not..."

She stepped closer, hands closing over my shoulders. "A few centuries are nothing and yet..."

"It is everything," I finished for her. "Especially when one assumes it will be eternity."

The perpetual breeze of the in-between rustled her hair, her feathers tensing in the wind to balance her. I flinched as mine did the same, a familiar flexing of my muscles, as natural as breathing. But I could not find it within myself to even reach back and touch them, let alone take to the skies. Because if I did only to have them ripped from me again when I woke...the agony would be unfathomable.

Asteria's delicate brows furrowed, attention fixed over my shoulder. I thought she was inspecting my wings until she frowned, a murmur slipping through her lips.

"What is she doing?"

I turned, tucking my wings in tight so I would not hit my mother, in time to see Oralia with three unfamiliar people. Two had their hands around one arm while another held her wrist. Samarah was at her back, fingertips pressed to my mate's spine as if pushing her forward.

"Do you recognize them?" Asteria asked.

Shaking my head, I moved closer to the space they were passing through. It was mere moments, not long enough for Oralia to truly see, but in another heartbeat, she and Samarah stepped through again. The latter sent me a concerned glance before they vanished.

On and on, Oralia walked close to thirty people through the in-between toward Infernis. At the end, I could have sworn it was her adopted brother, Caston, Prince of Aethera, with her, supporting another man under his arm. None wore the armor of the Golden King—not a single gilded helmet to be found.

"She must be gathering warriors," I muttered, sliding a hand through my hair, heart thumping through my chest.

We were close, then. I eyed my mother, the look of worry resting on her brow. "We need to figure out a way to get you back."

Asteria frowned, exhaling slowly through her nose. "I do not think such a thing is possible."

A muscle ticked in my jaw. It was a circular conversation and one we'd had a few times since my arrival into this realm. "Not before, no. But now I am here... We have learned much about this realm. With Samarah's help—"

"I have accepted my fate, love." The softness of her words rankled.

This was not the woman I'd known. The god who had railed against my father and his mad ways, who would not stand idly by and see humans enslaved by gods. That spark had died within her, withered away by loneliness and despair until only a shell remained.

"Well, I have not," I answered, unable to keep the bitterness from my voice. "Do you not want to leave this place? Do you not wish for Typhon to face his crimes?"

She pursed her lips, throat working with a swallow. "Of course, I do."

I raised a brow. "You do what? Want to leave this place? Or want Typhon to face justice?"

"Both. Of course, both."

Her answer fanned the ever-present fury. My nails bit into my palms as I clenched my fists. "Does it not horrify you what he has done?"

Asteria blinked at me. "How could you ask me such a thing? Of course, I am horrified."

I shook my head, a bitter laugh slipping through. "Because you have walked beside me on this path for however long I have been stuck here, content merely to wander, to listen to my fears, yet never once have you shown anger at what has befallen me...befallen *us.*"

"It was a long time—"

"Days ago, Mother," I cut across her. "Perhaps weeks, maybe more, but it feels as if it was days ago that Typhon strung me up and tore me apart piece by piece. And do you know what? I knew every second of that agony. I lived every moment of that torture until my heart was ripped from my chest and my head disconnected from my body."

Asteria turned from me, but I followed, tugged her hands from her face, and forced her to look.

"A bolt through each arm and each leg. Another through my chest." I touched the space between my ribs. "And then the killing blow through my neck."

Midnight eyes, identical to my own, glistened up at me, crimson staining pale cheeks. "Could you have stopped him?"

I nodded. "I could have, but I used my final reserves of magic to send Oralia back to the shores of Infernis."

Because my mate would always come first. I would die a thousand more deaths if it meant she was safe. Asteria's throat worked again, swallowing back whatever emotion she fought.

"You have seen the havoc he has wrought, and it was not millennia ago. It was yesterday, and the day before, and tomorrow, and the next." I cupped her face in my hands. "Do you not see?"

"My anger burns, but it consumes only me," she whispered. "I learned centuries ago my anger is useless in the face of so much time. Typhon is untouched by such a fire."

I leaned down to eye level. My hands dropped to her shoulders. "Then make him feel it. Choose to leave this place, to find a way to watch him burn."

She shook her head. "And then what would I be? The world has no need of the *Great Mothers,* as they call it."

I straightened to my full height, gaze fixed upon the point where Oralia had passed through.

"You would be the blade in the hand of the one who brings him down. A dagger shoved into his side by surprise. Place yourself in the service of my mate." Turning back to her, I noted the slight shift in her gaze, her lips parting in surprise.

"Because her magic is the thing that changes *everything.*"

CHAPTER

THIRTY-TWO

Oralia

"I think I have lost something..."

The words were quiet, barely audible over the crackling fire. Sidero sat beside me on the window seat of Ren and my room, both of us staring in companionable silence out into the darkened grounds.

I spent most of the evening with Thorne and Horace, questioning Caston's soldiers. Though Horace lacked Caston's power to see truth within the words someone spoke, he could weigh the weight upon someone's soul. When taking the measure of their character, he had seen nothing within the thirty-two humans and demigods to raise concerns. Only wariness and hesitation along with a desperation to do *good*.

After Caston's soldiers had been housed and fed, I'd all but retreated to my rooms where Sidero had found me. I was relieved they did not speak but were merely content to sit beside me as a weak sunset turned into twilight and twilight into night.

"What is it you think you have lost?" Sidero murmured when I did not continue.

"I did not hesitate to kill," I breathed, fingers flexing around the lining of my dressing gown. "And when Caston asked me to spare one of his men... When he begged me to take him to Thorne...I could not find an ounce of compassion inside myself."

I looked at Sidero, their mouth thinned into a line. When their eyes met mine, it was not wariness I saw, but the emotion I could no longer find.

"Instead of rushing to heal him, I weighed the cost of bringing him to Infernis—of saving him. Someone who I have never met, one whose allegiance had been assumed and yet not proven." I turned back to the window, resting my head against the cool glass. "Even now, I cannot find regret, only a...calm acceptance of what took place. As if it was nothing more than a conversation instead of gazing down at a man's innards spilled across the floor."

Sidero shifted in the corner of my eye, their mouth tensing, then relaxing. "I understand what you are saying. It is common to lose one's..." They paused, searching for the word. "*Humanity,* though I do not know if the word can truly apply to a god. But I know all too well what it is like to weigh a life in your hand as if it were fruit, ripe for the taking. It is hard not to lose a piece of yourself when your life is nothing but killing, nothing but endless war and bloodshed."

"How did you find it again? The compassion?"

They rolled their lips together as they thought, head tilting to the side. "Time. It is the greatest balm on a wound, even if it feels like torture in the beginning."

Recently, it was as though time was the answer to everything. Like if only I could be patient, then the questions I had would be answered. But I did not have time—not to wait for Ren to be resurrected nor for this wound within me to heal.

"Ren would understand," Sidero murmured. "He would not blame you for such things."

I nodded. "I wish for his comfort above all else."

Their warm hand covered mine, squeezing once. Early on I'd discovered they were immune to my power and the way it threaded through souls. The happiness and contentment my touch brought did not reach them, and I could only guess it was because they were already content. Sidero had faced their crimes centuries upon centuries ago for the wars they'd fought and forgiven themselves long before I ever crossed these shores.

In fact, they could have ascended centuries before I was ever born but chose not to. Their loyalty to Ren and this kingdom was too great.

"Tell him, speak to him, and perhaps, he will hear."

I did not answer. I had not told anyone about my visits to the in-between, nor had Samarah. It was too intimate to reveal I'd seen Ren, spoken to him, held him, in the strange place between worlds. But they were right—perhaps speaking to Ren would assuage the fear I had.

They did not press further or question what else happened that morning in the Western Reaches. It was a long time later when I sighed, rubbing my fingertips to my lids while I asked if they would find Samarah and bring her to me.

The God of Nightmares slid through the room like a shadow and bent to press a kiss to the top of my hair.

"I thought you would kill me that day in the swamplands," I murmured, unable to tear my gaze from the rocky plains of Isthil.

Samarah hummed, gathering her skirts with a click of bones to settle beside me, one hand reaching out to wrap around my ankle. "I would have, sweetling. In a heartbeat."

"What made you change your mind?" The question was passionless. I did not truly care, and it was a mere preamble to the request I would make of her.

But her lips pursed in thought, violet eyes glittering in my peripheral vision. "Why does anyone change their mind? Because I saw in you what I thought would never come. There, nestled in the mud and muck of my lands, was a fire I could not snuff out, snarling and screeching at the mere mention of the absurd last name Typhon gave you and his heir like an illness. *Solis*, ridiculous." She sighed as if the memory was a sweet one.

"And now you call me *little queen* and press your lips to the hem of my cloak," I muttered.

The hand on my ankle tightened before disappearing, nails sliding over my chin to pull my face to hers. "Yes, I do. You are *myhn latska lathira, myhn Lathira na Thurath.* And you are what I have been begging the universe to provide for longer than you can fathom."

But I did not get to ask what it was before she drew her claws across my cheeks, the sting of pain flashing across my skin. And then she pressed two fingers to her lips, licking my blood from the tips.

"The light and the dark. Sunrise and sunset. The first breath and the last and each in between. Made by the universe and chosen for your circumstance, you have basked within the light of a realm most will never see. Life. Death. Fire. Rain. Ice. Shadow. You are *ih rhyonath.*"

I dipped my head to brush my cheek against the shoulder of my dressing gown to wipe away the dried blood. "I do not know that word."

Samarah pressed a finger to the space between my brows, smoothing them with a gentle touch. And her face was so solemn, so filled with feeling, she was unrecognizable as her hand dropped away to hover between us, palm up.

"You are the reckoning."

Samarah sent me to the in-between with a light kiss to my temple and words of comfort.

I will be here when you wake. You will not be alone.

Ren's wings were the first thing I saw, flexing as he walked up the mountain. He stumbled when he caught sight of me on the path, reaching out at once to pull me to him. "What has happened? I saw—"

"I almost killed a man today." The words spilled from my lips like blood from a wound, and it was a relief to see warmth there as I told him everything I'd told Sidero. "I cannot find remorse within myself, Ren. I cannot find the compassion I used to set my soul upon. Caston asked me: *Where is your heart?* And I do not know. I can find yours, but I cannot find my own."

The last words broke with the tears burning in the corners of my eyes. I pressed my face to his neck, breathing in the scent of him, though this was not his true body. But his magic smelled like him, like *us*, our bond. It soothed the panic twisting through my belly.

"I do not blame you," he whispered.

A muscle in my jaw twitched, and I burrowed my face deeper into his neck. "You do not?"

His hand smoothed over the back of my head, his lips brushing across my temple. "If our roles were reversed, that boy would be dead right now, and if it had meant getting you back, I would not have blinked an eye—even if it meant I grieved for him later."

When I drew back to search Ren's face, it was to find it set in hollow lines of grief, so ancient in his despair I experienced the weight of his timelessness I did not often feel. His thumb traced the curve of my lower lip before he pressed his brow to mine.

"I do not care if it makes me monstrous. I do not blame you for what you did or did not do, and you should not for a second blame yourself."

I gripped his wrists tightly, struggling to find the words to reply.

Ren hummed, filling the quiet space between us with the sound of his understanding before brushing his lips against my cheek, offering me comfort even when there was none to have. "You are close. I can feel it."

My laugh was hollow, merely an approximation of humor. It did not feel close—it was as though we had miles and miles to travel before we could rest. Ren had been gone for a month, perhaps more, and yet, it was an eternity etched across my soul.

"What is next?" he asked.

Blowing out a breath, I slid my hand up his chest, palm pressing over his heart. "We travel to find the final piece of you. Though Typhon grows restless, according to Caston, I do not know how long we have until he tries to invade our shores."

His expression darkened. "Use his recklessness to your advantage, *eshara*. Make him believe he has a chance to destroy you and then cut him down."

"Do you think he does?" When his brows drew together, I clarified, "Have a chance to destroy me?"

Ren smiled softly and shook his head. "No, my heart. It would be easier to bring down the entire universe than destroy you."

CHAPTER
THIRTY-THREE

Oralia

"May I come in?"

I knocked again on Caston's door, waiting for his muffled invitation before pushing through. It was the dark green room I'd stayed in when Ren first brought me to Infernis, and the sight of it made my throat burn at the memories lingering within. Caston was seated at the window as I often had been, one knee up on the cushion, dressed in a simple white tunic and dark trousers.

When I took a step in, he rose, but I waved him off, crossing the space to settle beside him. "If you put on any more formalities, I think I might be sick."

He huffed, shaking his head. "Old habits."

I hummed. They were difficult to kill, especially growing up in Typhon's court and then in his armies. Caston's life had been filled with pomp and circumstance. His entire existence had been a choreographed dance until the moment his father shot a kratus arrow through his heart.

"Do you think he knows?" I murmured.

We did not say his father's name aloud, but there was no need. His throat bobbed with a swallow. "If he does, it makes no difference to him. I am no more an heir than he is a father."

Carefully, I covered his hand with mine, running a gloved thumb over his knuckles. "I am sorry."

"Do not be. I have learned more about the man who sired me than I ever could have wished to, and it makes me want to set fire to the blood running through my veins."

I did not know what to say, so I squeezed his hand, wishing Ren was here. He would have the right words.

"Did you know he never intended for you to keep your magic?" Caston asked bitterly, his attention sliding to me from the window.

My throat clicked with a swallow. "Yes, I did."

A small part of me had always known, even when I'd fooled myself into thinking otherwise. But now, after everything, I knew for certain.

The small sound of disgust flying from his mouth spoke louder than any word could. "Those healers he brought...they were not there to *heal* you. They were trying to do what he has finally accomplished with this sun-forsaken weapon. All this time, he was trying to strip you of your magic in order to take it for himself."

"I know," I murmured. "Believe me, I do."

To Typhon, I had been merely a cup on a shelf, a vessel to hold the power he knew lived inside of me. I did not know how long ago he had realized I contained this power. Perhaps he had even known the night I was bitten. But it did not take a seer to connect the dots.

"That is why he kept you weak. He feared what would happen should you learn to control your power."

All I could do was nod again as emotion played across his face. "I do not blame you."

Caston slipped his hand from beneath mine, scrubbing at his face. "Give me a task. Tell me what to do. I am powerless here."

His words were a relief. They were the reason I'd come here in the first place.

"Come with us today. This last piece feels strange. More treacherous than the others. I have this feeling..." I trailed off, pressing the tips of my fingers to my breastbone. "There is a knowing inside my power that tells me I need you there."

We stared at each other for a long moment while Caston read my face. His magic fluttered against my skin, featherlight and unobtrusive as he searched for the truth in my words. Finally he squeezed my wrist, giving me a small smile.

"Of course, I will come, Oralia. I would follow you to the ends of the world."

I flipped my hand over to grab his. "Well...that might be exactly where we are going."

"Come, children," Samarah crooned in her singsong voice, tugging Drystan closer to me.

Nerves fluttered in my chest. Here before me was the final piece, save for Ren's wings. But I hoped I could retrieve those too before long, even if he must be revived before then. Drystan's hand closed over my elbow, squeezing gently.

"There is no rush, Oralia," Drystan murmured. "Take your time."

I relaxed at his words, even though I wanted to rush headlong into whatever was waiting for us on the other side of the in-between. But it was a relief to know I had those at my back who cared for me, who wanted me to come out of this alive, even if I could not find it in me to care for it myself. Because deep down, I would gladly sacrifice myself if it meant returning Ren to this world.

Shadows twined over my shoulders, rising to wrap around my waist and out to cover my companions. Aelestor stood at my right, holding my elbow, while Drystan held the other. Caston's hand was on my shoulder, and Samarah's hand was on my waist. Though I did not think I needed it, Samarah's magic bolstered my own, deepening the darkness around us until it was as easy as breathing to carry the four of them. I kept my eyes wide open as we stepped through the dark, looking for a glint of a silver-capped wing in the night.

Ren and I locked eyes for the briefest of moments, and my heart clenched at the small nod he gave. More intimate than any kiss, prouder than any word. He believed in me when I could not believe in myself and was so sure of my path I had no choice but to continue to travel it.

I would not let him down.

The shadows dissipated slowly, salty spray misting over my face, sunlight breaking through the last of the dark. The hands over my arms tightened, and the tips of my boots hung over the edge of a rocky ledge. A collective gasp cut through the roaring waves. The water before us was an endless expanse, obstructed only by an island covered with mist so thick I could only make out the ragged cliffside.

"*Great Mothers,*" Aelestor cursed.

"Yes?" Samarah asked, turning with raised brows.

Shaking my head, I wiped the spray from my face, leaning over the edge of the cliff to eye any sort of way down. Drystan kept a hand around my arm, holding me steady as my stomach swooped with the vertical drop. There were enough handholds to maneuver down the rocky cliff, though the mist from the ocean might cause us difficulty. I wished I had Ren and Asteria's wings so I could fly us over the water and to the island where the silver thread tugged.

Wreckage caught my eye on the shore below. Battered pieces of wood, waterlogged by the ocean, were strewn across the black sand. How many had tried to traverse these waters and how would we get across to those shores when others had failed?

"Where are we?" I eyed the shimmering waves, calmer farther out toward the island.

Magic rippled across my skin. Power rumbled through my veins. Something within this place called to me, beckoned me forward and into the water. I was unsurprised when no one answered for a long moment, transfixed by the undulating mist across from us. I could have sworn I saw figures twisting and writhing in pain within the fog so much like our mist within Infernis. Was that a shriek I heard? A scream? And then silence, nothing but the sounds of our breaths and the churning of the ocean.

It was Samarah who eventually spoke, a strange mix of grief and longing in her words.

"Welcome, my darlings, to Iapetos."

CHAPTER
THIRTY-FOUR

Oralia

The descent was more treacherous than I had originally assumed.

No one commented on our location or what might be waiting for us on the other side of the churning water. We merely conferred about the best way to get across and agreed swimming was our only choice.

"These are waters you have never seen before," Samarah said, gesturing to the wreckage below. "No boat or craft will float. It must be crossed by will and will alone."

Caston was the first to descend after her ominous pronouncement. Aelestor followed before Drystan and Samarah insisted they were next until I was the last to climb down. The waves roared in my ears as I struggled to find handholds on the damp rocks, sometimes so brittle they shattered between my fingers. Each foothold was perilous, and I was blind, even looking down was impossible when hanging on to tenuous ledges.

"Almost there," Caston called, but his voice was distant beneath the waves.

By the time my boots hit the black sand, my arms were trembling, and my fingertips ached. But there was no time for rest. Even now, the tide was rolling in and less of the beach was visible than when we had first begun. Aelestor shucked off his cloak. Caston and Drystan secured their weapons tighter across their chests while Samarah observed with pursed lips.

"Your blades will be no match for what we will encounter next," she said, gathering her hair up onto the top of her head. "Best to leave them behind."

The three men stared incredulously at the God of Nightmares, but none of them removed their weapons. Nor did I—I was loath to part with Ren's weapons. Samarah merely shrugged, turning back to the water with a click of her bone corset, and I wondered how she would manage swimming in her heavy skirts before she walked into the water as if it were merely a corridor.

"Come then, children. Let us see what horrors they have in store."

"What a wonderful way to begin this next adventure," Aelestor muttered.

I shrugged off my cloak and left it beside the others.

Caston huffed a laugh, and Drystan murmured his agreement while he fell into step beside me as we edged our way into the waves. Samarah was already a few feet out, her head bobbing and ducking below the higher swells as they rolled in. I was sure this was not the right moment to mention I had never really swam before—unless one could consider wading in the small pond near the palace of Aethera swimming. But then Drystan was there beside me, hand extended.

"Let me help you," he said, low enough for the others not to hear.

My chest ached with affection for him, and I moved closer as he curled his hand beneath my arm. There had been a time before I was bitten where he'd tried to teach me to swim in the deep lake near the palace grounds, but the daemoni attack had stopped any hope of learning.

As the sea deepened, so did my dread, the waves crashing over my face and shooting up my nose. But Drystan's hand did not stray from my arm, dragging me above the surface again and again.

"Kick with your legs," he instructed, moving his grip to the baldric around my back. "Good, now use your arms to push the water away."

I tried my best, able to at least tread water as we pushed farther out toward the island, even as the tide tried to drag us back to the rocky shore we had just left.

"Oralia!" Caston called, turning around to ensure we were following.

I could not answer, but Drystan raised the hand on my back quickly to grab his attention before holding on once more when I fell below the waves.

"It is calmer here," Aelestor encouraged, swimming back and pausing to wait for us alongside Samarah.

Already, I was panting, embarrassment heating my cheeks as I struggled toward them. We were barely past the shoreline and into open water. I could not imagine how long it would take me to cross.

"You should have told us you cannot swim," Samarah chided, wrapping her hand above Drystan's to give him a break from holding me up.

"I did not..." My voice trailed off.

She guided me forward, tugging me a little faster than Drystan had. "The only one who suffers when you do not speak up is you."

I bit the inside of my cheek, hating the truth of her words. "I did not want to appear weak."

With a hum, she nodded, the skirts of her gown trailing behind us, occasionally brushing against my leg. "Weakness is believing that one must be someone other than themselves in order to be strong."

"Oralia..." Caston called.

I sighed, turning, ready to see Caston and Aelestor far ahead of me, but my blood ran cold. They were not looking at me at all but at the water ahead. Giant bubbles broke free from the surface, flicking up into the air and twisting around themselves. We paused, and I struggled to keep my chin above the waves, even with Samarah's help.

"*Back! Back!*" Aelestor cried.

But a crash echoed through my skull as a creature exploded from the water. It flew high into the air, claws encircling Drystan and ripping him from the surface along with it. Its body was long, fluid like a snake's, with wide, arcing wings pushing it higher. And yet, I could not see any true shape beyond, the body all but transparent and shimmering in the sun.

"Ah, *serapha*," Samarah observed.

"*Drystan!*" I called desperately as the creature flung him higher into the air, only to catch him again in its tail.

Spluttering, we swam forward, only for three more creatures—or *serapha* as Samarah had called them—to burst from the depths. A strange, garbled screech ripped through the world. They were identical, save for the shape of their snouts, some long and curved and others short and rounded. But each possessed wide wings, their sinuous bodies weaving across the sky.

One dipped low toward Caston, who dove beneath the waves to avoid the creature. Beside me, Samarah tightened her grip, pulling me faster toward the opposite shore which was drawing farther away with each passing moment.

Water filled my mouth, and I spluttered, wincing at the strange taste coating my tongue. This was not salt water as I knew most oceans were, and yet, it did not taste fresh either. But the first pass of water into my mouth made my lips and tongue tingle, and my power stretched within my chest.

The *serapha* holding Drystan descended toward the surface, and I pushed forward to make my way into their path. Samarah appeared to understand, dragging me into the line of the monster as it dipped low.

"Hold me above the water if you can," I instructed a moment before I raised both hands, focused my attention fully upon the creature, and surrendered to my magic.

Flames burst from my palms, colliding with the *serapha* right as its jaws descended on me. A screeching wail ripped through my ears before the fire consumed it, leaving merely steam in its wake, and Drystan crashed to the surface.

"*Aelestor!*" I yelled, gesturing to where Drystan had fallen.

I accidentally gulped down more water, and my magic shivered. But I turned toward the next creature, who deftly avoided the flames, another right on its flank. Samarah laughed beside me, the sound slightly mad, but I could not turn to look at her. Instead, I spread my arms wide, pushing the fire out in opposite directions to hold back the *serapha*, even as the third closed in.

"Oh, Belinay, you have grown torturous with age." Samarah's voice was amused as she reached out to drag her fingers over the belly of one before it twisted away at the last moment.

A wave overtook us as one crashed back into the ocean—the force so powerful Samarah's hand slipped from my baldric. I kicked, pushing my arms through the thickening water, the glimmering surface only a few feet above. My head spun even as magic prickled at the back of my neck, tapping on my temple and sparking through my mind. But embers burned within my chest, and black spots bloomed within the corners of my vision.

I took an involuntary breath, more water filling my lungs, only to find the burning begin to wane. Slowly, I forced my limbs to relax, allowed the ocean to cradle me as Asteria had that long-ago night when I had first been bitten.

This is not water, I said, though no one could hear me. *This is magic.*

And the last thing I heard before I was dragged to the murky depths was a woman's voice laughing in my ear, saying: *Yes, it is.*

CHAPTER
THIRTY-FIVE

Oralia

A gush of water spilled from my nose and mouth.

I tried to take small sips of air, but my lungs were already full. As I choked, my fingers grappled at the slick stones beneath me, my vision so coated in blackness I was sure I was on the bottom of the ocean. But slowly, my lungs cleared, and my breaths came in raw gasps whistling through my throat.

Not on the bottom. As I blinked, I traced the edge of the wide stones beneath me, green grass grew between them in perfect lines before meeting tall walls of the same material. But the sun shone overhead, casting carvings on the walls into relief.

I was alone.

"Drystan?" I cleared my throat. "Aelestor? Caston?"

Their names echoed off the stone, reflected back as if taunting me. I pushed to my feet, limbs aching and tired, wincing at the squelch of my boots and the heavy leather clinging to my skin.

"Samarah?"

It was a courtyard of sorts, the center inlaid with an olive tree heavy with fruit. I could not make out an entrance or exit, merely four looming walls of stone inlaid with incredible detail. The closest wall depicted a group of people gathered within a circle with a woman standing in the center, her eyes closed and arms raised. She was beautiful, even within the stone, hair swirling around her shoulders, full lips soft in an expression of contentment. This woman radiated an intensity in whatever it was she was doing, surrounded by what appeared to be other women protecting her. I thought I recognized a few of them—including one who was now my companion on this journey.

The next was a forest, a few trees on their sides, in the process of decay. A fallen fawn lay beside the trunk, fur peeled back to expose its ribs. And there, kneeling next to it, was a god I knew all too well.

His wings were relaxed within the carving. Even in stone, his hair appeared soft, waving around his shoulders, brushing the shoulders of the robes that pooled at his feet where he knelt. It was an impeccable rendering of Ren's face, down to the furrow between his brow, fingertips outstretched to brush against the fawn's head in the perfect expression of grief.

I could not help but reach out to trace the curve of his jaw, anguish burning in the back of my throat and across the bridge of my nose. The image was so real. For a moment, I thought he might turn to me, the torn expression bleeding into one of joy. But this god before me was young. I could see it in the smoothness of his brow—the clarity of his eyes. He had yet to see the horrors in store for us all, to carry the weight of so much death upon his shoulders.

This moment was merely the beginning: the first death.

More and more scenes, some with gods I recognized like Horace and Morana and Samarah, all depicting what I thought might be the beginning of time, the cycle of the seasons, and all centered around the largest carving of them all. A woman dragged toward a great tree by two faceless gods, her face contorted in fear and pain, reaching out toward the viewer in panic.

Asteria and the creation of the first kratus tree.

"She did not scream, not even once." The voice was mild as if the comment was not heart-wrenching but merely a fact.

I whirled, my wet braid slapping against my neck. A man stood a few feet away, arms clasped behind his back, staring at the image of Asteria, mouth soft beneath his thick black beard.

"How would you know that?" I could not help but ask.

The man did not look at me, but he did step closer, the sunlight gleaming upon his deep olive skin. His robes were similar to the ones depicted within the stone, but a deep red, fluttering around his sandaled feet with each step he took.

"Asteria fought bravely, without pleading or tears, and to be honest...she almost won."

Somehow, it made the story all the worse—to know she had almost gotten away. The man suddenly appeared beside me, taller than Horace or Ren, but he might as well have been alone within the courtyard for all the attention he gave me or my question. His thick black hair flowed down his back like a waterfall as he tipped his chin up toward the carving, hands twitching behind his back.

"Where are my companions?"

After another long silence, he turned, ruby-flecked eyes impassive in their stare. "This is what you ask? Not '*Where am I? Who are you? What do you want from me?*'"

My power sparked, reacting to my frustration, but I quelled it with a breath. "I know where I am, and from your musings, I am sure you will eventually tell me who you are and what you want from me. Therefore, I ask what is important to me in this moment: where are my companions?"

The corner of his beard twitched with amusement, head tilting ever so slightly to the side. "You are quite the *latska lathira*, are you not?"

Little queen. The name had been affectionate on Samarah's lips, but on his, it rankled. So, I merely raised an imperious brow in imitation of the title he bestowed.

"And you are quite high-handed for a coward."

The words were met with a ringing silence, the ruby of his irises brightening a fraction before he gave a bark of laughter. I did not join in as he turned, wandering toward the center of the courtyard where an olive tree overflowed with blossoms. He stopped before it, weighing one between two fingers.

"You call me a coward and yet you bent your knee for centuries to a tyrant?"

It was my turn to laugh, though I did not follow him. "There is a difference between ignorance and cowardice. It comes down to the choices one makes once they understand the game. You ran from a tyrant while I turn and fight him."

With a click of his tongue, he nodded before plucking the olive from the tree and smashing it between his fingers. A breeze ghosted across my face, the drying strands of my hair lifting to itch my cheeks.

"You know, when I first learned Renwick had found a mate, I wondered if you were strong enough to withstand his volatile displays." He sighed, the branch snapping back when he plucked another olive from the tree. "Ren had so much emotion and so little control. Or at least...that was how he used to be. I've heard in recent years he lost much of his fire."

My jaw tensed, vision narrowing onto the god as he turned on the grind of a heel to look at me.

"That magic cunt of yours must have been a relief for him after centuries of feeling nothing. No wonder he bonded you."

Shadows slithered from my chest, over my shoulders, and down my arms in reaction. But I did not send them forward, only stared at him with an approximation of the look I'd seen on Ren's face when we first met. I did not allow this god a moment of my ire or my pain—both of which he was looking for with such a hollow jab.

"Are you the God of Bastards, then?" I asked, ice dripping from each word.

His head tipped back toward the sky with his laughter, arms spread wide as if he could embrace his humor. I blinked, and we were suddenly nose to nose, a silver-tipped dagger pressed to my throat.

"I quite like the look of his head upon my mantel. Shall I add yours too?"

A small smile curled my lips, shadows sliding from my arms to his. I ducked beneath his hand, shadows and fingers twisting around his wrist to jab the blade to his own throat, my lips at his ear.

"No, but I quite like the idea of yours upon my own."

Kratus resin gleamed on the edge of the blade—heavy enough I could scent the earthy tang of it. My gloves had been lost within the ocean, and my palm pressed to his skin without damage. Timeless, then, as I'd figured he would be. He laughed again, patting me on the hand as if we were merely playing.

"All right, little one, peace now between us."

But I did not release him, I only tightened my grip and my magic. "Where are my companions?"

"You are wiser than you appear. Release me and I will tell you."

My shadows curled tighter around him, the blade pressing into his skin, though it did not break the surface. Something like pride shimmered around us, his approval a tangible being in the space as if it were stroking my cheeks.

"Very good, Oralia, *Lathira na Thurath*. They are waiting for you within the great hall, alive and well."

"Take me to them," I commanded.

He nodded. "You might be his true match after all. My name is Gunthar, little one. You would do well to remember it."

Before I could respond or push him forward, the god made a slash through the air with his arm. My shadows and the knife in my hand disappeared as if they were merely smoke. He twisted in my hold, pushing me back with a slap to my chest and forcing the air out of my lungs with an *oof*. Suddenly, I found myself on the pitch-black ocean floor, choking on water.

And then my heart stopped.

THIRTY-SIX

Oralia

I blinked and bright sunlight streamed across my face. The air hung heavy with spices, the rustle of a crowd in a market. Smudges of color came into focus like wildflowers climbing a mountain.

Mycelna. The human realm.

Shaking my head, I caught sight of the great ships at my back. Humans were gathered in a line, receiving barrels and crates stacked onto a narrow wagon. Around them stood what appeared to be warriors, hands resting on weapons in their holsters. As one turned, a flash of silver glimmered against their throat, as if someone had pressed a coin deep into their skin above their pulse. A warm breeze caught my hair and rippled through the thin fabric of my gown.

"Oralia?" The scarred god's voice was familiar even after all this time.

But when I turned to face him, I flew backward. My arms flung out, and my knees hit the stone floor of the courtyard in Iapetos with a *slap*. Volleys of water poured from my nose and lungs, magic tingling at the back of my neck. Two sandaled feet stood before me. The god, Gunthar, grabbed me by the hair, dragging me to my knees as I continued to retch.

The knife in his hand glimmered in the weak light of the court-yard and, though my shadows spooled up to meet him, he broke through them easily, plunging the knife into my chest. I gasped, bowing over the blade as blood slipped from my lips and onto the stones. One beat of my heart. Then another.

Blackness crept into the edges of my vision, and I wheezed. But the kratus resin was too potent as it ate away at my bones. Gunthar's hand closed over the hilt and wrenched it out with a jerk of his. hand. A cry slipped from my lips as tears rushed down my cheeks—agony, that was what this was. I could not catch my breath, could not see. Blood rushed up my throat, and I fell into darkness.

I jerked upright with a gasp and blinked into the bright light. My heart pounded in my ears as I struggled to find my bearings. My hands slipped across the worn wood beneath me. Fear reared its head like a monster, and I bit back a scream. But when my fingers scrambled over my chest toward the gaping wound, it was no longer there. I raised a hand to shield my eyes from the sun before it was blotted out by the face of the scarred god.

"What is happening?" he pleaded, falling to one knee.

But I did not know. I only knew the torture of my heart stopping. I gripped the front of his tunic, staring up into bright, mismatched eyes.

"I think I—"

Another jerk as I was wrenched forward this time. Beneath my hands, the pool of my blood was wet as was the blade clutched in Gunthar's fist.

Someone new cupped my face. I spluttered as they pulled me

upright, and two milky white eyes stared into mine. This god before me was all sharp angles, even down to the bow of her lips and straight auburn hair catching on my wet cheeks from the breeze as she prodded my face.

"What do you see?" Gunthar asked, his grip tightening on my head.

My hands slipped off the god's wrists, and, though my shadows danced in my vision, sliding around myself and Gunthar, they could not reach her. I pushed my power out, forcing the shadows into flames.

"*Enough,*" he commanded, rattling my head with a jerk of his arm.

The god appeared unaffected by the display and only continued to trace the planes of my face, humming to herself. Overhead, the sun shined but weakly. It was so different than the sun in Mycelna had been—colder somehow. But I squinted against the glare all the same. She shimmered before me, the courtyard shifting first to the dock where I'd been only a moment before, then to the wide field of Aethera's palace, and back to the courtyard again. I blinked, and the castle of Infernis appeared in the distance, the sound of metal clashing ringing through my ears, and then the quiet of the courtyard, only my heartbeat and the breathing of the god.

My voice was barely more than a rasp. "Let me go."

"Petra, what do you see?" Gunthar said over me.

The castle winked again before my eyes, and I thought I could see a figure in the distance, blood running down their hands, chest heaving. Were those wings on their back or were their arms secured behind them, creating the illusion? Beside them, blood fell like rain and screams rent the air. And then the courtyard, the god, whose mouth flattened further in concentration, a rosy blush deepening the freckled skin of her cheeks.

"Who was that?" I asked, slipping on the stones as I tried and failed to push myself to stand.

Gunthar's grip tightened, and his free hand closed over my shoulder. He was grumbling at me to be calm, to be quiet, but I only stared at the god. "What was that? It looked like—"

"Infernis," the god answered.

Her voice was a shroud around us. Even the sun in the sky dampened. Fingertips brushed my lips before her hands fell away like leaves fluttering from a tree.

"The universe converges around you. It pours its energy into your fount, its magic. There is no stopping what will come, and no changing what has already come to pass. Light and dark, fire and shadow, sun and rain, life and death, ruin and reckoning." Her head tilted up, milky irises sliding to the god above me.

"All the power of the universe," Gunthar murmured.

The god—Petra, Gunthar had called her—hummed again, nodding. "As powerful as a timeless god—more powerful even. It is as you thought. She cannot die."

I gaped at her. "No...that is not true."

Gunthar huffed a laugh, tugging at his thick beard. "Oh, it's true, little one. I've killed you twice in the span of a few minutes and Petra drew you back."

No—no, it could not be.

"What did you see when you died?" Petra asked.

My brows pulled together, and my skin itched with the drying water on my clothes. "The human realm, Mycelna."

Gunthar made a small noise in the back of his throat. "The same as Renwick always did. It is her all right."

But I shook my head as much as the hand in my hair would allow.

"But I have seen that place before, long before I ever came here."

The god before me gave a soft smile. "That day in Infernis your power consumed you."

"How do you know about that?"

Her milky eyes glazed as she touched my cheek. "We know everything that has come to pass."

Stars. I was not sure if I could believe it, and yet, my magic pulsed with understanding. It had been so painful. I could recall the memory perfectly.

The grip on my hair lessened. I wrenched myself away and rose to my feet. Both gods stared at me, at the shadows pooling at my feet, the clouds gathering overhead, and the flickering flames dancing at the ends of my fingertips. If they wanted to see all the power in the universe, then I would show it to them.

"Take me to my companions," I commanded.

In another breath, Gunthar and I were nose to nose, but I ducked before he could strike again and send me catapulting back into the water. My shadows wrapped around his ankles, jerking him back so he fell with a *crack* on his face. But he only shook the blow off, rising with a manic grin pulling at his beard.

"Do you think you are special now, little one?" His tone was soft as if he was speaking with a misbehaving child. "That it means something, this power?"

I ducked as he swung out, his fist connecting with empty air, but his next punch landed in my ribs. Though he did not send me back into the water, the breath rushed from my lungs, and I was unable to answer him.

"Do you think this means you were *chosen?*" A bitter laugh echoed off the stones.

Behind him, the god who had pronounced my power observed without expression, milky eyes flicking back and forth between us, her hands clasped lightly in front of her bright white robes.

"I do not care what it means," I gasped, sending my shadows forth only for him to brush them away. Gritting my teeth, I pushed my power harder, firming my magic until one tendril struck, sending his chin to the side.

"So humble, our *latska lathira na thurath,* but I see you." His voice dropped low. His hand flicked out to wrap around my throat and drag me up to the tips of my toes. "You think the universe chose you for this power, but it did not. You are merely a convenient host—one who was there at the right time and the right place. If Typhon had not taken you in the woods that night, you would have never been bitten, and the power would have never been yours."

"But I was," I rasped, "and it is."

The wind shifted my wet hair, and a chill flicked up my spine. My fingers dug into his wrist even as his tightened over my throat until the air was thin. I fought against the hold. But, I did not look away from the red shards within his brown eyes, I mirrored the ruthless grin spreading across his cheeks.

"Yet you are no closer to your goal than before. You are a child playing at being a soldier in a war among titans—your power will not save you, little one."

My shadows crept up behind him, gripped his head, and jerked it to the side with a crack. Gunthar fell into a heap at my feet, and I wondered how long it would take for his broken spine to heal.

"We will see about that."

CHAPTER
THIRTY-SEVEN

Oralia

ake me to my companions."

The words were not said with anger or fury. Only a moment later did I notice the cold settling over my shoulders, the ice crackling through my chest. Petra gazed impassively at me for a long moment before dipping her chin once and gesturing toward the wall to the far end of the courtyard.

We were silent as she pressed her hand to one of the smooth sections of stone, which gave way in a plume of white smoke to an ornate arch. The courtyard was situated on the edge of the cliffs, deafening waves crashing below. From our vantage point on the rolling green hills, it was easy to see the tiny island from which we had started. The mist surrounding Iapetos could only be seen from the outside, but did not restrict their view from within.

Petra gestured toward a collection of buildings settled at the end of a short, serpentine stone path lined with wildflowers and frothy leaves. The air was fragrant with the scent of meat and spices, mixing with the fresh ocean breeze. As we passed the first few buildings, all gorgeously carved stone depicting the seasons, the stars, and the forests, I noticed a few people milling about inside.

They could have been humans or demigods, though all lacked any true power I could sense. A few wandered within a small building stuffed so full with books even the windowsill was stacked with tomes. In the next, a woman sharpened a blade against a whetstone while another carved into the carcass of a great beast.

"They are not gods," I observed, peering at one who stood before a loom.

"They are not," Petra replied. "Humans occasionally end up within the ocean, and sometimes, we decide to keep them. A few are demigods, the results of dalliances between ourselves and those who come to find themselves here."

Dalliances. Internally, I scoffed at the word but did not reply.

I spied a few instruments through the window of the next building, the curtains drawn save for one. There were only perhaps two handfuls of people, a strange contrast to the lavish buildings surrounding us.

But as we walked, I could not shake the coldness settling into my skin, the icy rage zinging through my skull every few moments. My retribution had not been fed, and my magic was hungry. Even now it was awake, the shadows that usually dissipated after a fight lingered around my shoulders like a cloak.

"Where are the others?" I asked, thinking of the timeless gods Ren had described fleeing after Asteria was imprisoned.

"Waiting for you," Petra answered, nodding toward the columned doors straight ahead.

At our approach, the doors inlaid with carvings of flowers and stars swung open. It was as Gunthar had described: *a great hall*, with its glittering white marble floor and towering walls. The roof, however, was not stone, but swaths of gauzy fabric strung from one side to the other. The deep blue sky peeked through the breaks and I could barely catch sight of a taller building beyond.

"Where is Gunthar?" a voice called, deep and resonant.

"I snapped his neck and left him within your courtyard."

There, in the center surrounded by timeless gods, were my companions. At the sight of them so surrounded, my power roared, shadows flicking out to wrap around those who caged them in. Bodies skidded across the marble, a few hitting the smooth walls while others stumbled. A few I had not touched merely stood in horror as fire flicked from my fingers to surround my companions in a circle, high enough no one could reach them but the heat would not touch my fellows.

Aelestor, Drystan, and Caston stood with wide eyes, their mouths agape. But it was Samarah who called my attention, lips tugging downward as she shook her head. My body vibrated with the fury rushing through me, power sparking like stars around my shoulders. Overhead thunder rolled through the sky, lightning crackling from one cloud to the other.

One god stepped forward, waving blonde hair tied back at the neck, hands raised in supplication. "Peace."

"I fear I have no taste for it while my companions are bound."

The god's blonde eyebrows ticked up. "The only bonds they suffer are yours, Your Grace."

I blinked, looking back at my companions to see they were, in fact, unbound. All three men carried weapons strapped to them. Caston loosely held Ren's axe I'd brought with me and thought I'd lost within the waves. But my power did not flicker, not even as Samarah stepped through the fire with a look of sadness etched into her perfect features, her hands upturned as if to receive a child.

She closed the distance between us, palms cradling my face. "Oh, sweetling, this rage is not for you. It is eating you from the inside and will reduce your soul to ash."

And yet, I could not let it go, not even as the anger roiled inside my ribs, banging against the prison of my heart. I flinched away from her touch, only for her to hold tighter, violet eyes boring into mine.

"They have taken something from me," I gritted through my teeth. "And I will retrieve it."

Samarah lowered her face closer to mine, her voice dropping to a whisper. "They did not take it, and nor do they keep it from you. You will have all restored, my darling. All in good time."

"It was a mistake to allow Gunthar to test her," another god murmured, hands gathering their messy brown curls atop their head.

"It was a mistake for her to be tested at all," the god with the blonde hair answered before gliding to Samarah's side.

"Back, Cato," she hissed before turning back to me. "Shh, sweetling. They are not a threat to you."

The blonde god's blue eyes widened in surprise, flicking between us before they nodded, taking a step back with a hand over their heart as if in supplication. It did nothing to cool me. There was no balm for the burning inside my chest. Sickly sweet, Samarah's magic slid across my tongue until I wanted to retch, and I squeezed my eyes shut, shaking my head.

"No, *no.*"

But when I opened my eyes, Ren stepped between us, midnight eyes glassy as he replaced her hands with his upon my face. His touch was featherlight, like the breeze, but I leaned into it all the same.

"Breathe, my heart," he said, thumbs stroking my cheeks.

"I cannot," I gasped.

A murmur slithered through the room, but his wide wings blocked the rest from my view. I could only see him and though I tried to find his scent, there was nothing, as it was when I went to wrap my hands around his wrists only to find empty air sliding through my fingertips.

He was not here, not really.

"I know what it is to give into the fury, to the blood lust. To gather it around you like armor so no light can enter. But this is not your burden to carry alone."

So I took a breath as his mouth brushed across my brow. My shoulders loosened, and with it, the grip on my magic until the shadows restraining many of the gods in the room vanished, along with the flames.

Ren's smile was soft, but grief clung to the corners of his eyes as he nodded. "These gods are not your enemies."

I shook my head. "They abandoned you."

"But that does not mean they are irredeemable, *eshara*. Forever is an unfathomable amount of time, and though we grow to be more truly who we are, there is always opportunity for change." Ren lowered his head until we were eye to eye. "You need them."

Heat pricked at the corners of my eyes, and his face swam in my vision. "I need *you*."

With a nod, he leaned forward to press another kiss to my brow, the feeling like a feather brushing across my skin.

"Not long now."

CHAPTER
THIRTY-EIGHT

Oralia

en vanished in the next moment, and I was left trembling in my sodden clothes, staring at the timeless gods as warily as they observed me.

Cato, the blonde god, stepped forward, their face full of understanding. I had not realized before that over their shoulders were gilded wings, tucked tight to their back. The light green robe they wore was gathered at the shoulders, short enough to catch sight of the gold sandals strapped to their feet as they moved closer.

"Peace," they repeated, hands raised palm out.

Samarah stood beside me, but I shook off her touch. Instead, I nodded once at the god before me.

"I acted rashly..." I began, my voice trailing off with uncertainty. My attention flicked to the gods who were making their way to their feet, brushing off their robes and looking no worse for wear. The words were uncomfortable, sharp as knives as they crawled up my throat. "You have my apologies."

"And you have ours," Cato answered, reaching forward to offer their hands.

A muscle ticked in my jaw, but I tentatively placed my hands in theirs. They exhaled, chin dropping a fraction before they squeezed once and let them drop.

"You will have Gunthar's too before this day is done," a feminine voice called.

"Perhaps two days," another answered with a grin, sliding a hand over strawberry-blonde curls a shade or two darker than mine, "if it is true you snapped his neck."

I rubbed my hands together absently. Caston and Drystan surged forward, the former reaching out and drawing me into his arms, while Aelestor stared up at the storm dissipating from the sky with brows ticked up toward his hairline.

"We were so worried," Caston breathed.

I took a deep breath, finding the scent of the ocean on his clothes. "How did you get here?"

Caston huffed a laugh, and over his shoulder, Drystan ran a hand over his damp hair. "Those sea monsters carried us."

He released me a moment later, and Drystan stepped in, cradling the back of my head as he drew me into his embrace. Aelestor's hand came to rest on my back, offering me his own relief. When we drew away I sighed, careful not to brush their skin with my palms.

Two other gods flanked Cato, the one with dark reddish-blonde curls and the other with pin-straight black hair and coppery feathered wings. They were opposites in every way, from their varying skin tones to their hair to their countenances, but the three of them somehow fit.

"I am Brio," the one with the strawberry curls murmured, his wide shoulders rolling back. He gestured to the god on the other side of Cato. "And this is Delia. We will take you to what you seek."

Delia, the god with the pin-straight hair shorn tight on one side, gave me a soft smile, her face pure and innocent in its beauty. The other gods—the ones who had not stepped forward to offer their names—murmured among each other, casting looks in our direction. But it was Cato who moved first, striding toward a door at the opposite end of the room opening to a narrow hall lit by wide-open windows, the same billowing fabric hanging from the edges.

Though they had offered peace, my distrust lingered. I noted the way Brio and Delia took up places at the back of our group, their arms linked with Samarah's. I wondered for the first time why Samarah had not stayed here with them. Truthfully, I'd been so preoccupied with Ren and the pieces of him I had never thought to ask.

We came to a steep stairway, and I gave Cato some space to climb the first few steps before following, mindful of the robe sliding across the rough stone and their wings flaring with each step. Gunthar had said he kept Ren's head upon his mantel, and I wondered if that was where Cato was taking us now. But when we reached the top and turned left, it was to find a room shrouded in night despite the day outside the walls, glittering stars hanging below the ceiling.

In many ways, the room reminded me of our bedroom at home with its dark wood and deep blue walls. But this chamber was sparsely furnished. Only a few chairs sat beneath what I assumed was a magically perpetual night sky. The rest of the dark marble was empty, save for an obsidian table atop which Ren's head had been lovingly placed, shrouded by a piece of shimmering black fabric.

"Gunthar said..."

"He said what he thought would provoke you," Cato explained

in a soft voice as if we were in a place of worship. "Though we abandoned Renwick in his time of need, we do not harbor hate for our God of the Dead. He is one of us."

I stared at their profile, the slight curve of their nose, and the set of their lips. "Those are pretty words, but they mean nothing while you continue to abandon us to our fate."

Cato turned, a golden brow raised, and I thought amusement might have flashed in their eyes. Behind us, the low murmur of conversation between Delia and Samarah was merely a hum, but it was Drystan who stepped to one side of me, Caston to the other.

"You are not abandoned," Cato answered, gesturing with an open palm between us.

I scoffed, shook my head, and turned to gaze instead at the plinth housing the final piece of my mate.

"You do not ask why we left?" Brio murmured, stepping closer to slide a hand over Cato's arm and resting his cheek on their shoulder.

Rather than answer, I strode forward to remove the final piece of Ren from the table, only to find the circumference blocked by a powerful ward. Panic prickled through my veins, my heart picking up a faster beat, and I whirled to stare at the gods.

"Tell me the meaning of this," I demanded.

"Not until you are ready," Cato said. "Not until you understand."

Caston stopped me with a hand on my shoulder before I could rush the gods, a snarl ripping through my teeth. But he could not stop my shadows as they spun outward only to make contact with empty air—the space around the gods as solid as stone.

"Ah, so this is it," a new voice murmured, footsteps ringing through my ears.

The god who entered looked vaguely familiar with her hooded

eyes and waving hair. Her frame was willowy, fluid as she moved, the deep blue of her robes as rippling as the blue-black sheen of her hair, as dark as her skin. This was the god I had seen etched in stone, surrounded by others, her arms stretched high into the air.

With a confidence I could not fathom, she strode forward and took my hands. "I admit I was hoping for another time, one in which we could embrace and meet as friends."

I grit my teeth. "Who—"

"Yes, of course. I always forget you hate to be kept in the dark. I am Harleena."

My brows furrowed at her words. "We have met before?"

She tilted her head from side to side. "Yes and no... We have met many times, but not yet."

Samarah stepped forward, wrapping a hand over Harleena's shoulder. "She is the God of Time."

I blinked, taking a step back. No one had ever spoken of a God of *Time*. In fact, I had been told that Typhon and his father had been the ones to create it. Ren had alluded to the Great Mothers, but he had not had an opportunity to explain such things when preparing for war had been more important.

"I am much like you, Oralia. Created by the power of the universe to make great change. Though I daresay my task was much less weighty than yours."

These words were said with kindness, and I softened toward her even as I fought it. She spoke as if we were friends. As if we knew each other's secrets and shared a trust forged through centuries.

"There were other options? Other ways in which we might have met?" I could not help but ask.

Harleena's full mouth pursed, strange flecks of gold and silver in her irises dancing across my face as if reading a page of a book. "Too many to count, but I had hoped for one in which your soul was not so mangled. Perhaps in which you brought our long-lost king to us. But this is what has come to pass, and now, the path is set."

I reeled, wondering in what world Ren and I would have traveled to Iapetos together, and I found myself longing for such a timeline. But then I thought of the final piece of him over my shoulder, barred from me by this god.

"I am the reason we left," Harleena continued, spreading her hands as if to encompass all of her fellows. "Because if we had stayed, the battle between us would have ripped the world in two. I saw it as easily as I saw my next breath. Leaving was the only way to avoid such a fate."

Any piece of me softening toward this god hardened. "And so you consigned Ren to his fate. Did you do the same for Asteria?"

At this, Harleena's face crumpled, eyes growing glassy in the twinkling starlight. "Time is a burden, and sometimes, sacrifices must be made."

"But you could have saved her," I pressed.

The God of Time sniffed, lifting her chin as a tear slipped down her cheek. "And in doing so, I would have sacrificed your mate and half his court. Gunthar might have said you were merely a product of circumstances, but nevertheless you were *meant*—one of many possibilities upon the horizon. I chose not to stop Daeymon then in favor of you someday coming into this world and obtaining your power. That would not have happened if Ren had been destroyed."

I shook my head, clenching my hands into fists. "Ren cannot be destroyed."

She clicked her tongue, attention flicking over my shoulder. "His resurrection is a cycle, Oralia, like the moon or the seasons, but it can be halted as anything can. As one thing is created, another can be destroyed."

Ice dropped into my stomach. "And that is a power you possess."

With a slow nod, she stepped forward.

"As do you."

CHAPTER
THIRTY-NINE

Renwick

My head spun as I was flung back into the in-between.

I groaned, clutching my temples, and waved off my mother's assistance. Oralia's face was burned into my mind, the empty coldness in her expression a mirror to the feeling I'd carried with me for so long. Her power had rippled across her like a storm. It had been unfathomable to stare into her eyes and feel the deep well of magic inside her, ready to spill over. I could understand why Samarah had plucked me from the in-between, but it had cost us both. Even now, I was panting, my magic depleted, and I could feel each tear in my body as if Typhon was once again ripping me apart piece by piece.

"Where are they?" Asteria asked.

Rolling to my knees, I propped my hands on my thighs and let my head hang. My wings flexed, steadying me with the movement, and I squeezed my eyes shut so I could not see them skimming the ground behind me.

"Iapetos. With the others." My voice was as cold as Oralia had been.

Asteria gave a soft sound that might have been a gasp or a hum, but she did not press me for more. She only stroked my hair from my face and smoothed the shoulders of my tunic. The magic of the in-between had altered my clothing as I'd worn it for centuries—the two slits in the back open for my wings and closing with magic.

I described the state in which I'd found Oralia, the icy rage, the blank look in her eyes before it faded into grief. Her desperation.

"It is much to hang upon one soul," Asteria murmured.

"She is not alone," I rumbled, unable to keep the venom from my voice.

Oralia was not alone and would not be alone. This was the final piece, I knew, and soon, I would be restored. Soon, I would rise from this grave to seek retribution for all Typhon had taken...starting with my mate's gentleness. I was not sure there was much left in her now, not with the trembling rage. As Samarah had catapulted me back into the in-between, I thought someone had said she'd snapped a neck while another murmured of her violence and how well-suited we were as a pair.

"And what will you do when I am gone?" The question was a tired one, but one I could not help but ask as I had countless times before.

Asteria shrugged, silver wings mirroring the movement while she finger-combed her long black hair. But her expression was distant. Asteria did not fidget, she did not pace, she merely stood, head tilting ever so slightly to the side, lips moving as if she were singing to herself.

"We need to find a way to get you out of here," I pressed, gesturing to the landscape around us.

She did not answer, though I thought I caught a snatch of the song she hummed beneath her breath. The old language was liquid on her tongue, an echo of one I'd heard countless times in my existence. It was the same song Oralia sang when she brought life, a song my mother had taught her when she was merely a child.

But nothing could be changed here in the in-between. How many times had she told me that? For thousands of years, Asteria had endured, wandering aimlessly through the world in search of a way out, only to find nothing but loneliness broken by brief moments of connection with the outside world. But she'd had none for centuries, not since Oralia had been fevered in her bed and traveled into this realm unknowingly.

Asteria's left hand spread wide, fingers fluttering as if she played some phantom instrument. I observed for a few long minutes, wondering what it was she was doing. But as those minutes lengthened, I caught the glimmer beneath her hand, starlight glittering through her fingertips.

"Mother..." I rose to my feet and made to grab her wrist.

Beneath us, the ground shook, cracked, and a rumble of thunder clapped overhead.

The everlasting twilight plunged into midnight darkness.

CHAPTER
FORTY

Oralia

o you understand now, Oralia?" Harleena gazed at me with those strange eyes as if the entire universe was contained within her stare.

Truthfully, I was off balance from her pronouncement that I had the power to destroy Ren or any timeless god. I never wanted to know how in case the knowledge fell into the wrong hands. For the first time, I thought I understood the burden of so much power—of realizing you could crack the world in two and stand in place as the pieces fell.

So perhaps, in a way…"I do."

"So now, I must also ask once more for your forgiveness," she murmured, voice soft and sweet like a lullaby. "It was I who sent Typhon his father's ring, his father's chains."

A muscle ticked in my jaw, and shadows and flames flared across my shoulders, but she raised her hands for patience.

"If he had not believed he had the power to take Infernis, so many more would have died—*you* would have died before you found the power of resurrection through the suffering he caused you, and Typhon would have placed Ren's crown upon another's head."

I shook my head, laughing bitterly. "Through suffering strength is found."

"Yes," she breathed.

"It is barbaric," I snapped. "You placed a weapon in the hands of a monster who then ripped Ren apart piece by piece."

Such a perfect expression of sadness there on her face. Her eyes were damp with grief, it rolled off her in waves with her power. "I live in many worlds, Oralia. Many times. A multitude of universes. Petra sees what is to come within *this* life and *this* path once the choices have been set—I see what might occur within each and every timeline, each and every choice." Cool hands cupped my face. "I fight on the side not of goodness but of peace, of harmony, and sometimes, it means terrible sacrifices must be made for the greater good."

The God of Time released me before she crossed to the plinth where Ren's final piece sat, gathered it in her arms, and passed it to me. I did not take off the shroud, unable to look upon the face of my soulmate in such a state. But it was a relief to have him in my arms, to know soon we would begin the work to resurrect him.

I had no words for her treachery, no forgiveness to offer her even if I understood. Time was a fickle thing, and I could no more understand the path than I could go back to change what had already passed.

"What she speaks is truth," Caston said behind me.

Harleena touched her fingertips to the curve of my cheekbones before rising to her toes to brush her mouth across my brow. I shivered, magic spreading out across my skin as if I had been dipped into a warm bath.

"This path is treacherous and treasonous," she said before dipping down to press her lips to the top of the bundle in my arms. "The way forward is split into two, and I cannot yet know what the outcome will be. But there are horrors ahead, regardless of what road you take."

I looked at my companions who lingered at my side. Drystan's gaze was fixed upon the woman before us while Caston had eyes only for the bundle in my arms. War was imminent, and I could feel his impatience to resurrect Ren—as acute as my own. And though I could not offer her forgiveness, I could find it in me to offer her something much more valuable in the face of such pain.

"Peace," I said, dipping my chin.

Harleena gave a small bow, pressing a hand over her heart before she stepped away. "*Myhn lathira.*"

My laugh was bitter. "I am not your queen."

But the god merely raised a beautifully arched brow. "You are the queen of death, Oralia. And death comes for us all."

We stood on the grassy hillside overlooking the sea where Petra had first led me from the stone temple. The wind whipped through our hair, swirling up our cloaks and mixing with the sea spray. None of us had spoken as we made our way from those strange rooms where timeless gods wandered without purpose—the way the souls in Pyralis and Isthil often did.

The final piece of Ren was heavy in my arms, and I was desperate to return home. Yet I hesitated, turning back to look at the stone path winding through Iapetos. There, a few of the gods were gathered, observing us warily.

There was Delia, her silky hair blowing in the breeze, hand in hand with Cato. Petra was there as well, a frown on her face, beside a god with a shock of white hair, matching wings, and deep bronze skin. Harleena stepped between the small gathering, placing a hand on one god with skin so dark it reminded me of night, their hair cropped close to their skin and full lips pulled into a seductive smile.

"Would you allow some to join you on this road?" Harleena asked, raising her voice.

My companions all looked at me. I frowned at the group. The Gods of Youth, of Wisdom, of Prophecy, of Time, and a few others I did not know.

"The one beside her is Kaemon. His magic is steeped in pleasure," Samarah murmured, leaning close. "And the one beside Petra is Felix. They are the God of Luck."

Luck. I thought we could use some of that right now. And what was the harm in allowing them to come unless they planned to betray us?

"Caston," I said, gesturing toward the group.

He nodded and, without a word, strode forward with Aelestor close behind, forearm resting on his pommel. We followed, Samarah's bones clicking with each step. Drystan took up the rear, and I could feel his discomfort, the worry curling through the air alongside the wind.

When we reached the group, Caston and Aelestor stepped to the side to allow me to move to the head, bowing in a way I'd seen others do a thousand times in deference to Typhon growing up.

I squared my shoulders. "Before we leave, I would like Caston to ask you a series of questions. That is how we will decide who will join us."

A few of the gods frowned while others, like Petra and Harleena, nodded in understanding. After another moment, I turned toward Caston, gesturing to begin. He had reached prime only half a century or so ago, but his magic was strong and growing stronger with each passing day. He took a breath before turning toward the gods we had not met yet.

"Your name?" Caston asked the one with midnight skin.

The god took a step forward, a curved brow rising. "Kaemon, and yours?"

His voice was smooth, the way silk felt beneath one's hand, drawing an unexpected flush to my cheeks. Caston, however, was too deep within his magic to notice, his attention fixed on Kaemon.

"Why do you wish to join us?" he questioned.

The god tilted his head, light green-flecked eyes traveling the length of Caston's body and back up again. "I wish to see the end of Typhon."

"That is not your only reason," Caston pressed, and his tone was different, magic heavy in his voice.

Kaemon grinned, pink tongue darting out to slide across his bottom lip. "And I like the look of you, Prince Caston of Aethera. I want to see more."

Finally, a flush did creep up Caston's rose-gold cheeks, and he cleared his throat, turning to me with a nod.

The God of Pleasure would be joining us.

All of the gods were questioned in a similar way, though with slightly different wording. Cato and Harleena alone appeared to have no ulterior motive, though I was hesitant to allow the God of Time to come after what she had done. Petra wanted to see her son, Thorne, and Brio, Delia, and Felix, the God of Luck, all wished to see the world they had built after so many millennia of hiding. Belinay, the God of Water and Zayne's mother, wished to see her son, and the same for Kahliya, the God of Love, who did not say who her child was.

In the end, they would all join us in Infernis. My stomach flipped with the realization that soon Ren would be restored. Soon, he would be home. An itch spread out across my palms, my power stretching and reaching for it.

"We will take you in groups, I think," I said, deciding I would split my companions up to stay behind with each set I shadow-walked.

"Wait," a familiar voice grunted, footsteps crunching behind us.

"*Stars*," I cursed, turning as Gunthar made his way toward us, a hand running down his thick beard.

He must have been more powerful than they'd let on to have already healed. There was steel in his eyes, sharp as the blade he'd killed me with, and I could not help but remember the tang of salt-water on my tongue, the burning of my lungs as I choked with it.

"I will join you on this journey," he announced.

Biting the inside of my cheek, I turned to Caston who looked back, bewildered. With a sigh, I turned again toward the god whose neck I'd snapped.

"Why would you join me?"

The God of War grinned the way I was sure a thousand warriors before him had on the battlefield when the thirst for blood ran wild through their veins.

"Because when one finds a worthy opponent, sometimes it is best to make an ally rather than an enemy."

CHAPTER
FORTY-ONE

Oralia

By the time I was back in Infernis, it was as if I'd been gone for a century.

The timeless gods we'd brought with us gazed at the bones lining the castle walls with tears standing in their eyes. Felix stepped forward to place their hand over one, whispering in the old language. I could only pick out a few words—*brother, love, rest.*

Horace and Thorne appeared only moments later, mouths falling open in shock at the gods they had not seen in thousands of years. It was Kahliya who bridged the gap, pulling Horace into her arms and kissing his cheeks as if he were merely a boy.

"*Maelith,*" he murmured. "Mother..."

Petra and Cato approached Thorne. He gathered them up into one embrace, his booming laugh echoing off the stone. It was joy as I had not seen it in so long. Even Morana drifted toward us from Isthil, gazing impassively over the group before she was swept up into Harleena's arms and kissed soundly.

I cradled the last piece of Ren as I skirted around the reunion and climbed the steps to the castle. Sidero waited inside, a beaming smile on their face I so rarely saw. They did not offer to take the bundle from me, but joined me on the walk down the corridor toward Thorne's rooms, linking their arm through mine.

"The last piece was in Iapetos then?" Sidero asked, eyeing the dark fabric covering Ren's head.

I nodded, pushing my magic forward to open the doors.

"What was it like?"

Blowing out a breath, I paused before the threshold. "It was what I sometimes imagined the tunnels to be before Ren destroyed them. Horrible and strange and yet...beautiful?"

Sidero hummed their understanding. "It was both a haven and a prison for them, I expect."

"Yes, exactly," I agreed before stepping into the room.

Thorne had laid Ren's body out on the large table, a sheet covering most of it. I swallowed the lump forming, circling the granite slab to place the bundle in my arms down above the shoulders and neck.

"Are you ready, *myhn lathira?*" Thorne's resonant voice was quiet for once as he stepped into the room and shut the door behind him.

I swallowed again, unable to find the words, and nodded instead.

"At each break, I have repaired the damage," he explained, drawing back the sheet to show the faintly raised scars on Ren's shoulders. "But without his heart..."

Without his heart, he would not rise. I nodded, stepping back as Thorne unwrapped his head. But I stared at my feet, at the mud caked on my boots, instead of at his work. This was an image I did not want seared into my mind. I was not sure if I could have survived it.

"Oralia..." Thorne murmured.

I looked up. There Ren was, lying upon the granite table as if he were merely sleeping. A thick red scar circled his throat. Where before there had been many silver threads drawing me toward each piece of him, there was only two now, one pulling me to the edge of the stone and the other to the beyond where the in-between lay. With shaking hands, I smoothed back his hair, combing through the tangles, blinking quickly each time my vision blurred. He was pale, as lifeless as a corpse, yet I could feel his magic within him and within me.

"Will you get me a knife," I breathed. "One that will pierce my skin. And Samarah."

Heavy silence followed my request until there was the clatter of a drawer opening, metal sliding against metal, and a dagger pressed into my palm. A few heartbeats later, the door swished open. The gentle *click* of bones announced Samarah's presence. She did not touch me, but I caught her sweet earthy scent as she came closer.

Ren's magic curled around me, the same strange tug now tapping at my skull, encouraging me to bring the dagger to my wrist.

"Oralia..." Sidero started.

"Quiet," Samarah hushed.

I slashed the vein, blood blooming against my pale skin before I pressed it to Ren's mouth. His throat did not work, but I used my free hand to massage the muscles, encouraging the blood down.

"Keep the wound open and my wrist at his mouth," I instructed, unable to tear my attention away from Ren's lifeless face. "Now, send me to the in-between."

Her sickly sweet magic coated my tongue in the next breath, and the world went dark. I blinked. I was standing halfway up the mountain I'd seen whenever I shadow-walked while Ren stood a ways off at the base, staring up at me with furrowed brows.

"It is time to go, love," I said, walking down the path to meet him.

His wings flared, pushing himself toward me as he gathered me up in his arms. "You did it."

Not a question, only a confirmation of what he'd believed all along.

I breathed deep, nodding into his chest before moving back and keeping a hold of his hand. "We need to go. I do not have your wings, but—but soon, I promise."

Ren touched his fingertips to the curve of my cheekbone. "It does not matter, *eshara*, as long as I am with you."

Tilting my face to his, I rose to my tiptoes. He smiled, meeting me halfway to brush his lips against mine.

"Where is Asteria?" I asked as we parted, looking around for her silver wings.

Ren frowned. "She has returned to the tree she was imprisoned in. She said there was something she needed to see."

There was more to the story. I could read it on his face. Guilt was swimming in his eyes, and his mouth firmed into a line. But I did not press him on it, only nodded and turned toward the mountain where a small, dark archway now waited. The silver cord connecting us tugged me through the arch and into the dark.

I took a step toward it, only for Ren to pull me back, his hand on my jaw as he pressed his lips to mine once more.

"I fear what I will become when I rise," he breathed against my lips. "That I will be hollow and cold as I was when we first met."

"Then I will recover those pieces as I did before."

Those midnight eyes softened as they looked into mine. "And what of your lost pieces? Are they to be mended?"

Wrapping a hand around his wrist, I pressed a kiss to his palm. "I hope so."

Our foreheads touched, and I longed for when this would be real, when his scent could surround me, and inhabit my world once more. We broke apart, our hands linking together before we stepped into the darkness beneath the mountain.

Pitch black. There was no other word for it. A blackness beyond darkness surrounded us as we walked. I could not see nor hear, and if Ren's hand had not been in mine, I would have been sure I was alone. This could have been death. Perhaps if we lingered, it would have been. But Ren's thumb brushed against mine, and I pushed forward with a confidence I could not truly feel.

I knew I should not look behind me. To look back at Ren would mean to resign us both to this darkness for an eternity. So we walked in silence, not even our breaths audible in my ears. The dark was thick, molding around my arms, my legs, and even the curves of my cheeks and lips.

Each step was the same as the last. I might have screamed, but if I did, the sound was swallowed by the dark before it ever reached my ears. After a while, however, there was the barest shimmer of light, like the sun reflecting on water high above. It brightened little by little, growing more vibrant until I was shielding my eyes from it, blindly walking into the light.

The scent of the sea hit me first. Spices. Wheels turning over cobblestones. I blinked, and color assaulted me from every angle. Mycelna. Standing a little to the side was the scarred god with the streak of white-blond in his hair. The half-skull mask was affixed to his face, ominous and bone-chilling.

"You are well?" he asked.

I nodded. "I am."

He hummed, staring between us as if he could see through our skin and down to our bones. "You have found a way to restore him?"

"The blood is the key," I answered.

The scarred god blinked a few times before nodding slowly.

Ren reached out a hand. "Talron, my old friend."

But it was strange, though I heard the name Talron, it looked as if Ren had said another name entirely, and I'd sworn the other had been spoken beneath it at the same time.

The god, Talron, shook himself before clasping Ren's with a familiarity that spoke of lifetimes. "It is a relief to see you and know the cycle begins again."

Then he gestured for us to follow him up the winding path toward the temple he'd once taken me to. The streets were packed, and occasionally, we stopped to allow a cart to pass. Once, we stepped to the side as a procession of worshippers led by those with tinkling chains hanging around their faces wound their way up the mountain ahead, blue ash flicking from their fingertips. The midday sun beat against my bare shoulders, and as we waited, Ren's fingertips slid across my upper back, touching the gold pins holding the strange dress in place.

"You look like a sacrifice," he murmured, pressing a kiss to my shoulder.

Looking down at the pleated fabric, I frowned. I did look like a human maiden to be sacrificed. It was the same clothing from the other times I'd been here. Ren, too, was dressed in unfamiliar leathers, the same as the god who led us. His wings were gone, perhaps because I had not retrieved them. As we continued in the processional's wake, with every step Ren took his face paled until he was breathing heavily, and I was supporting most of his weight.

"Come, friend." Talron circled back and ducked beneath Ren's other arm. "Your world awaits you."

The heavy stone doors slid open, pulled by two women shrouded by gauzy fabric, delicate chains hanging over their faces to hold it in place—one of them was the same priestess who had led the group. They did not truly see us and, when I looked over my shoulder, it was to realize we had been leading another crowd of worshippers into the temple.

"Why are they following us?" I breathed, looking across Ren to the god.

He frowned, the movement pulling at the scars across his left cheek. "Many were lost this morning. Most of Mycelna is now in mourning."

"It has begun?" Ren wheezed. Talron gave a soft noise of assent, and Ren gripped the god's shoulder comfortingly. "Have you found her yet?"

We maneuvered around those gathered beneath the monstrously large statue in the middle of the temple, covered in a similar shroud to the ones the priestesses wore. Our companion guided us toward another small alcove before sighing heavily.

"Yes, though the fates have not deemed me ready. Another has been offered in her place."

"Who? What is happening here?" I asked as we paused before an altar. A curtain swayed behind it with a phantom breeze.

The god ducked from beneath Ren's arm, steadying him with a hand on his shoulder before moving around the altar to drag back the curtain. Darkness curled around the stone threshold like the shadows we knew all too well.

"What must happen for this world to right itself...or fall into ruin," the god answered. "Go. Perhaps we will meet again in the future and all will be well."

We stepped toward the darkness, but Ren paused and the two men gazed at one another. Ren lifted a shaking hand to curl around the god's neck, pressing their brows together.

"You are ready," Ren murmured. "She will accept you."

Talron did not frown, but the heartbreak written across his features made my throat clench. I knew that look, had felt it when Ren had died. "I am afraid the price will be too high and her heart too cold."

Ren shook his shoulder, and there was nothing either of us could say. We did not know this world or how it worked, and this god was bound by a power I could not understand. The fates, he'd said, as if they decided the path of the world. But he and Ren broke apart, and I slid beneath my mate's arm once more.

"Thank you," I murmured as I passed him, helping Ren through the threshold.

Talron nodded, pressing three fingers to his brow. "Open your heart, Oralia, it is the only way."

The darkness swallowed us whole.

I blinked, the room coming back into focus, Samarah tapping my cheek with furrowed brows.

"Where did you go, darling?" Samarah was asking in a hushed voice, as if she wished not to wake the dead. "I could not find you."

With a start, I jerked my arm toward my chest and cradled the wound on my wrist. But I could only look down at the god prone on the marble slab before reaching out to touch Ren's face.

He had not woken.

"He is close, but he is waiting," Samarah murmured, running a hand over Ren's long hair.

Waiting for his heart to be returned. My pulse pounded in my ears—1 had taken his heart, imbibed his power, and though the blood I'd given him had paved the way, he could not cross the final threshold.

"Take it," 1 rasped.

She blinked up at me. Over her shoulder, Thorne wore a similar expression of confusion. My hand closed around the knife lying on the table, similar to the one Gunthar had used to send me to Mycelna.

"Open my chest and take half my heart. It is the only way."

CHAPTER
FORTY-TWO

Oralia

I pressed my ear to his chest, my breath catching in my throat.

A heartbeat, soft but *there*.

But his chest did not rise with breath. His lids did not flutter. He was the lifeless corpse I'd left before sliding into the in-between.

At my command for them to take half my heart, Thorne had roared his negation, all but ripping out his hair. Samarah had not spoken, nor had I as he raged until the room fell quiet. I could not die—I knew that now. And perhaps the power had been gifted to me for this exact moment, so I could give Ren half my heart.

I had not given them more time to argue before I'd plunged the dagger into my chest and sat with Talron on the docks of the sea, toes brushing the warm water. We spoke of everything and nothing: his mate who had a wanderer's soul and a fearful heart, Ren's path through the in-between, and so much more. But when I'd woken, there was a deep, angry scar across my chest, and my magic hummed through my veins. Even now, I could feel the piece of me regrowing, faster than ever before.

"Ren," I murmured, brushing my thumbs across his cheeks.

No sign of life other than his heartbeat. He lay as still as before, though there was a soft flush rising in his cheeks. His skin was perhaps a degree or two warmer than before—like the weak winter sun heating a stone.

"Ren," I repeated, a little louder, tapping him as Samarah had me.

Nothing. Fear prickled at the back of my neck, and I swallowed thickly, tapping him a little harder before my fingers curled into his hair.

"Ren." It was more of a gasp, this time, desperation clawing its way up my throat, and I dipped my head down to his chest. "*Please.*"

Hands closed over my shoulders, and Samarah shushed me in words I could not understand, something about patience and hope. But I could not find either.

"I have done something wrong," I rasped, the sheet covering Ren's chest damp with my grief.

A wide hand covered Ren's chest, auburn hair tickling my hands as Thorne lowered his ear to Ren's mouth. "You have done well, Your Grace."

I pushed myself upright, heartbeat thudding through my skull as Thorne pressed his fingers to the base of Ren's throat before drawing back his lids to observe the whites of his eyes.

"Why will he not wake?"

Thorne ran a hand down his beard. "His resurrections have always taken time, and this is no different. Perhaps this will take even longer since he was apart for so long. He needs time for his heart to grow, as you need time for yours."

I nodded, shifting on the cold stone beside Ren, but Samarah clicked her tongue.

"You need rest, *myhn lathira*," she said, soft enough it did not feel like a reproach. "Renwick will be here, watched over by Thorne, and you will need your strength for what is to come."

It was on my lips to refuse, but Sidero came forward, offering me an arm. Reluctantly, I slid from the table, pressing a kiss to Ren's cold lips, knowing I would not be able to rest until he was revived.

"The borders?" I asked Thorne, turning in the doorway.

He sighed. "More of Typhon's men have found their way through. It's a slow trickle as if they are merely testing whatever method they might have for breaking through the mist. Any who found a way through has been destroyed before they could report back."

"Do you think..." I could not say the words, could not voice the fear that perhaps Ren's magic was fading from the kingdom.

Thorne did not appear to need me to finish. He shook his head emphatically, placing a hand over his heart. "On my magic, I swear to you, it is as strong as before. Typhon has found a way through some sort of a loophole, but Ren's magic is rooted in this world. Someone has discovered a path, or else is being taken by another who once had favor with the kingdom."

"Or perhaps it is Daeymon's ring which allows him through," I murmured. "Perhaps it allows him to bestow favor upon others to find the path."

Sidero and Thorne nodded together as if this was something that had been discussed in my absence. Weariness clung like a second skin, and I sighed, rose to my feet, and scrubbed a hand over my face before I left the room with Sidero close behind.

"You are troubled."

I could not help the bitter laugh rising from my throat. "Ren will not rise, and he is our only hope of survival. Typhon wields a weapon that might have given him a way through our defenses. There is much to worry about."

"What can I do?"

Slowly, I rested my head on their shoulder, linking our arms. "You are doing it. You are here."

They placed their hand over mine, squeezing once. We turned the corner into the entrance hall as Mecrucio slipped through the doors. He was disheveled, brown curls tangled in his lashes and cheeks pink. Even from this distance, I could hear his ragged breathing, and he stopped to rest his hands on his knees, coughing, yet at the sight of me he rose at once, placing his palm over his heart.

"*Myhn la—*"

"Rest a moment," I interrupted, raising a hand.

He nodded gratefully, leaned against the far wall, and raked a hand through his hair to smooth it. I looked him over as he caught his breath. He was haggard, deep blue bruises beneath his eyes no doubt from sleepless nights.

"Are you well?" Mecrucio asked after a minute or so, no doubt noting the same wan features on my own face.

I grimaced. "It is nothing."

He took a step forward as the doors opened once more and Aelestor came striding through with a similar look of worry. The God of Storms inspected me as a general might for injuries.

"Thank the stars," he breathed, lowering to a knee and pressing his hand to his heart. "You are alive, *myhn lathira.*"

Thorne had raged loud enough I was unsurprised Aelestor had heard from wherever the others waited. "I am."

Mecrucio frowned between us. "What do you mean? What is going on?"

Sidero shifted uncomfortably beside me while Aelestor and I exchanged a look. But there was no harm in telling him now, not when all the pieces of Ren had been found and he was in the process of resurrection. "We have found the pieces of Ren—"

A gasp slipped through his lips, a similar relief to Aelestor's brightening his features.

"—and pieced him back together. But...but he will not rise."

The corners of my eyes pricked with heat, and I swallowed again, my hands clenching into fists at my sides. Aelestor gave a soft noise of pain, disappointment clear in his features.

"Do you have any idea why?" Mecrucio asked, looking between us.

"It will take time," Sidero murmured. "Time is all he needs."

Mecrucio frowned, and I could see his mind working. He crossed his arms over his chest, eyes flicking back and forth on the stones at his feet as if he were reading some invisible message upon the stones.

"What is it? What are you thinking?" I pressed.

He pursed his lips. "Perhaps he will not rise because he is not fully pieced back together. His—"

"His wings," I finished for him.

It was a fear I'd had from the beginning. Perhaps because he'd had his wings in the in-between, his magic would not recognize him as fully reassembled.

"I do not think so," Sidero said, looking between us. "He has been without them for centuries. And before, when they were taken from him, he reanimated. Timeless gods are different, as are their wings. They do not bend to the laws of this world. You know this."

But I could not let go of the fear and, when I looked at Mecrucio, the same was written upon his face. What if Sidero was wrong? What if Ren would never resurrect without his wings? Could we risk it with so little time left?

"Oralia..." Aelestor started, my name a warning.

We needed Ren. It was his magic feeding Infernis. Selfishly, I needed him too. I did not know how to stop the tide of this war without him and could not stomach the idea of running into battle while he lay cold on the marble slab. I did not want to wait any longer.

"Where is Typhon?" I asked, voice so soft it was barely a whisper.

Mecrucio blinked while Aelestor cursed and Sidero stiffened. But I kept my eyes trained on the God of Travelers.

"He is at the Western Reaches for the next few days, ensuring no battalions have been left unaware. Caston has not yet reported home."

Not in the castle, then. It was the perfect opportunity. My heart raced in my ears, magic sparking in my veins, and tapped at the back of my skull I paid it no mind. Instead, I took a deep breath and nodded.

"Take me into Aethera. My king needs his wings."

CHAPTER

FORTY-THREE

Oralia

N o."

Aelestor's voice boomed through the entrance hall, but I paid it no mind. Not when Mecrucio looked uncertain. When his loyalty to his king weighed so heavily on his heart.

"It is the only way," I pushed.

"It is not," Sidero argued. "We can wait—"

"We do not have time to *wait*," I cut across them. "It is only a matter of time before the trickle of soldiers becomes a flood, and Infernis needs her king."

"Oralia..." Aelestor stepped between Mecrucio and me, leaning down until we were eye to eye. "Ren will resurrect, but it takes time."

"Yes, but how much time? You cannot guarantee—"

His hands closed over my shoulders, squeezing tight. "Nothing is guaranteed in this world except if you cross the border, you will die."

I shook my head. "No, I will not die. I cannot."

A bitter smile crossed his face. "It is more certain than his resurrection. Give it time, another day even, to see if he will—"

I stepped around Aelestor, pinning Mecrucio with a look. "Smuggle me into Aethera. That is an order from your queen."

Mecrucio blinked at me, indecision warring across his features. Aelestor blew out a breath, knuckles bleached white as he clenched them into fists. We did not have time for this argument. Soon, Samarah would be on her way to find me—or else Horace or Thorne. Dimitri and Drystan were down with the warriors who guarded Infernis, but they might seek me out as well.

It had to be now.

"Yes, *myhn lathira*," Mecrucio replied, though his voice was tight.

I extended my arm for him to take. We would shadow-walk to the river so we would not be stopped. Vakarys would shepherd us across, bound as she was by the magic of this world to provide crossing to anyone on shore.

"Oralia, do not do this," Sidero pleaded.

I shook off their hand on the arm I extended toward Mecrucio. "I will not sit idly by and wait for Ren to revive. I will do what I can to ensure his survival."

"I am coming with you," Aelestor growled.

"No, it is better—"

"It was not an offer," he cut across me, hand closing over my arm.

All right. Perhaps this was a battle I would not fight, not with our limited time. I refused to look at Sidero, knowing the disapproval in their expression might sway me. Instead, I nodded to Mecrucio, who took my arm hesitantly.

"You have a way to get us in without detection?"

"Yes, through the side door of the keep. It is usually unguarded in the daylight hours."

Which meant we would have to get through the fields without being seen as it was day, but Aethera would be too heavily guarded at night.

"I will send his wings first," I told Sidero, chancing a glance over my shoulder.

Their face was stricken, shoulders bunched toward their ears.

I swallowed back the fear curling in my gut, refusing the thought trickling through my mind asking if I was making a mistake. "We will be back before nightfall."

I gathered the shadows around us and stepped into the dark.

Water lapped at the boat, around the bodies of the water shepherds hugging close to the bow. The mist was thick here, so dense I could barely see my hand in front of my face, similar to the day Ren had taken me back to Aethera. The last day I had been me, really.

"Vakarys," I called.

"Yes, *myhn lathira?*" the skeletal woman rasped.

I could barely make out her form in the mist, lit as she was by the blue flame of the lamp. "Have you been taking the soldiers across the river? The warriors from Aethera who seek to invade our shores?"

Mecrucio and Aelestor turned as well, and I wondered if they too were trying to make out her face beneath the cowl and the mist.

"No, Your Grace, I have taken none who were not meant for this land or granted favor by the king."

With a frown, I looked down at the water shepherds, the bits of flesh and hair dragging in the water as they guided the boat. Any who touched the water were dragged to the bottom, cursed for the rest of their existence to guide this vessel.

"Then how are they getting across?" The question was more for myself than her, but Vakarys gave a small wheeze, shifting her weight to push the staff into the water.

"As I told Lord Horace, there are small sections of the river one might cross by foot. But those are heavily guarded by the king's magic. One must have his favor to cross, and even then, the river is guarded by our warriors. Whoever is letting them through has ample knowledge of this realm and its inner workings."

There were only a few who had such knowledge. Dimitri to be certain, though he could not leave these shores as a soul. Thorne and Horace would, but they never left Infernis. The boat slid smoothly to a stop on the opposite shore, Aelestor stepped out first, offering me a hand on my elbow as I stepped off the boat.

"Thank you, Vakarys."

She placed a hand over the hole in her chest where her heart used to be. "Of course, *myhn lathira*."

Mecrucio was the last to disembark, leading us through the forest until the mist thinned and the sunlight streamed through the trees. The warmth of it was like a heavy blanket over my skin. I craved the cool mist and dark of my kingdom and wondered if I would ever seek out the sun after this was through.

I did not think I would ever be able to stomach the sight of it again.

"We will go around to the east," Mecrucio murmured, gesturing toward a winding path. "Pull up your cowls and stay close."

With each step toward the golden castle, my magic roiled, as if it was pulling me back to Infernis. My heart tugged in my chest, but I took a breath, pulled up the cowl of my cloak, and rounded my shoulders as we stepped into the field. There were a few trees here that provided cover as we made a serpentine path toward the door I'd first escaped out of.

This had been the path I'd taken when Ren had found me. The memory made my throat burn as we walked the route in reverse. Wildflowers swayed in the breeze, the scent now reminding me more of blood than sweetness. I wondered if I were to look for it, if I could find Ren's and my blood within the field. Perhaps it had helped the flowers grow.

We ducked from one apple tree to another, skirted the edge of a vegetable patch, and found the side of the palace. The sun was so high in the sky, heat radiated off the gold in waves, as if it, too, warmed this world.

"Quickly." Mecrucio darted to the door and opened it.

I curled my hand around Aelestor's fabric-covered arm where we were ducked behind a wide tree, gathered the shadows around us, and stepped through to appear within the doorway on the opposite side. Mecrucio jumped but only gestured to us to continue. The three of us had grown up in this castle. Though by the time I was born, both men were well into prime, but we knew this palace like the back of our hands.

It was easy to slip through the hallways to the library. Almost too easy, not even a servant in sight nor a guard like the last time I'd been here.

"Where is everyone?" I whispered, tugging the gold handle of the library open.

Mecrucio did not answer as we crept into the one place I'd once thought of as my sanctuary. There, above the gilded mantel, were Ren's wings, as they'd been for the last three centuries.

Quiet. Too quiet.

"I do not like this," Aelestor breathed, hovering at my back, though he was turned to the room as I approached the hearth.

Metal zinged as Aelestor unsheathed his weapon so close to me, his shoulders brushed the back of my head.

With a frown, I reached out, fingertips sliding over the gold frame. "The ward Typhon placed upon his wings is gone..." I'd thought I'd have to break through it and had been preparing to fight my way through the ward to the wings.

"Quickly, let's do this and go home," Aelestor pressed, reaching back to place a hand on my hip as if there were invisible enemies looming over us.

I took a breath, shadows pooling at my fingers before sliding beneath the glass until the wings became invisible through the dark power. Closing my eyes, I focused on Thorne's rooms, the space beside the table, and forced Ren's wings through the in-between. It was the same magic he'd used to transport Drystan, Aelestor, and me.

Magic rushed through my ears like the wind. It was a wonder Ren had managed this, strung up with cables and bleeding. This was infinitely harder than shadow-walking, and every part of me wanted to move with the wings, to follow them home.

"Mecrucio, come. We're leaving."

Footsteps echoed through the room.

The hand wrapped around my hip tightened painfully and I stiffened, eyes flying open. The wings were gone, in their place only the white backing they'd been pinned to, and Aelestor was pushing me farther behind him.

"*You bastard,*" he spat through his teeth.

I turned, eyes widening at the sight of gleaming gold armor filling the library. Everywhere I looked were gilded soldiers, some coming from the entrance, others slipping from between the stacks. We were surrounded, and the scent of kratus resin was so thick in the air I wondered how I had not scented it before.

There, in the midst of it all, Mecrucio smiled sadly at us with a hand pressed to his heart as his chin dipped. "My apologies, *myhn lathira*."

Before I could so much as call my magic forward, metal whirled through the air and the first bolt struck Aelestor straight through the heart. My shadows rose, but the next bolt pierced my shoulder, a dark metal chain tugging me forward. The shadows flickered, strengthening again before the next flew and the next...and the *next* until I was pierced through each limb as Ren had been.

Aelestor screamed. His eyes were not fixed on the bolt through his chest but on me. I jerked, a sickening pop echoing through the room as my shoulder dislocated, and I fell to my knees beside him. His scream was dying out, replaced by his lips moving again and again in the same pattern.

A name whispered as each tendril of his magic leached away, as his veins blackened and the resin pumped through his system. Blood tinged with the poison dribbled out the corner of his mouth, and with each breath, more fell until it pooled beneath him.

My throat burned as I tried to reach for him only to be stopped by the chains. Each of his breaths was agony made audible, and a slice across my heart for the god I'd grown to trust with my life. A sob wrenched out of my throat before I could call it back.

"I will care for Josette," I rasped, holding his gaze since I could not hold him in death, leaning down enough to press my brow to his. "I swear this to you, my friend."

Merely a hollow, rattling breath, then a sigh of relief, before

Aelestor's eyes, the whites tinged a sickening gray, slid from mine to the ceiling, and I was wrenched away. I hated that I had enough magic to feel his power leaving his body and yet not enough to save him. Hated that I could sense his soul hovering around me for a heartbeat before he slipped away and yet could not comfort him in this final moment.

My eyes stung with tears I did not want to shed in front of these monsters, and yet I dug my heels into the rug as they jerked me upright and tried to pull me forward.

"Aelestor Thyella, your soul is set free from this mortal casing. Cast off your sorrow, for now, is the time of reckoning." My voice caught on the last words, and I found myself repeating them as I looked up at Mecrucio, who stared back with wide eyes.

"For now is the time of reckoning."

CHAPTER
FORTY-FOUR

Oralia

I stared at the back of Mecrucio's head as I was dragged through the castle.

Aelestor's body had been left on the library floor, blood soaking into the white rug, but I knew in my heart he had left this world, felt it as I had spoken the words. Even now, his magic had returned to the earth to begin again, as gods had no need to stop on the shores of Infernis. I tried not to think of Josette and the way losing Aelestor would tear her apart.

He had only wanted to protect me—had *died* to protect me. I would not let his death be in vain.

White-hot agony seared through my limbs with each step. I'd given up on fighting the soldiers, not with my magic drained. Even now, spidery black webs fanned out across my skin around where the bolts lodged within my arms and legs. Flashes of gold made my head spin as I was marched through the halls and up a flight of steps, each bounce of the metal in my limbs another crackle of agony.

This was what Ren had endured. I could not stop reminding myself of it. And, somehow, it was right that I experienced this agony too—that in this we would be connected.

So I stared at the back of Mecrucio's skull as if I might be able to burrow into his brain and find the answers there. The question was there on the tip of my tongue: *why?* And yet I did not think he deserved to voice his reasons, to make his case, no matter how feeble it might be. He would die for this.

I would see to it personally.

The doors to the throne room slid open at our approach. It was Mecrucio who glided in first and fell to his knees before the gilded throne where Typhon sat with a cruel smile on his face. Every soldier around me fell to a knee until I, alone, stood before him.

"The prodigal daughter returns," Typhon boomed, wings flaring as he shifted to rest his elbow on the arm of the throne.

I lifted my chin but did not speak, only savored each drop of my blood onto the floor, a dark mar against the sickening splendor around me. But Typhon did not appear to mind my silence as he nodded at Mecrucio.

"Well done, son," he murmured.

Son... I blinked, looking between them. Was it merely a term of affection between the two? There were no similarities there, save perhaps the bronze threads through his brown hair. But Mecrucio was gazing up at Typhon as a human might look at us, with reverence which bordered on obsession. A flush crept up his throat until his cheeks were bright red, and I was surprised he did not fall forward to kiss the Golden King's feet.

I could remember a time in which I had done such a thing, though it had always been in relief and not reverence. Relief that my punishment had not been so painful, or his retribution not so severe. And Mecrucio had been present so many times as I'd been pinned to this floor by countless healers, as I'd screamed for mercy as they'd tried to banish the dark magic from my heart.

Now I was sure those hours of torture were merely a means of torture for Typhon to avenge his cuckolding while trying to take the power he so desperately craved from the child his wife and her lover had created.

Typhon rose to his feet, and the soldiers who had hold of my chains jerked until my knees fell to the floor with a familiar *crack*. With each step he took, my magic struggled against the kratus resin until flares of shadows appeared around my chest and arms. Gold eyebrows ticked up as he observed, a greedy grin twisting his features.

"Just as I had hoped," he mused. "You have returned to me stronger than ever before."

"Ren has been restored," I gritted through my teeth.

White wings flared with his shrug. "It was a sacrifice I was willing to make to ensure you would find your way home. The moment you stepped into the Western Reaches, I was alerted to your presence. Why do you think those men only ever slipped through his borders while you were gone?"

I did not answer as he circled me and my captors slowly.

"It is easy enough to sense when you have left Infernis, as powerful as the connection between you and my brother is. Mecrucio here informed me himself each time after happening upon you leaving."

"He was the one who guided them through," I murmured.

There was no rip in the mist, no weakness in our defense, save for placing our trust in a god who did not deserve it.

"Do you not wish to know why?" Typhon mused, looking between us.

Mecrucio's back was to me as if he feared looking at my face.

"Not particularly," I answered, fighting back a groan as one of the soldiers jerked on the chain attached to my right shoulder.

A laugh rumbled across my skin, and my stomach turned at how close Typhon was now. I could scent the sunlight on him, his strange magic, and my fingers itched to reach out and destroy. He brushed back my hair, and my lids automatically squeezed shut, muscles tensing out of habit as I braced myself for his wrath.

"I am to be the new king of Infernis," Mecrucio announced, pride dripping from each word while he turned on his heel toward me.

I couldn't help it. I laughed. I laughed until my hands were splayed across the marble floor and tears mixed with the blood. I laughed until Typhon snapped at his guards, who pulled the chains taut, wrenching me back upright.

Every god had a price, and it was clear Typhon had found Mecrucio's. But I did not think for a second he would actually get his wish. No, Mecrucio was merely another pawn, another piece on the board.

"You laugh at your new king?" he all but growled.

"I laugh at your stupidity," I countered. "For believing a man who lies more than he tells the truth."

The God of Thieves rushed at me, grabbing my hair to jerk my head back. "You speak of what you do not understand. He has sworn an oath that I will take the throne."

Nodding, I could not help the maniacal smile tugging at my cheeks. "Ah, *an oath.*"

The Golden King flexed his hand, the ruby of his father's ring dancing in the light. "All I need is your magic before it descends to the earth."

I hummed my understanding. "And you would give this volatile power to another? You would allow another to rule in your stead?"

Mecrucio's hand tightened in my hair. "He would."

But Typhon hesitated a beat too long before he answered. "Of course. Mecrucio is to be my heir within Infernis. He is perfectly suited for the task, all will follow him."

"And why would they follow him, follow *you?*"

He gestured, and in an instant, I was dragged across the floor toward the throne room doors.

"Because I will bring you to their doorstep and slit your throat for all to see. One rules by fear more effectively than they ever would through love."

I stood on the bank of the river, staring across the shallow water to the shores of Infernis, dread trickling through my veins.

The mist was heavy around my shoulders, invisible hands wiped at the tears falling from my eyes unbidden. Pain was only a distant memory now as Mecrucio guided the first battalion of soldiers across the ankle high water. Then the next. More and more followed until most of Aethera's army crossed over the border of my kingdom.

"Come, Lia," Typhon crooned, wrapping an arm around my waist and careful of my chains. "Take me across."

I dug my feet into the slippery rocks, thrashing in his hold, and yet I was dragged along like a puppet on a string. The water did not rise to wash us away, water shepherds did not crawl from the depths to drag us under—because I guided them, however unwillingly. We stepped onto the shore of Infernis, and I grit my teeth against the sob lodged in my throat.

"Forward," Typhon commanded, gesturing with the flat of his hand.

Like a flock of birds, they all moved as one toward the castle in the distance, toward my home. I could barely see the lookouts Thorne had erected to watch the river and the soldiers there. All I could feel was the same tugging in my chest and the grief I carried with me of Aelestor's death. The knowledge that soon, I would bring more destruction to this world.

Perhaps it was for the best, for this world to be ripped in two.

Heavy feet crunched over the dead earth, the golden armor of Aethera glinting in the weak sunlight filtering through the mist. Typhon smiled with satisfaction each time he caught my eye, all but dragging me on his hip like a child. And though my hand slapped over his again and again, my magic had faded until I wondered if, like this, I could truly die.

But as we approached, it was not to see the silent green grasses I'd grown, dotted with asphodel flowers. Typhon's army was greeted by a sea of soldiers, outfitted in deep black armor. And there, toward the center, I picked out Caston and his battalion dressed in the same black, faces half obscured with black curved visors.

Thorne headed the vanguard and never had the God of Healing appeared so threatening than at this moment clad in black, only the bright green of his eyes visible beneath the helm. But it was him. I could sense it as he spotted Mecrucio. Beside Thorne, Dimitri and Drystan wore similar expressions of shock, their attention flicking from Typhon to Mecrucio and back again. But Sidero was the only one who saw me, their face paling until for once they truly looked dead. Their lips formed my name, but it was lost in a roar of outrage.

"*Traitor!*" Thorne boomed, slamming his staff down on the ground. The world shook around us as if the earth might crack in half.

The soldiers of my kingdom answered the call, hitting their swords against their shields until my ears rang. Color drained from Mecrucio's cheeks and he took a step back, but Typhon prodded him to the side.

"I am here to take what is mine," Typhon announced over the din, stepping forward as if he were merely at a banquet.

"And how will you take it, Golden King?" Thorne called. "You have no power here."

"No, I do not. But she does." Typhon gestured with an open palm, and at once, I was jerked forward, dragging on my knees beside him.

I bit my tongue to hide my cry of pain, but it would have been lost beneath the cry of outrage from my people. As one, they crouched into a fighting stance, shields raised and swords ready. I met Thorne's gaze, noting the kratus staff in his hand, then searched the crowd for the timeless gods, but found none.

Had they turned tail and run when Ren did not resurrect?

"A new light dawns upon Infernis," Typhon boomed, raising his short sword high. "And it begins with the death of your queen."

An arrow flew through the air, slicing cleanly through Typhon's upheld wrist. He screamed, the sword falling at his feet. I turned, jerked myself from his other hand, and fell to the grass. His cry echoed off the mountains as blood poured down his palm, and he wrenched the kratus arrow from his flesh.

The Aetheran army attacked. More arrows flew, black mixing with gold, and as one, shields rose, protecting those in their path. The soldiers holding my chains converged behind me until my arms were tightly bound behind my back, and I could only look on in horror as gold surged forward to meet black. The clang of metal filled the air and I blinked.

This was the scene I had witnessed when Petra touched my face—this moment here, the clash of living against soul, the cries of those who might be killed as a sword found its home. Chaos broke out around us until my captors dragged me backward, Typhon at my side. I twisted, refusing to give in to the agony as I tried fruitlessly to be freed.

Screams, cries. Far off a burst of flame flooded a quadrant of the field and, in its center, Zayne stood with his hands outstretched. The calm and peaceful expression I'd known had burned away into something as murderous as the flames itself. They rippled, great beasts of flames leaping into the sky to dive down upon gilded soldiers, but the heat did not touch our own.

Yet in horror, I watched a soul while they were pierced through the heart with a gilded sword, the tip blackened by kratus resin. And as they fell, their body evaporated like the mist curling through the fields. I might have screamed—I opened my mouth but no sound came out. Not as another chain wrapped around my throat, as blood pooled at my feet and my magic seeped back into the world.

Souls everywhere fell, and I could not tell who was winning. But I turned from the carnage toward the god who had raised me, rearing back with all my strength and snapping my teeth. Typhon only laughed, shaking his head before he pinched my chin between two fingers.

"No better than a common dog," he tutted.

I blinked when a haze filtered over my eyes. But as I tried to clear my vision, I realized it wasn't a haze at all, but the mist deepening. A shadow fell over us, so dark it might have been night. There was a cry, but whether it was fear or elation I could not tell, not when the tip of a blade was pressed into my cheek, slicing slowly through my flesh until blood ran down my throat.

A *boom* echoed through the clearing. A few of the soldiers holding my chains jerked in surprise and wrenched me backward. We twisted toward the noise, toward the looming shadow rising from the ground.

Night-black wings stretched wide encompassing the world itself. Power dripped from the silver talons of his wings to the sharp planes of pale cheekbones. Fingers rose, but they were tipped in black now as Talron's were, drawing a curved axe from its sheath, and those dark blue eyes I knew as well as my own fixed upon Typhon.

A deadly smile curved Ren's mouth.

"All that begins must end."

CHAPTER

FORTY-FIVE

Renwick

Hours Earlier

I nodded at Talron. His scarred face and mismatched eyes made my blood run cold every time I saw them. I gave a silent prayer to the fates of this world he would find some peace after all this time. We had been friends, brothers of sorts, before time was made—he and countless others had been ripped from us and spread throughout different worlds. It was always a comfort to see him during my resurrections and the god he had become.

Oralia stepped into the darkness before me, her hand wrapped around mine tight enough I wondered if we would ever be parted. But I gave it a squeeze as I followed her into the dark.

Suddenly, she was gone.

"Oralia?" I called, but she did not answer.

I stepped forward, or perhaps I did not. It was difficult to tell, swallowed as I was by the dark. My body was not my body. There was no extension of my consciousness outside of the mere thought that I was alone. Alone as I had been for millennia, though surrounded by others—now I knew the true meaning of the word.

But there, in the dark, there was a burst of silver magic, the thread leading me home to *her*. It rippled out before me, widening into a path beneath my feet, illuminating a way out of this nothingness. With each step I took, my magic greeted me, rushing up my spine and settling in my chest.

I took a deep breath.

Then another.

Only to find my chest expanding in an unfamiliar way. My muscles ached, my lungs burned, the scent of mist and ash flooded my senses. I shivered, and the movement rustled fabric around my middle. A hand covered my shoulder, shaking me, and with a gasp, I wrenched myself upright, blinking in the bright light.

"Ren," a familiar voice rasped. "*Ren*."

I scrambled against his grip, shaking my head to try to clear it. At my back, my muscles screamed in protest, and I groaned.

"Steady, brother. Take a breath," Thorne rumbled.

A breath. My head spun as the room came into focus. Thorne's eyes were rimmed in red, his cheeks ruddy to the point of matching his auburn beard. Behind him, Sidero wore a similar expression of grief, their hands clasped tightly around themselves before they rushed forward.

The muscles in my back twitched again, and I froze.

"*Great Mothers...*" I cursed, turning to look behind me. "She did it."

My wings were tucked in tight to my sides, though they flared as I turned. Unlike in the in-between, here, my back protested their weight, despite the cloak I had worn for centuries to keep it strong.

It had been nothing to the actual weight of my wings, and with each breath, the muscles spasmed and protested.

Oralia had done this. I scented her magic clinging to them as they flared, clinging to *me*. Our power was now so completely intertwined I could barely distinguish between what was hers and what was mine. I pressed a hand to my chest, breathing in once more, searching for what might be lost now. Was it my compassion? Or perhaps my love?

But the more I searched, the more I found myself whole.

Voices murmured outside the door, a mix I could not quite place. I frowned, twisting my legs off the marble table.

"Take it slow," Thorne warned, keeping his grip on my upper arm.

I nodded. "Who is here?"

Thorne's chuckle reminded me of thunder rumbling. "You will not believe it until you lay eyes on them. Oralia outdid herself."

As I looked around the room, my brows pulled together, and something like fear sparked deep in my chest. "Where is she?"

She should be here. It should have been Oralia at my side when I woke, not Thorne.

His face fell, and behind me, Sidero gave a groan of pain. When I turned to look at them, their eyes were trained on the marble slab, lips turned down at the edges.

"Where is my wife?"

Thorne pressed clothing into my hands, but I paid him no attention as I slid on the trousers, unsteadily standing upright to do up the placket. I stared at the soul who was more than merely my most trusted spy within this kingdom. They took a deep breath, their wide chest trembling with the movement.

"She is gone, Your Grace. Mecrucio, Aelestor, and Oralia

returned to Aethera to get your wings, and though your wings have returned..." they trailed off, apology clear in their eyes when they looked up at me.

"She has not," I finished for them.

"I tried to stop them, Ren. I told her to have patience, but—"

I raised a hand to silence them. "But she had none. I do not blame you, Sidero. Oralia is queen of this land. She does as she wishes."

Oralia was gone. I reached for the connection between us, the soul bond stronger than ever before. She was there on the other end, I could sense it, and I tugged in hopes she might use it to find her way home. Fear slid down the bond, mixed with pain so great I leaned into Thorne's hold, gasping for breath.

"She has been alone with her pain for much too long," Thorne added.

The door burst open. Of all the gods I expected to see, I had not anticipated Harleena, the God of Time, to enter first.

Her eyes were wild as she looked me over, hands outstretched to wrap around my elbows. "She has been captured, Ren."

I had so many questions, especially as Gunthar and Cato strode in after her, followed by countless other timeless gods I'd never thought to see again. Kahliya, my mother's closest friend, gazed at me with shining eyes, while Felix's wings flared in greeting as they bowed. It was as if this were any other day—as if they had been gone to explore the human settlements or giant encampments and not holed away for millennia.

Kaemon strode in last, arm linked with Caston's, though Caston shook him off at once, striding forward with all the air of a general. I blinked, realizing a beat too late he was clad in Infernis armor, down to the starburst sigil at his shoulder signaling his rank.

No, all I could think was that Oralia was captured. All I could focus on was the pain rippling through the bond, the fear, and—strangely—the humor briefly flaring through it. Dimitri and Drystan followed behind Caston, their attention fixed on me: soldiers ready for their king's bidding.

"Tell me what you know."

It was simple, really, once the pieces were explained, to understand who it was Typhon had promised Infernis to. Mecrucio had always been cunning, keeping his cards close to his chest. More than once when he had first arrived looking for a purpose, I'd wondered if one day he would turn against me. But that had been centuries ago—so long time had proven his loyalty. Or so I'd thought.

No one knew when Typhon had first offered him the bargain, but he'd been feeding information to the Golden King for centuries, perhaps longer. Yet it was clear he had been planning for any eventuality. He truly was the God of Thieves—as conniving as they come. Typhon did not know everything. Something I was sure should the tide change, Mecrucio would bring to his defense in a heartbeat.

But Mecrucio would not live long enough for that.

"This whole time..." I breathed, looking at Horace.

He nodded, face stricken with grief. I knew there had been something between him and Mecrucio, a sort of repressed longing for one another at least.

"My magic is imprecise, unlike Caston's," Horace explained, shaking his head. "I saw the conviction in his heart, the righteousness in his actions, and believed it when he said he was loyal."

I crossed the space between us to place a hand on his shoulder, wincing as my wings flared. "Do not take this blame on yourself, old friend. We all trusted him."

His mouth opened, then closed, ruby eyes glazing with regret.

"It was Mecrucio who let the soldier in this winter to steal Oralia away," Dimitri explained when Horace's voice failed. "And I believe he has been guiding soldiers through a shallow point in the river ever since."

There was no weakness in the mist, then. For weeks, Morana and I searched through my magic, attempting to find the failure within the boundary line. But there was no failure—only that Mecrucio was able to shepherd Aetheran soldiers across, shrouding them with the favor I'd given him.

"Where is Morana?" I asked the group, looking for her but coming up empty.

"She and Samarah have gone to visit your mother's tree," Belinay answered, her voice as smooth as the water she conjured. Her bright blonde hair was swept back from her face. Beside her, her son Zayne stood, staring at her with a mix of wonder and heartbreak.

I thought I understood the expression when I thought of my mother. A ripple of grief ran through me as I realized I'd been unable to bid her farewell. She had gone off alone to visit her tree within the realm.

"Go to Rathyra and ensure all souls stay within their quarters," I instructed Sidero. Those within Pyralis, Isthil, and the Tylith would stay sheltered by their boundaries, but I could not risk any who did not wish to fight stumbling on a battle.

Sidero bowed and rushed from the room before I turned back to Dimitri and Drystan.

"Ready the warriors," I commanded, catching Thorne's eye as well. "Position them at the edge of the kingdom so we might intercept Typhon and his army before they get too close."

Drystan's white eyebrows ticked up in surprise. "You believe he will strike so soon?"

But it was Caston who answered, his voice bitter. "My father has Oralia. He will use such a thing to his advantage before she can turn the tide herself."

"Go," I pressed, gesturing toward the door. "I will be with you shortly."

Dimitri stepped closer. "I believe it wise to wait to be seen, Ren. Allow Typhon to believe you are incapacitated or yet resurrected. It will make him act rashly."

I remembered all too well his arrogance from the last time his soldiers entered these shores before the mist was made. With a nod, I clapped Dimitri on the shoulder, shaking him once. "You are right, I will do as you say."

Dimitri gave me a rare smile, gripping my elbow. "It is good to see you again, old friend."

Though the warmth was there in my chest, it was eaten by the dread sliding through the mating bond. But I managed a smile all the same. "And you."

The four gods left the room quickly, leaving only the timeless behind. We stared at each other in silence, millennia of hurt heavy between us.

"Has your prison become so boring you wish to witness the wreckage you have wrought firsthand?" I asked coldly, grabbing the old tunic Thorne left on the table, the slits for my wings gaping in my hands.

They all looked similarly abashed, save for Gunthar, who grinned madly. His presence I understood, as bloodthirsty as he was. But the rest? The rest I could not fathom why they were here.

"No," Cato answered, their face grim, hands steepled before them with their fingers pointed toward the floor. They took a step forward, and my throat ached with long-forgotten grief.

Again, I could not shake the feeling that the last few thousand years had been a dream I'd woken from. They had stayed the same, while I was something unknown to them.

Time had changed me but had not touched them.

"Then why is it you have returned?" I snapped, sliding the tunic over my head and tensing my wings to slide them through the slits.

Gunthar's grin widened, and they spread their hands wide in front of them as if to receive an offering. For the first time, I caught sight of the weapons strapped to his sides, the long steel-tipped whip and curved swords within their scabbards.

"We are here for the golden prick's downfall."

The world was silent, save for the echoing rumble of soldiers making their way through the mist. I stood toward the back of our battalion, nodding at the souls who occasionally caught my eye before they turned forward once more. The ancient bow I had not used in millennia was light in my hand, kratus arrow nocked and ready.

Caston's band of warriors spread out before the souls in the perfect formation of Aetheran soldiers. But it was strange to see the heir of the Golden Kingdom outfitted in Infernis black and to catch the scent of bloodlust slipping from his small battalion and know it was not directed toward me.

"Steady," I murmured as gold glinted in the weak light.

But there was a rustle of astonishment rippling through the crowd before Thorne's voice boomed through the clearing.

"*Traitor!*"

Through a gap in the formation, I caught sight of Mecrucio, his skin blanching as he stared upon the consequences of his actions.

"*I am here to take what is mine.*" My brother's voice was loud, a gloved hand pushing the traitorous god to the side as if he were merely a boy.

The souls around me froze, indignation shoring up their ranks. Mist curled around their shoulders as if the sentient extension of my magic was preparing each of them for the task ahead.

"*No, I do not,*" Typhon boomed. "*But she does.*"

My blood ran cold, wings flicking out as a roar crawled up my throat. Oralia was dragged toward the crowd, her face wan with blood loss, spidery black veins creeping up her neck from the kratus resin and my father's magic in her system. My mate, my queen. At my roar, gold clashed upon black like a horrible gilded tide. I lifted the bow, string pressed against my cheek.

"*A new light dawns upon Infernis, and it begins with the death of your queen.*"

My arrow flew. The scent of blood stained the air, but I could only growl when my mate was jerked back, even as she surged forward with hatred in her eyes. And then, as a blade sliced through the air, as her blood spilled down her cheeks, I pushed into the sky.

I landed with a crash before them, and I could only look on my brother, who I had once been desperate to love. Who I had once sheltered from the wrath of our father until Daeymon understood which of us could be molded into his image.

His eyes widened in surprise before he controlled the expression, gripping the heavy sword in one hand and short knife in the other. I tilted my chin up before I withdrew the axe from my baldric, shadows slipping down my arms to slither across the ground. A cruel smile curled my lips.

"All that begins must end."

I did not rush him as he expected—only held my axe at my side while my shadows slipped over Oralia. Her groan of pain was not audible over the tumult of the fighting around us, but I felt it through the bond, followed by the relief of her magic slowly finding its way back to her as the last of the resin was purged from her blood and her shackles fell to the ground. She would be weak, but she was strong enough to fight and hold her own on this battlefield.

Typhon, however, had eyes only for me. He took a step forward, sword rising into position.

"I am relieved to know you are revived, Brother. It would not have been satisfying to take your lands without taking your life too."

I chuckled, the sound like ice even to my ears. Behind him, Oralia rose to her feet, taking me in greedily before her attention slipped to Typhon. The soldiers behind her all looked at each other in confusion, holding the dark chains loosely in their hands. They would not want to kill her, not when her power was what Typhon needed to control Infernis.

"Yes, well, there is nothing I love more than dying," I answered, weighing the axe in my hand.

Behind him, Oralia turned toward the soldiers with a similar cold smile on her cheeks. Her shadows, darker and sharper than I'd ever seen before, flashed out. Blood sprayed from necks, soldiers gasping as their hands flew to their throats, crumpling to the ground before they could even take a breath.

More soldiers barreled toward her, but she crafted her darkness into two deadly blades, swinging them in an arc and taking down two in the next breath. My attention slid back to my brother as he rushed me.

Metal clanged against metal. His sunlight recoiled from my shadows. The memory of our last meeting like this burned in my mind. The boot he'd had pressed to my throat before I'd shoved it off. The burning heat of his magic curled around my shoulders as my shadows wrapped around his arms.

I ducked beneath his blade, ramming his chest with my shoulder to unbalance him, his wings spreading wide to counterbalance his weight. He laughed, leaning forward to strike once more, only to find my axe meeting the blow. I pushed his sword to the left, forcing him to stumble forward.

"You cannot kill me." Typhon spun with the next breath, his blade catching my thigh.

The pain burst bright across my skin only to die, the kratus resin barely impacting against my strength. My magic ate it away in the next moment, faster than it ever had before. Oralia was at my back, and we were close enough to touch now as she met each new fighter with a dizzying speed. I could make out her panting breaths, the groans as each demigod or human pushed forward, and through the bond, I could feel her despair. Not at their deaths, but at her hunger for *more*.

Thorne was right. She had been left alone in this pain for too long.

"Of course, I cannot," I answered Typhon, grabbing his mangled wrist with the next blow and sending his short dagger skittering off to the side as I turned his back to my mate.

He grunted, swinging out with his sword in his other hand, but

I twisted, the blade merely skittering across the skin of my throat as my wings balanced me. Oralia's voice was wind chimes in the dark, the burst of dawn across a never-ending night sky.

"But I can."

CHAPTER
FORTY-SIX

Oralia

I pressed the tip of Typhon's dagger to the seam of one white wing within his armor.

He froze, wings flaring wide as if it might shake me off, but I only pressed harder, beads of blood appearing across the gold. What was it Samarah had said what felt like centuries ago when we had first met?

Horrible thing, to be stripped of one's wings. It is the easiest way to subdue a timeless god, you know.

To rip the wings from a timeless god was a tragedy. That was why Typhon had done it to Ren centuries ago.

The ground rumbled beneath our feet, but I paid it no mind, not even when in my peripheral vision I caught sight of a whole band of Aetheran warriors frozen in place, eyes wide and horrified, with Samarah in their midst. A spray of rocks and earth flew high, molding, twisting, and changing before plummeting back to the earth in the form of her demon Hezanah.

The blade sank another inch into Typhon's skin. Around us, his men fought wildly, consumed by the flames Zayne conjured or falling prey to Samarah's pet throwing soldiers into the air as if they were treats for the taking.

Typhon's hands flew back as if to stop me, but he was impeded by the span of his own wings. His father's ring caught my attention, the glittering gem of Daeymon's blood taking on an unearthly glow.

"You kept me weak," I gritted through my teeth as my blade sliced through a tendon. His rasp of pain was a balm upon the raw spot in my chest where the scared child within me still knelt on his throne room floor. "You kept me afraid like one might keep a pig before it is ready to be slaughtered."

Another slice. Another gurgle. Ren fought efficiently beside us, allowing me room with Typhon.

"I think I would like to see your fear." I dragged the blade down.

He cried out as his wing fell at our feet, and he pitched forward onto his knees.

"Perhaps, through this, you can begin to understand what it means to truly suffer."

I gripped his remaining wing, slicing down cleanly through bone. He jerked. His scream was loud enough to rattle my teeth and sweeter than the softest melody. But when I wrenched the last of the sinew and muscle away, throwing the feathery white mass to the side, he only reached one hand forward toward his golden sword.

To find a delicate foot placed upon it.

I could barely hear my gasp over the fighting, but I thought perhaps Typhon made a similar noise.

"Hello, boy," Asteria murmured, gazing down upon Typhon as if he were the child she had once known.

Typhon's hand jerked back as if burned. Her silvery wings glittered as she stretched them wide. A gilded soldier rushed through Ren's defenses, and before he could reach me, my shadows snapped out, slicing his head clean from his body. He was a good few feet from me when his body tumbled to the ground, but I only had eyes for Typhon.

"*Asteria,*" Typhon whispered in a rasp, pressing up to his knees with shaking arms.

Asteria toed the hilt of the sword, flipping it off to the side and out of his reach. "I have no taste for war or for the violence you seek. I merely wished to gaze upon you one last time before your magic was sent back to the world to begin again—hopefully in someone better suited." She leaned down until her mouth brushed the shell of his ear. "Death is a mercy I am not sure you deserve."

Her lips brushed his cheek, fingertips passing over his hair, before she launched herself into the sky with those silvery wings. Typhon stared, slack-jawed, at her retreating form before he unsteadily rose to his feet, laughing bitterly.

"You— You do not have the power to kill me, girl," he wheezed as he turned to face me but it was clear he was rattled, that Asteria had unseated him.

I smiled, weighing the dagger in my hand. His father's ring glimmered on his finger, reminding me I should not use my shadow magic for fear he would take it. Around us, the cries of the fallen swelled to a fever pitch, dirt and dust mixing within the mist, tendrils of it winding around my legs and shoulders. The scent of death was everywhere, cloying and sickening.

One step forward, and he matched it. Then another. Another. He reached for me, wide hands going for my throat, but I slashed at his hands, metal wrenching through leather and bone sending the cursed ring flying off into the mud. Blood sprayed across my face, but I did not move to wipe it away before I sent a wreath of flames forward to twine around his neck.

His sunlight exploded from his skin, working to slice through the fire only to find no purchase. This was not the darkness he could dissipate. My free hand clenched into a fist as I drove the dagger into his belly.

He roared, swiping out wildly. Knuckles caught my chin, snapping my head to the side, and I stumbled. But my flames did not flicker. Blood exploded from my mouth, but I only turned with a smile to spit it across his face.

Typhon screamed as I lifted my hands, placing them over his cheekbones.

Black veins crept up his neck, spiderwebbing across his cheeks. Here was the true monster I had grown up with, the façade tarnished until I could see him clearly. And I would never forgive him, regardless of how I knew it would haunt me. But I would try my damnedest to forget.

"Now is the time of reckoning."

My hands pressed to his face.

His gold eyes widened, the inky veins spreading out across his skin. The cry of agony on his lips was short-lived as his body twisted. The sword in his grip clattered to the ground, and I dropped my hands from his face as his skin curled into ash.

The world went silent. Typhon's body cracked and fell as his magic was swept up into the wind and carried off into the sky. But I could not find relief in the sight, only some maddening lack of satisfaction, some wish for his blood to coat my hands.

I might have screamed—perhaps I did, because I was spun in place, tugged forward into a wide chest. The scent of sandalwood and ash filled my lungs, and I cried out again, clutching at Ren's tunic, my knees buckling beneath me.

"He is gone," he murmured, hand stroking my hair. "You are free."

Free. I did not know the meaning of the word. But I clung to Ren, all the same, savoring the feel of his true body against mine. All around us the battle continued to rage, Typhon's men unaware of his destruction. But the fighting did not touch us for this brief moment, not as Ren drew back to peer into my eyes, his thumbs brushing against the dirt on my cheeks, mixed with my blood.

Far off, someone yelled in triumph, and I thought it sounded like Gunthar. Another cry echoed the first, until around us golden soldiers fell to their knees, their swords upraised in defeat.

"We are free." Ren leaned down and covered my mouth with his.

The kiss was not merely a kiss. It was a revelation. The moment his lips touched mine, my heart cracked open. Power flooded my body as if light was filling my veins, sliding through the cracks in my soul until none remained, filling those lost parts of me. I gasped against his mouth, long-forgotten warmth spilling into my chest with each pass of his lips over mine, each swipe of his tongue.

And when he pulled back, he wiped at my tears with a smile, tracks shining down his cheeks. He was so beautiful with his night-dark wings spread protectively behind him. His dark blue eyes filled with so much love it made my chest ache.

"I missed you," I breathed, raising a shaking hand to cup his cheek.

His forehead met mine, and all around us, the sound of fighting faded, not from magic, but from the sweeping tide of victory and the endless cacophony of death. Even now, I could sense the souls gathering on the far side of the river, waiting for Vakarys to shepherd them home. But such things could wait a while longer, I thought, as we breathed in each other's scents and reveled in the bond thrumming between us.

Ren leaned into the touch, cradling my palm. "And I missed you, my heart."

CHAPTER

FORTY-SEVEN

Oralia

The Aetheran soldiers who had not yet surrendered lay down their swords at the sight of Caston removing his helm, gold hair gleaming in the dying light.

"Your king is dead!" he cried from across the battlefield. *"Lay down your arms before you give up your lives!"*

Asteria was cradled in the arms of Kahliya, who spoke in soft whispers, apologies not meant for our ears. Ren and I pushed through the throng, each black-clad soldier stopping to drop to one knee, spear their sword into the earth, and bow their head. The Aetheran soldiers gazed among each other before the first hesitantly dropped, followed by the second, third, on and on until all bowed before Caston, Ren, and me.

"Your king is dead," Ren echoed, louder than ever before, hand hovering over Caston's shoulder before it gently dropped onto it. "Long live your king!"

There was a tentative cry of "Long live the king" among the

Aetheran soldiers before it quieted into a hush as Caston turned to Ren, dropping to a knee to press his forehead to my mate's knuckles.

"Forgive me for my father's crimes, King Renwick. Forgive me for the cruelty my kingdom has wrought upon you and your queen."

My heart twisted, and I blinked back the haze as Ren cupped Caston's cheek and bent to press a kiss to his brow.

"Peace between us, Nephew." Ren assisted Caston to his feet and drew him into an embrace.

The soldiers of Infernis banged their fists against their breast-plates, the tumult ringing in my ears as I breathed a sigh of relief. It was a word I had not truly understood until this moment, with Typhon's gleaming sword removed from our necks.

Peace.

Caston turned to me next, and I gave him a watery smile as he gathered me up into his arms. I pressed my cheek to his, sighing as he put me down.

"There is much to be done to rebuild Aethera," he murmured. "Promise me you will visit often, that you and Ren both will help guide me."

Ren's arm wrapped around my waist, his hand closing over Caston's shoulder as I nodded.

"We promise."

But we did not part from the new king, not right away. Instead, we made our way through the throng of soldiers, speaking with the wounded and offering them my gift of healing. Some did not take it, preferring for Caston to deliver the killing blow so they might begin anew within Infernis, to atone for the horrors they had acted out for their *Golden King*. Most, however, refused or lifted their weapons to fight us, but as we fought each outcry of loyalty to Typhon, I knew we would welcome their souls into our fold when they made the journey home.

The ones who accepted our help tended to observe Ren with uncertainty as he moved through the dead, wings tucked tight to his sides. He would pause over one form or another to release their soul into the afterlife or a demigod's magic back into the world with a gentleness bordering on reverence. Ren picked his way through the crowd but stopped before a crumpled body, a muscle ticking in his jaw as he reached out with a trembling hand.

Slowly, I pushed to my feet to join him and then froze as the body of Mecrucio—mangled and twisted—came into view. Ren was speaking softly, though it was clear Mecrucio's magic had already been released back into the world. And I knew he was releasing whatever lingering hold his soul might have kept upon this life. Within the act, Ren offered his forgiveness and acceptance of the betrayal Mecrucio had wrought.

Ren joined me as I knelt at one soldier's side, the wound on his stomach gaping, hands scrambling to keep his intestines from spilling out.

"Breathe," I murmured as the human man grit his teeth from the pain, light brown skin paling further.

Ren's face fell as he looked at the man before falling to his knees beside him. "What is your name?"

The soldier froze in shock, his body trembling, but he stammered out his name clearly enough, "Firo Grayson, Y-your Grace."

I closed my eyes as they spoke, the song trickling up my throat, a warm light of healing magic settling around my shoulders like my shadows. The man sighed in relief, his body relaxing toward the ground.

"Had you a brother? Or a son?" Ren asked.

The man cleared his throat and grief filled his reply. "A b-brother, Jesper. But he was killed months ago."

Guilt trickled through the bond, and I opened my eyes to see Ren's face stricken, a muscle ticking in his jaw. The magic pulsing with each beat of my heart was working on Firo, knitting the ruined pieces of his stomach back together, the color returning to his cheeks.

"I am sorry." Ren's words were soft.

Firo's throat worked with a swallow as he nodded.

But Ren shook his head, running a hand back through his hair in a way that told me even more than the bond and the nervousness he had. The guilt weighing on his heart.

"Would...would you like to visit him?" Ren offered, glancing over his shoulder toward Rathyra.

The man's eyes widened, and he nodded mutely before his attention flicked back to me. I managed a small smile at him as one of Ren's warriors approached.

"You will be fine," I murmured as Ren instructed the soul to escort Firo to Pyralis so he might see his brother.

The soul assisted the man to his feet before he bowed his head toward me, pressing three fingers to his brow. "Thank you, my lad... Your Grace."

I extended a hand to Ren to draw me up when the man was out of sight. "That was a kind thing you did."

He frowned down at our hands, squeezing mine. "His brother begged for death, to be released from the guilt of his life in Typhon's army..."

"Just like so many here."

Ren wiped his face with his sleeve and sighed before tugging me into his embrace. I went willingly, breathing in his scent as he tucked me beneath his chin. This was home, here in his arms, where everything made sense and the world was right. Even now, his magic—our magic—was working on me, filling in the cracks of what the resurrection had taken from me.

"How are you?" I asked into the leather of his baldric as he slid a hand through my tangled hair.

"I am...tired," he answered, drawing back to look at me. Slowly, he leaned down until our foreheads touched, taking a deep breath. "And desperate for a moment alone with my wife."

A grin pulled at the corner of my mouth, reflected on his face. His mouth covered mine, and it was another relief to have him draw me tighter into his arms, to have the darkness slither around us and swallow us whole.

Our bedroom came into view, though I paid it little attention as he walked us back into the bathing chamber. The tub was filled with steaming water, the clean scent cutting through the acrid smoke and blood clinging to us from the battlefield. Weapons and straps and boots fell to the floor with a clatter as we stripped each other of our fighting leathers. Ren touched me softly, reverently, tracing the line of my collarbones, the curve of my jaw, the hollow of my throat. And then, his hand pressed to the space between my breasts, my heart pounding into his palm.

"Beautiful," he whispered. "My beautiful *eshara*."

He guided us into the tub, tucking his wings in tight, and I shivered at the warmth as we sank into the water. Immediately, Ren tugged me onto his lap, my knees resting on either side of his hips, before he threaded his fingers through my hair and drew my mouth back to his. Teeth grazed my lower lip, his tongue pressing forward to steal my breath. I whimpered as his mouth moved to my cheek, down to my jaw, before he kissed the space below my ear.

It was overwhelming to be touched by him after so long apart. The hollow cold in my chest had lasted weeks, but it had felt more like centuries. I could not begin to imagine how it had been for him to be without a body for that time, to be stuck within a realm that time and space had no hold on. Perhaps it had been longer for him—millennia trapped in that place.

"Are you hurt?" he murmured as he pulled back, hands sliding over each inch of my skin.

I shook my head, tracing a line down the white scar on his chest, the twin of the one on my own. He pressed a kiss to my scar.

"I have your heart." It was not a question, but he raised his brows all the same.

I nodded. "A piece of it, yes."

He hummed. The ends of his wet hair dragged across his shoulders as he tilted his head. "And you have mine."

My eyes burned. "Yes."

Ren's smile was blinding as his thumbs stroked my face, and he leaned forward to cover my mouth with his. His presence here in these rooms was like breaking from the surface after drowning, like the first deep breath of unencumbered air.

"I am yours," he vowed, pressing his brow to mine.

"And I am yours."

For once, the prospect of lying down to sleep did not fill me with dread. Not when Ren cradled me in his arms, tugged back the sheets,

and arranged me beneath. Especially not when he followed, frowning as he arranged his wings a bit awkwardly.

"Is it strange?"

He shifted again, rolling a little more onto his side to face me fully and resting his head on his hand. "Stranger than I hoped it would be."

Tenderly, I brushed the furrowed space between his brow with my thumb. He caught my hand, flipping it over to press a kiss to my palm. "Rest, *eshara*."

Though I shook my head, hands hungrily roaming the planes of his chest, my lids drooped with exhaustion. His fingertips skimmed the length of my jaw, over my brow, before guiding my eyes closed.

"I will be here when you wake," he promised.

It felt like only moments later I opened my eyes, but the pale morning light was sliding through the window, whose drapes had not been shut. Hands skimmed across my belly, over my hips. A whimper slipped through my lips as a hard length slid against my backside.

"Ren," I moaned as one of his hands slid between my thighs, and I arched my back. His answering groan was hot against my neck, mouth nipping at my shoulder. "I need you. Do not make me wait."

But when he did not take what was his, I turned in his arms. His brows were furrowed once more, and though his cock jutted between us, the head already shining with the evidence of his need, his hands were gentle on my waist.

"I do not want to hurt you," he breathed, thumb skimming the underside of my breast.

I brushed my hand across his face, rising up to press my lips to his. "The only way you could hurt me now is if you stop."

His eyes fluttered shut, and as I pressed another kiss to his jaw, I traced the line across his heart, down the hard ridges of his stomach, before wrapping my hand around his scorching length. My name was a prayer on his lips as I ran my thumb across his slit, midnight gaze snapping open as I brought it to my lips, licking his taste off my skin.

"Is that what you want, *eshara?*" he all but growled. "Because once I start, I will fuck you, fill you, claim you, until you are dripping with my spend and screaming out my name. Once I start, I will not be able to stop."

With those words, he rolled me onto my back, sliding my knees apart and settling between them. His wings flared out behind him, and I could not help but marvel at the sight of him—the power of him fully restored. And then his mouth was on me before I could answer, diving between my thighs and devouring me until I was screaming out his name.

Every kiss, every touch, every roll of his hips was another spark of power between us, another strengthening of our bond until our magic danced between us. Sunlight and shadows and flames, the power of the universe echoing throughout our room.

Later when our bodies stilled and we exchanged languid kisses, for the first time in my entire existence, I found I understood the meaning of freedom, of peace, of forever.

"I love you."

Ren touched a knuckle beneath my chin, eyes glittering.

"And I love you, *unendingly.*"

EPILOGUE

Renwick

A Few Weeks Later

The dawn was quiet.

Mist rolled across the green grass of Infernis, at the edge of the forest surrounding the western edge of the kingdom before the Cyvon Sea. Within the forest was tree my mother had torn herself from after millennia stuck within the in-between. A few days after the battle, when all had settled and Oralia and I were content to leave our marriage bed, Asteria told me the story.

She had cut her wrists in the in-between and bled upon the tree. Her blood had opened a space within the trunk, and she had traveled through unfathomable darkness to reach the other side. It was a darkness I understood, a darkness both Oralia and I could easily recall.

I am sorry, my son, that I did not try sooner, Asteria had apologized again and again.

But there was nothing to forgive.

I'd asked her if, in the darkness, she'd seen another place—perhaps a scarred god with mismatched eyes. But she'd said it had merely been the blackness of oblivion and then the sliver of light from Infernis, the mist slipping through the crack in the tree beckoning her out along with Morana and Samarah.

Neither Oralia nor I knew how to get back to Mycelna and Talron, though I worried about him often—the scarred god who always stood vigil with me during my resurrections. Who had so often knelt beside me as I cried out in anger, or horror, or grief and offered me reassurance in whispers of the triumph that comes through pain.

I could only hope when the time came for the fates of his world to guide him to his mate, she would accept him with an open heart.

Oralia's palm slipped against my own, fingers tangling together. Her throat clicked with a swallow, and when I looked at her, it was to find her eyes brimming with tears, cheeks ruddy with the effort to hold them back. Her mouth worked as she fought the sob in her throat, the grief heavy in our bond.

Josette stood within the circle of souls ready for ascension, a look of heartbreaking hope on her face. At the news of Aelestor's passing, she had been inconsolable, begging once more to drink from the Athal to rid herself of the unending pain. She had screamed her pleas to anyone who would hear until she had accepted her fate and resolved to ascend, to join Aelestor in the beyond to begin again.

I could not imagine what pain it must have been—to remember after centuries the god you loved only to have him ripped from you once more. My lifetime spanned past time itself, yet I was not sure I had ever experienced such an agony and hoped I never would.

She did not cry, not anymore. Josette merely stood with her arms hanging loosely at her sides, gazing up at the mist above as if Aelestor was already waiting for her in the beyond. Who knew? Perhaps he was. But such things were beyond me and the realm we ruled.

I did not know what lay beyond death.

Magic hummed in the air, and my power rushed to the surface of my skin. Through the bond, I sensed Oralia's power reacting similarly. There was no need for words. This ritual needed no guidance, no pomp or ceremony. No, it merely needed a witness, and I was the one who must shoulder the burden.

But not alone. Oralia's shoulder pressed against mine, and everything within my body sighed. We were not alone, no matter how often in the night she woke screaming for me, her hands outstretched or clawing at the sheets.

Time was the only bandage I could offer, though it did not feel like enough.

Her moon and star crown glimmered at the first soul ascending, their magic shooting bright white into the sky. Another, and another, until it was tempting to shield my eyes against the glare, but we did not. We stood witness for those who would begin again.

And when all had given their magic back to the world and the light had dimmed, Oralia and I stood vigil for a few minutes longer, breathing in the crisp morning air.

"What do you want to do now?" she asked in a quiet voice, turning to me with a smile on her lips.

I cradled her face in my hand and pressed a kiss to her brow.

"Live."

AUTHOR NOTE

I can't believe our journey with Ren and Oralia is finally over! I first wrote *Ruin* back in September of 2022 and to now find ourselves here is an absolute dream. Thank you for joining me on this ride.

I have other exciting things on the horizon! If you'd like to stay up to date with my upcoming books (including a spicy vampire romance coming soon) you can follow me on social media (@gillian-eliza) or join my newsletter at www.gillianelizawest.com. I also have a Patreon where I share exclusive behind the scenes, art, bonus chapters and more a www.patreon.com/GillianElizaWest.

Either way, from the bottom of my heart thank you for reading.

xo—Gillian

THE
LANGUAGE of
INFERNIS

Myhn Ardren (m-YN ar-DREN) | *My King*

Myhn Lathira (m-YN la-THEER-ah) | *My Queen*

Eshara (eh-SHAH-rah) | *love, life force*

Maelith (MAY-lith) | Mother [formal]

Thurath (THUH-rath) | Dead, death

Lathira na Thurath (la-THEER-ah n-AH THUH-rath) | Queen of the
   Dead

Naturhum Rhyonath | "Your reckoning."

Latska (lat-SHKA) | little

Kalimayah (kah-lee-my-UH) | *beautiful*

Cahrdren (kar-dh-ren) | *Prince*

THE
INFERNIS DUOLOGY
CHARACTER LIST

TIMELESS GODS

Renwick | God of the Dead, brother of Typhon and son of Daeymon and Asteria (he/him)

Typhon | God of the Sun, brother of Renwick and son of Daeymon and Delia (he/him)

Horace | God of Judgement, son of Kahliya (he/him)

Asteria | God of the Cosmos, Mother of Ren (she/her)

Daeymon | God of Creation, Father of Renwick and Typhon (he/him)

Samarah | God of Nightmares (she/her)

Belinay | God of the Sea (she/her)

Kahliya | God of Love (she/her)

Morana | God of the Night (she/her)

Harleena | God of Time (she/her)

Delia | God of Youth (she/her)

Petra | God of Prophecy, Mother of Thorne (she/her)

Gunthar | God of War/violence (he/him)

Chenin | God of Wine (he/him)

Kaemon | God of Pleasure (he/him)

Brio | God of Music (he/him)

Felix | God of Luck (they/them)

Cato | God of Wisdom (they/them)

Talron | God of Death (he/him) trapped in the human realm

GODS

Oralia | God of Life, daughter of Peregrine and Zephyrus (she/her)

Caston | God of Truth, son of Typhon (he/him)

Thorne | God of Healing, son of Petra and Cato (he/him)

Aelestor | God of Storms (he/him)

Mecrucio | God of Travelers and Thieves (he/him)

Zayne | God of Fire, son of Belinay (he/him)

DEMI-GODS

Drystan | Favored by Typhon, Oralia's guard, Dimitri's brother (he/him)

Hollis | Favored by Typhon and his right hand man (he/him)

Ilyana | Gardener within Aethera (they/them)

SOULS

Sidero (they/them)

Dimitri, brother of Drystan (he/him)

Josette (she/her)

Lana (she/her)

Jesper (he/him)

ACKNOWLEDGEMENTS

First and foremost I want to thank YOU for picking up this book and for following Oralia and Ren in the conclusion of their journey.

Thank you to my husband, Dan, for your unending support, sometimes usable suggestions (you're getting better!), and belief in my abilities even when I don't always believe it myself. I love you so much and am so grateful I get to do this life with you.

To Angie. I said it in *Ruin* and I'll say it here again—thank you doesn't feel like enough. You have been with me every step of the way, reading each word I wrote of Ren and Oralia and pushing us to be the very best we can be. I love you so much.

To Farrah, without you this book would never even be a thing. Thank you for always encouraging me to take a break even if I don't do it and for always believing in me. I love you!

To my brother, Chris. We are walking a tough road, but we will get through it together. Love you.

To my cover artist KD and my map maker/interior designer

Travis—your incredible artistic skill has brought this series to life. I am so incredibly grateful to have you on my team and helping to bring this baby into the world.

To my editors Eleanor and Jen, thank you for turning this mess into something readable. I was so afraid that I wasn't a strong enough writer yet to pull this off and thanks to y'all, I think I did it.

Thank you to my beta readers for this series: Lauren, Dani, Brooke, Brit, Jessi and Rachael.

To my personal assistant, Ann Marie, thank you for picking up the pieces I fumble, for your unending organization, and constant positivity. Knowing you were there on my team to help me if things got to be too much helped to keep me sane.

To my Patreon subscribers, thank you for your continued support so I can keep doing what I love and bringing you these stories.

Thank you to the dramione fandom for believing in me back when I was just a random person with an idea for a dark fic and continuing to support me all the way to now. I feel like I will say it forever, but from the bottom of my heart *thank you.*

ABOUT THE AUTHOR

Gillian Eliza West lives in Austin, Texas with her husband. With a passion for mythology that has taken her around the world (despite her fear of flying), she strives to infuse her own stories with a similar kind of wonder and magic. Her first foray into writing for an audience came through fan fiction, allowing her to hone her skills as a storyteller. When she isn't working on her debut duology, you can find Gillian snuggled up with her dog, Walter, and a book or her favorite fanfic.

To stay connected, you can join Gillian's mailing list via her website: www.GillianElizaWest.com or follow her on social media:

IG: @gillianeliza

TT: @gillianeliza_

For bonus chapters, sneak peeks into upcoming projects, and first looks, you can join Gillian's Patreon: www.patreon.com/GillianElizaWest

Made in the USA
Coppell, TX
02 May 2025

48961493R10184